IZVALTA
J W Murray

ISBN:
978-1-9161209-0-7

CHAPTERS

CHAPTER 1
ALONE IN COMPANY

It's his last cigarette.

Amazing it's lasted this long really – it's been calling to him from the side pocket of a backpack for two days. Now he's watching the line of embers creeping towards his fingers and despite the fact that two thirds of it is now ash, he's trying to convince himself that he still has over half a smoke to come.

It's not that it makes him look cool – cool is a thing that Terry Morton has never looked, never been, never so much as brushed past in a corridor. Awkward and unfocused, on the other hand, have always been close.

He's spent a good deal of his twenty-four years straining to resist the forwards motion of time, but there seems to be no way to stop the turning of the earth, no way to prolong a single moment to an infinite degree. He fears the inevitable, the cosmic pre-arrangement whereby Terry will one day be forced to assume responsibility for his life and compete with a billion millennials clutching at the disintegrating coat-tails of a previous generation.

And this is the allure of the solitary smoke: it has the marvellous quality of stopping time. Whatever happens, whatever he must do, he will only do after the last embers have disappeared from his cigarette. And then he might just manage to find another tiny moment to stretch out, long and thin like elastic dough in the hands of a pizza chef.

"Dollar! Dollar!"

The kid looks up at him, round face composed entirely of circles; a badly drawn caricature – eyes, mouth, nose, and even his ears, which stick out in flat planes from the sides of his head, all beaming with hope.

"No dollar." Terry scowls back. "No."

The circles crumple into other shapes, angular and annoyed, and Terry returns his lips to a burned out cigarette. The cold moves in, as if it was only being kept at bay by the smoke.

He twists his head slowly back and forth, eyes twitching along ragged lines of flaking houses, carts made of clapped out car parts, scabby animals roaming the streets, fighting over rubbish they've dug up from the snow. It's depressing.

This is the 'low town' of course. The other end of town, he's been led to believe, is littered with tourist shops, cobbled streets and subservient hoteliers. Tomorrow he'll find out whether that's true. He plods on through the slush, which is beginning to re-freeze under his feet. Not for the first time, he feels like a ghost, his life sucked dry by a Carpathian winter ravenous for warmth.

There's no street lighting and the stars, which he was assured by fanciful friends back in England, were going to be beautiful, are obscured by a thick grey mizzle. It's only by the daubs of light from behind curtains along the street that he is able to find his way to the bar.

"Tirig og Kam" proclaims the sign leaning against the side of the building. It's a little faded, but he can definitely make out a picture of a wild bear in the process of tearing apart an armoured knight. It's an alarmingly bloody representation – probably something from local folklore, although he can't imagine what positive message it might be designed to convey. Maybe 'don't mess with the bears'. Fair enough, he thinks.

The bar is a recommendation, in the loosest sense of the word, from none other than his commanding officer – a man he still hasn't figured out. He tells himself that he's only imagining the drop-off in conversation, that it's normal to hear your own footsteps in a busy bar. He tries meeting the eye of a shrunken old man with floppy lips and heavy eyelids, sitting on a stool nearby. The man simply stares back at him – there's no feeling of recognition, no sense that one human being is looking into the eyes of another. Terry is looking for a fellow soul, but his search stops at the impenetrable surface of the other's eyeballs. It's as if they were made of glass. God knows what the other man sees. Presumably he has some frame of reference – maybe he sees a foreigner, maybe a tourist ready to be exploited, perhaps a frightened animal. There's no mirror like the blank stare of a stranger.

Embarrassed, Terry looks to the opaque floor, wondering, for the sake of something to wonder about, whether there are floorboards somewhere under the mud. As his eyes resurface, he meets the expectant face of a man who might be the barman. There's no way of being certain because there is no bar – just a thin table the same height as the rest – but this man is the only one standing up.

"Uh... Zi... uh." He gives up – the words he's been repeating over and over in his head throughout the fifteen-minute walk are gone. "Tzuica. Please. Thank you." Some fucking interpreter. At least Izvaltese shares this one word in common with Romanian.

The barman turns towards a collection of old plastic soda bottles on the floor behind him. Alongside the cheery caricatures of pandas and turtles are English-sounding brand names like 'Sprint' and 'Croc'. He unscrews a blue plastic lid and slops a generous serving into a cracked glass tumbler. He says something like "Mic vlon" and Terry nods, smiles, fails to conceal his complete lack of comprehension and drops a note on the table.

The barman takes the note and Terry takes a slug of tzuica, which scorches the back of his throat. He looks away and masks his coughs with a fist. When it becomes apparent that the barman isn't going to hand him any change, he looks nervously around, trying to avoid meeting one of the many sets of watching eyes, and makes a beeline for a vacant seat within ten feet of the fire. In his head he tries to figure out what the exchange rate is and the value of the note he's just handed over. It seems to be an adage of travelling that a wallet full of small notes will go a whole lot further than a couple of big ones. He sighs and puts it down to experience, although that won't stop it bugging him – it must have been about three pounds he just handed over, in a country where drinks are usually fifty pence.

Perching on a stool, he looks out over the rim of his glass to further survey the room. It almost appears as if he's sitting in someone's shed – there's no decoration on the walls; not even a collection of horse brass or hunting trophies. Several of the chairs are flimsy plastic affairs that look like they are about to give up under the weight of their occupants. In particular, he can't help but stare with car-crash fascination at a fat old lady in the corner with her shoes off, revealing a pair of stunningly disgusting swollen feet. She's sitting next to a middle-aged man in a cowboy hat. The hat makes Terry feel slightly more comfortable; in a culture so unfamiliar, incongruities like this one are reassuring; even the old soda bottles go some way to providing a context he feels he can grasp.

Terry takes the measure of the rough beams in the ceiling and the flaking walls. He listens to the patter and lull of conversation and even taps his foot in time to a jaunty tune played on an instrument he doesn't recognise, like a harp laid horizontal, an old man hitting the strings with sticks. He exchanges nods and smiles and gets another drink. With some sadness he reflects that he feels almost comfortable here. The sadness is there because now that he's comfortable, where is the adventure? This is no longer undiscovered country. Before he opened the door to this place, anything could have been on the other side, from mobsters to circus performers to farmyard animals, but now that he knows what's here, the scope of what could be is just that little bit slimmer.

He tries to imagine that time when the world was surrounded by the unknown, where the limits of its dark seas were marked by leviathans and mermaids. Where the map ended the imagination roamed free, but in a world that's entirely knowable the imagination is locked into a tight cell. Which is why Terry feels a constant urge to shut his eyes and to stop taking it all in. Once it's catalogued in his head, he knows it will hold no more interest for him.

"You reckon you're bloody Faust, you know that!" That's what his girlfriend Lucy said. "You think there's some great unknowable truth behind it all and nothing else is worth a damn."

"Sure." He replied.

"Despite the fact that you barely even studied. The whole thing with Faust was that he'd put in the hours – he knew what he was talking about, but you – you're just poncing around trying to avoid doing anything with your life."

That's the bit that he finds hard to deny. The part of the educational process when he's supposed to have found his direction never really happened – perhaps because he kept on closing his eyes – just like he is now – and hoping that when he opened them again, there would be a different world looking back at him.

He opens his eyes.

There's someone new in the room and everybody is looking

at her – some surreptitiously; others blatantly. Terry recognises a fellow human being in distress, but she doesn't look like a tourist: her big wool coat doesn't have a Karrimor label – in fact it looks hand-woven. Her features are broadly Romanian, though her complexion is uncharacteristically pale.

And then she's gone. Out of the door as though she had an allergic reaction to the place. Her departure elicits a murmur and a chuckle from the drinkers – the same kind of noise he suspects will follow him out of the door too.

Even without the words, gossip has a recognisable aura, like bubbles popping over a simmering broth. Perhaps she was looking for somebody? Her husband? Her lover? It would certainly explain the ripples of amusement that are still sloshing back and forth around the room.

His drink finished, Terry gathers about him his coat and scarf and gloves – the outer armour against the cold, which complements the pleasant burning in his belly. Lanky and rickety he stands and straightens his back, surprising one or two of the locals who had completely forgotten the strange young man. Leerily they look up at him and perhaps exchange a word or two with a neighbour about his height and smile at the way he has to duck for the beams in the ceiling.

The evening ends fuzzily. The morning starts a blur.

Terry finds himself staggering into his trousers and tumbling into his shirt, finally emerging, blinking into the sun long after his room-mate and the rest of the camp. It doesn't seem to matter. His commanding officer has made it quite clear that Terry's role is to sit tight and be patient. "Anything you want me to be doing, sir?" he asked when he first met Captain Rogers. "You? No. There's a whole list of things I want you not to be doing though." That list had not included getting drunk at local hangouts or sleeping late. Even if it had, Terry has his doubts about whether anyone here cares enough to call him out on it.

Leaving the camp, he tells nobody where he's going and nobody asks. They don't seem to care, and that suits him fine. He's not here for them – he's here for money. And for Mr. Nevelson, Lucy's father, who was a field medic at Terry's age, saved hundreds of lives, earned a display cabinet's worth of medals, and "learned everything there is to know about the world". Active service, he'd suggested, and not learning some dead language, would give Terry a grounding in what was important. Terry protested, but without the prospect of alternative employment or the actual threat of bullets being fired on this mission, the most he could muster was that French was hardly dead, and that it had accounted for half of his course credits.

He walks slowly, savouring the feeling of discovery. His feet take him for the first time towards the high town. As he walks, the number of dogs scrapping around the streets thins out, as does the number of wood-plank carts pulled by ancient wheezing horses and held together by bits of frayed rope.

He crosses the market square, slotted in like a lumpy knee joint between high and low towns, and the cityscape changes: the mud-stained snow, dilapidated buildings and clapped out lanes give way to an altogether different and more welcoming city. As the street inclines, Terry begins to breathe heavily. The sharp air at the back of his throat feels good; the oxygen bathing his brain makes it tingle; he feels alive, as he spews plumes of body-warm steam from his mouth. When he stops to look back over the path he's just come up, he is transfixed by the beauty of the scene below. From here he can see over the crazy angles of the thousands of ramshackle roofs. Wintry wisps of smoke drift unhurriedly from the chimneys, and beyond them, plains of blue-white snow broken up by low fences stretch all the way along the valley floor to the base of the far mountains. That view changes his whole concept of Izvalta.

As he nears the apex of the hill, the high town becomes a complete inversion of the low: the smelly, unkempt animals are gone, replaced by well looked after cats that watch from pink granite window sills and purr obligingly when stroked, nuzzling up against Terry's hand. The people seem thinner and healthier too – less like the grotesque and lumpy people in the bar the previous night. They smile at him as he passes.

Nothing prepares him for the next surprise from the city of Svart. It looms up out of the cobbles that are laid so neatly into the delicate little plaza. There, like a burst blister on peachy skin, stands an enormous stone horseman. The stallion rears as if making a point of exposing an intricately carved cock and balls. The man's face has a fearsome aspect, his mouth open wide in mid battle-cry as he points a spear directly at the chest-level of anyone idiot enough to stand in front of him – as Terry is now.

It's completely out of place in the continuum of local symbolism, which is mostly composed of crosses, shrines and devotional symbols. These are omnipresent; hidden in tiny nooks and shelters by the roadside; at the tops of mountains; practically overwhelming the unsuspecting trees that were unfortunate enough to grow directly in the path of somebody's religious fervour. Unlike anywhere he's been before, there are simply no statues that aren't devoted to one little-known saint or other. Izvalta does little to honour its conquering heroes and hirsute statesmen – presumably it has none. But there is no way that the statue in front of him represents some meek martyr; this is like an incarnate spirit of war, a barbarian war-chief hell-bent on the destruction of his foes. The name at the base is 'Monterek' – a name he recognises. The reigning King of Izvalta.

"Bloody hell." he mutters to himself.

Terry wanders the rest of the high town in a daze,

overwhelmed by a torrent of tiny details: a hundred alcoves sheltering weathered murals with their cast of obscure biblical characters; the tiny window-slits in the roofs that look like little black eyes under tile eyelids; the winding lanes stuffed with curios and wooden knick-knacks, all beautifully tailored to some completely unknown purpose. He feels that he should try to avoid discovering all of the mysteries of Izvalta at once and save some undiscovered territory for later, but he can't help himself. The city is a many-veined mine that taunts him with untold treasures. It draws him in with tiny mysteries such as the English translations that adorn the souvenirs, more often than not just adding an extra layer of confusion to his understanding of the items on display. 'Tradizional pottere' makes sense, but what's a 'holy stick' or a 'festival bread mark'? With some restraint he resists asking any of the mostly absent shopkeepers. Some mystery must remain.

When he catches sight of the church, at first he doesn't realise what it is. It looks humble and functional, almost like a granary, but it radiates a peculiar power that the other religious buildings of Izvalta, while often impressive, do not share. The standard church surfaces are sheened with white glazed tiles, their gates wrought in artful forms. This building announces its grandeur not with a fanfare, but with a whisper. It has no tiles or gates at all – just a bare stone façade that is somehow far more imposing, and it looks ancient, like it was part of the landscape of this valley long before the city of Svart crawled into place beside it.

Opening the weathered wooden door, his eyes strain for clues as to the anatomy of the black hole of a room in which he finds himself. There seems to be only one light source in this building, which emanates from the top of the domed roof. By this light, other things begin to appear: wooden ornaments; flat, saintly faces rendered in dark pinks with deep azure clothes; and a screen at the end of the room that looks like a minor, but incredibly ornate, fortification.

Proceeding slowly and respectfully down the threadbare carpet, he is stopped short as he notices something even grander in the bay to his left. Here is something entirely out of keeping with the rest of the building: an enormous sculpture that appears to drip with gold, like a spray-painted model that hasn't dried yet. But this is no paint; this gold has *substance*. It's more solid than anything he's ever seen, yet it almost appears to be moving, the sculpted figures writhing like war victims struggling to free themselves from a cascade of golden napalm.

The centrepiece of the whole work is a particularly horrifying crucified Christ, which seems to change as he looks closer. It appears to convulse, racked with pain. The downcast eyes for a moment seem to tilt ever so slightly upwards to meet his own in a look of longing, begging the pain to end. What he's seeing is death and suffering – not a portrayal, but a fact. This is no thick-lined glass painting, with a colourful naïve style, this is the work of a master. Or a madman.

"Zja burevje?"

The shock of the voice against the silence almost knocks Terry over. A man with a startlingly white beard is looking at him. He wears a plain black cassock, a square-topped cloth hat, and he has a pair of spectacles through which he directs a vicious glare towards the intruder. Terry is grateful for those spectacles: without their shielding he may have already melted away under the man's fierce gaze.

"Ah. Ey vekk... ey vekka." Terry makes a stab at the language – and inflicts what appears to be a mortal wound. The priest's glare becomes even more scornful – if such a thing is possible.

"You are just looking, yes? Good, well I remind you that our donation box is over there." He adds a grimace that falls halfway between a smile and a sneer, then turns away.

Unwelcome as he clearly is, Terry feels he must ask a question. "Who made it?" he says.

"What? This?" A pause. "A servant of God."

"It's real gold, isn't it?"

The priest is silent. Terry has clearly outstayed his welcome. He drops some loose change in a wooden box on the way out as a way to ward off evil spirits like the one he's just encountered.

As he steps out into the chill of the early evening, he takes a look back towards the church façade. He stands there for a minute, letting the impression of the place sink in. It's one of those buildings that embodies something intangible – as if a bell was rung at the beginning of time and the echo was preserved here, resonating around the walls, bouncing around the thick stone dome, fading slightly but never escaping.

There is just a single brick that, now he sees it, looks completely out of place. Where the rest of the stones are grey and weathered, this one is deep black and polished to a shine. Inset in white are the letters "FVLCANELLI".

Izvalta's days are short in the winter and a gust of brittle, twig-snapping wind persuades him to zip up his coat and turn back towards the low town, where a warm sleeping bag waits for him on an unyielding army cot. There, in the halo of a flashlight he can curl up and flip through the many thousands of pages of classic literature neatly catalogued on his Kindle. That too is an undiscovered country, and one whose depths he couldn't hope to fathom even if he had several lifetimes to do it in. But those volumes document bygone eras – though the delivery mechanism is fashioned in ergonomic black plastic, the contents have mostly been rendered obsolete by time. They lack the appeal of the present.

As he passes 'Tirig og Kam', the bar of last night, he hears something that sounds suspiciously like televised football: the unmistakeable low murmur of metronomic trivia from the commentators; then a build; a crescendo as the spectators' voices grow louder and higher pitched; the isolated shouts from the bar punching into the game like a cymbal crash, crash, crash, building in tempo and pitch and – a breath as the world freezes momentarily... and then the moment spills into an eddy of shouts, coughs, sighs, the commentators bringing the piece gradually back down to where it started.

Terry's feet follow the sound, as if drawn by instinct to any point of cultural common ground between his world and this tiny Carpathian settlement. As he enters, he's hit by a wall of warmth, smoke and intense attention as everybody turns to him and three excitable men in their fifties jabber at him in Izvaltese, occasionally offering little clues as to what they're saying in English. A complete change from the atmosphere on the previous night, though the communication barriers are still very much in place.

"From? Yes? You from?" asks a red face lurking somewhere behind a haze of alcohol.

"Oh, uh – England. From England."

"Oh England? Ah! Ah! Manchester United? Liverpool?"

Another breaks in. "Chelsea?"

Terry squints at the screen, which sits precariously on a stack of firewood in one corner. Trying to assume a polite neutrality, he decides to pick a team that he knows for certain isn't playing and is unlikely to elicit any strong opinions.

"Uh... Southampton. Very small team. Uh Letze – very letze."

It's while he's trying to explain where he lives in relation to Manchester that he sees the woman again. She huddles at the abandoned fireplace, feeding it logs and restlessly stoking the embers as if trying to coax out every last morsel of heat from the flames. He watches as she prods and riddles then, at least marginally content with the job, she pulls up a seat, uncaps a large bottle of tzuica and takes a few enormous gulps.

Even in the firelight she's mostly a shadowy shape obscured by a bulky woollen coat and her own dark curls. The pale white of her skin occasionally flashes through underneath. She's in her forties, he thinks, though he really can't tell. Her face is hard, with the cheek bones pinching into acutely angled cliffs on either side, her eyes darting restlessly under arched brows. She can't be more than about five feet tall, and yet he feels that even without the nebulous surrounds of her coat, her presence would somehow fill a space much larger than herself.

She mumbles something at the bottle, then her restless eyes fix upon Terry. Despite a strong impulse to look away, he doesn't. The woman's eyes refocus as she brushes a few loose curls away to reveal a frown of curiosity. He's at the back of the football-watching crowd now, so it's only a matter of a few small steps to take him to the edge of the fireplace.

"Français? English?" she asks.

"English," he replies. "And you?" he adds, before realising that it's a stupid question, although on second thoughts perhaps it isn't.

"Izvaltan," she says, "But I speak other languages."

Her accent is strange; he's not sure he believes that she is actually Izvaltan – she certainly can't have been taught English at the same school as the men at the bar. He starts wondering if perhaps she's a French tourist who came here years ago and settled here, although he can't imagine anyone doing such a thing. Even her voice carries a marked difference from the local sing-song – it has a rocky quality – almost masculine.

"Vous n'êtes pas française?"

"Non," she replies with a thin smile. "Mais..." and then she seems a bit lost – like she doesn't know how to continue the conversation or if she should have started it at all. She just stares into the fire, as if looking for an answer there.

"Your English is very good," he offers.

"Yes," she says, and as an after-thought "Thank you."

"How did you learn? If you don't mind my asking?"

"How does anybody learn anything? Books. Books left by tourists. Other books are hard to find here. People don't read English."

"But I thought it was taught in all the schools?"

"I didn't... I didn't learn so much from school." She returns to her drink, swallowing a great gulp that would have made most people choke – she doesn't even seem to register it.

"It's uh – it's quite strong. You don't want to slow down?"

"It has to be strong. It drives out the cold. The snow stays on the ground for three months in the winter. You get used to the cold and the dark, but... not on your own. Not even..."

She says no more. They both turn back to the fire. Behind them, the crescendo builds again. Terry looks around at the screen – what he can see of it through bodies and elbows – which isn't much at all. The remote patch of green with the brightly coloured dots is far away from the Carpathian winter.

He looks down to see that his drink is finished, which probably means it's time for him to get back. Not that there's a stated curfew. He's reluctant to leave the sad woman; he feels some obligation to stay and comfort her, but he's not sure he has the words or the ability to do it.

"Well," he says. "It was nice to meet you. I have to be getting back to the camp now."

She nods silently into her tzuica, then after a second, looks up. There's fire in her eyes – an expression that makes Terry pause in the middle of putting on his coat.

"Camp?"

"Yeah."

"You're a soldier, aren't you?"

"What? No – I'm... well – I'm working with them. I'm just..."

And then she's in his face, almost hissing at him. "They were in my house today. Idiot children with guns, touching everything; breaking most of it. They ruined months, maybe years of work. Not that you'd understand."

She's standing now and despite the fact that Terry is about a head taller, he's starting to feel like a very small child who's done something very very bad. In common with many small children in this situation, he just doesn't know what it is he's done.

"What are you doing here? Are we being invaded? Have you come to take our oil, because I'll tell you now, we haven't got any. Are you spying on me? Is that why you're here? Come on – answer me, spy."

He thinks for a moment that she's going to hit him, and he flinches back, suddenly noticing the quietness of the bar. Somebody's turned the football off. He doesn't need to look around to know that all eyes are on them.

"I'm... I'm not a spy. I'm an interpreter."

"Vrasj unok Izvaltej?"

"Well, I'm not a very good interpreter." He tries a little peace-offering smile.

"You're a child – that's what you are." And she sags slightly. "Just a child." She takes the bottle by the cap, its bright colouring looking all the more incongruous against the pale skin of her hand, then she walks slowly past a murmuring clutch of people and out into the cold.

As the door bashes back against the frame, Terry tries not to look at anyone, but it's no good – they're blatantly staring at him. The old woman with the swollen feet jabs a finger in his direction.

"Fama yeva. U tupi vre gyep va ni svata gi gyep veh vs nys."

It sounds harsh and raspy and vaguely threatening, and on the back of the spying accusation it manages to really piss him off.

"What does that mean?" he says loudly. "Did you just curse me? Fuck you, lady. You know what? I'm fed up with this bollocks. I didn't do anything. It's not enough that I have to take shit from a bunch of meathead soldiers – now I have to take it from the bloody locals too!"

"Vresk, vresk – tch tch." The barman's tone is much gentler than the old lady's prickly words. He says something to the rest of the bar that produces an understanding chuckle, then walks over to Terry's fireside seat and fills Terry's glass a short way. Terry looks up in puzzlement at the barkeeper, whose knuckly hand has come to rest on his shoulder in what must be intended as a comforting gesture.

"What was she saying?" Terry asks, slowly so that he might just be understood.

"The old woman – she say that this other woman you talk to is um... the devil – yes. The devil. That she has the son who is..." he makes a gesture with his hands on his head.

"A demon?"

"Yes – yes I think. But she is old and mad. I do not want that you should stop to come to the bar, so I tell her quiet and I give you drink – we are happy, yes?"

"Who was that woman?" he asks.

"The woman – she comes in. She drinks. She drinks much. I do not know more. I do not think she is devil," he adds with a reassuring smile.

CHAPTER 2
NIGREDO

Captain Rogers is hard to read. He has a kind of perpetually harried look and a way of talking to Terry as if he's not in the room, like he's addressing an abstract concept. He's of average height and average build with a paunch threatening and hair greying around the temples. Terry can barely guess at his roots – maybe an ex-civil servant? He could quite easily picture him wearing a tie, sitting behind a desk and barking at an overworked secretary.

Terry sits in front of him, looking nervous, like he hasn't done his homework. Rogers fails to focus on him, but does manage a brief glance.

"At ease, Morton – you look like you just sat on something sharp."

Terry tries to smile.

"So how's the Izvaltese going?"

"Uh. Well, slow, sir. It's... there's... there are a lot of unfamiliar words. Sir."

"Hmm. Yeah." says Rogers, looking down at a sheet of paper in his hand. Terry keeps on thinking it's his report card, that it's sprinkled with phrases like 'could try harder to engage' and 'needs work'. It isn't his report card, and he isn't at school. The sheet is full of figures – numbers that are absolutely meaningless to Terry, but apparently hold a great deal of fascination for Rogers. Finally, the officer looks up.

"Look – I'll be honest with you. The language doesn't matter all that much. I mean, yes, it could be useful, but the way I see it we'd be better off with diplomatic immunity and a lorry-load of boffins, but hey – we use what we've got."

"So what do you..."

"So where does that leave you? Well not quite with a whole packet full of paid holiday, but something close. What I want is for you to keep your eyes open. Look around. See what you can see. If you pick up the lingo on your way, great."

"If you don't mind my asking, what do you need the um... the boffins for?"

"I do mind. That's not your concern."

"Well, um..." He hesitates. "It's just that it might help me if I knew what to look for."

Rogers looks him steadily in the eyes. There's nothing explicitly threatening in the look.

"It's just that – well I went to that bar that you suggested I... and... Well I heard that you were at a local woman's house. She said you caused some damage. She seemed upset – I mean, she was upset. I was just wondering..."

"Look, Morton. Maybe you didn't pick up on this, but I'm none too happy about you being here. I couldn't care less if you were knocking off royalty, let alone the daughter of a ranking officer. Some posh tosser with a knighthood and a pack of corgis does not get to tell me how to do things.

"For the record, yes, we did visit a local resident. Name of Fulcanelli. Lives in the middle of some woods out east. We'd heard a few things, so we paid her a visit. There was some unintended damage." He coughs. "If you happen to see her again, you can convey my apologies."

"But what were you looking for?"

"For God's sake, you prat, can't you take a hint? In the army – at least in this army – there's such a thing as knowing your place and there's a fine line between a healthy inquisitive mind and pissing me off. Actually no – it's quite a thick line. Now, I want you to keep an eye out for me, a general kind of eye out, but let me make it clear – no thought is required on your part. Understand?"

"Yes, sir."

"University educated, weren't you? Somewhere within spitting distance of the red bricks?" He doesn't wait for a response. "Well that's just dandy. Go find a rock to study. Dismissed."

Terry talks to himself as he comes out of the rickety office. "Why shouldn't I know what's going on? I mean what the fuck is there that's so damn secret around here? Fucking meathead wan..." He raises pair of angry eyes from the muddy snow and sees that he's not alone.

"Bee in your bonnet?"

The soldier who addresses Terry is older than Rogers. He's lent up against a wall smoking a cigarette. The fact that he isn't wearing a coat suggests that he's only just stepped outside. He has that bearing that makes him look completely at home – even when he's far away from it. It's reassuring.

"Ach. No. Unreasonable expectations I think," says Terry carefully.

"Sounds familiar. I've been lobbying for Tetley's for thirty years, but we're stuck with brand X. Tastes like damp leather."

He takes a box of cigarettes from his shirt pocket and offers it to Terry, who sheepishly grins before taking one.

"Old man Rogers can take some getting used to. If he ever pats your back, you just make sure you aren't standing on a cliff edge. This your first time with the forces?"

Terry pauses while he lights the cigarette with proffered Zippo.

"First time doing almost anything. I was studying. Then, well..." Rogers might have a point, he thinks to himself. Find a rock to study.

"Studying's good. Something useful? Practical?"

"French and Classics."

"I get ya. Got a son about your age. Same predicament. Plus he's a lazy tosser." The man grins. "Currently in Singapore living off stepdaddy's paycheck. Rather his than mine, anyhow." He holds out a hand. "Ethan Smith."

"Terry Morton."

"Yeah, I know. The tourist."

"Well it's a pretty lousy holiday so far."

"That it is. I missed Christmas and you can't find a turkey out here for love nor money."

"How long have you been here?"

"Seven months."

"Doing what?"

"You mean you didn't get the brief?"

Terry shakes his head.

"Not sure I did either – in any case, as I understand it, it's like it says on the tin – it's uh... brief." The older man grins.

"So what do you do? What's in that building?"

"Me? I spend my days peeling potatoes – we don't all get to wander around playing tourist."

"Potatoes?"

"Straight up."

"And the building?"

"Full of 'em."

"Right. And you can't peel potatoes in Leeds?"

"There's an idea. It's Liverpool, by the way."

"So you don't know anything about a raid on a local woman's house?"

Ethan Smith looks at him quizzically. "What woman?"

"I can't remember her name now. Something Italian-sounding. Big coat. Curly hair." He wonders how much he should tell Ethan about the meeting. "I heard in Svart that this woman's house had been um... invaded."

The man grins and breaks into a laugh that gives Terry the impression that this story is just too good not to share.

"Look," says Smith, dropping his voice to a whisper. "This goes no further, right? Right. So this place is in the middle of bloody nowhere – at least an hour's trek away. Little black house with this giant chimney – and Jesus does it need one – the reek of the fumes in there. I'm amazed anyone could live in a place like that and stay alive. Beakers and things everywhere – what are they called – alumbicks? You know – those glass things with the funnel tops. Coloured liquids and test tubes. It's like Hammer Horror eat your heart out.

"Anyway, we get there, we find the proprietor – your Italian lady, though I doubt she's Italian, and she's not much of a lady with the words coming out of her mouth. You know, you don't usually expect the red carpet when you do this job, but we *were* trying to be friendly. Anyway, all is relatively fine until Jim 'bull-in-a-china-shop' Sale starts knocking over the props.

"Some Jekyll-and-Hyde experiment goes off like a firework and the rest of the unit that's been waiting outside storms in to take up position, but they can't see anything because it's dark and there's smoke everywhere, so they take out a bunch more beakers and potions. Some of it catches fire, some of it just stinks the place out even more. Everyone winds up outside feeling very sorry for themselves, one or two nursing a couple of light acid burns." Smith chuckles – he seems to be taking it all so lightly.

"What about the woman?" Terry asks.

"Well, she screamed a bit. Shouted at us – and, well, we couldn't understand most of what she was saying. I guess we should've brought you with us, mister interpreter." He laughs quietly to himself. "You know, you get an interpreter in Afghanistan, they're asking 'Where is the bomb? Where is the bomb?' Out here in the arse end of nowhere it's 'Put down the chicken entrails. Step away from the goat.' Shouldn't complain, I suppose. It was pretty clear she was barking. So we left. She kept screaming at us halfway back here. She has a pair of lungs, I tell ya. Funny story, huh?"

"Yeah – I suppose. Odd though. I mean, why did she have all of those beakers and liquids? Isn't that something worth investigating?"

"Ah, it's just a bunch of pagan mumbo-jumbo. Sacrificing chickens to the earth god or something. Only idiot she had fooled was Sale – reckoned he saw a bogeyman in the shadows, but we cased the joint. I reckon he was making excuses for being clumsy." Smith takes a final draw on his cigarette before flinging it into a patch of dirty snow. "She's just another peasant in a country full of peasants."

It almost sounds to Terry like a lecture from Lucy, it has that same ring of dull plausibility. *Where did the wizards and witches and dragons go?* he once asked her in a moment of disillusion. *They got replaced* she said. *By bankers and corporations and things you can't just ride off on a horse and stick a spear through. They're better at hoarding than any dragon, and when they cast their spells, police appear at your door. So stay on the right side of them and get a bloody job.*

He has one of those now, but apparently that hasn't stopped him looking for dragons.

Terry is trying to find a place to sit and study. Finally, he finds an empty tourist coffee shop on a blocky street crowned by tangles of tumbledown satellite dishes.

The coffee shop is clearly closed for the winter, but he manages to attract someone's attention by rapping on the blinds. Inside, he sits rubbing his palms together and bathing his cold face in the warm steam of the coffee, before sipping tentatively at it, trying to decide whether it's crappy real or average instant.

The coffee shop is nice. Twinkly lights hang from wooden beams and mismatched chairs compete for space under the low ceiling. Stacks of ancient issues of Cosmopolitan inhabit the corners, eagerly awaiting the passing interest of a passing tourist, for whom they will give themselves completely, exposing their lush glossy interiors with a whiff of elegant decadence. Terry blows dust off the top issue, then puts it back down.

His mind is swamped with thoughts of the woman at the bar. There's something other-worldly about her, even without the tales of bogeymen and experiments. She doesn't belong in this place – not in Izvalta, not Romania, not Europe. Not even amongst the glamorously airbrushed Cosmo girls – she doesn't seem to belong anywhere at all. And despite that alien quality, he knows that when he met her, he felt a connection – like she understood him and maybe he could understand her – if only she hadn't taken exception to the company he keeps.

How could he explain to her that he is anything but a soldier – not even the interpreter that he's currently claiming to be? That he's here because of Mr. Nevelson's insistence that Terry should experience the world, and perhaps also because Terry is the albatross around his beloved daughter's neck.

With a sigh he returns to the task at hand, the acquisition of the local language. There are no books that teach Izvaltese – at least none written in English – which leaves only two ways to learn it. Either by talking to the locals, who insist on trying to speak to him in their abortive English, or by carefully analysing the local newspaper in an attempt to decipher what it could be saying based on the one or two black and white pictures. With another sigh, he lays out a copy of *Valta* – named after the only sizeable river that in the region – and has a go at scrutinising it.

"Why are you reading *that*?" says the café owner in rather good but slightly sneering English.

"Um – why shouldn't I?"

"It is in Izvaltese."

Terry feigns shock, though his sarcasm is lost on the café owner.

"It is local politics – that is why it is in Izvaltese," she expands. "It is not for tourists."

"Really? Try me. I'm not a tourist as such – I'm trying to learn your language."

The woman laughs, which sets her ample sides shaking. "Well you are the first one. It is a dying language now – everyone from my generation speaks English, like the rest of the world. Izvalta is more progressive, you see, than some other countries."

But this only makes him wonder more – why isn't *Valta* written in English then, if everyone is supposed to be able to speak it? Is there something the publishers want to hide from the rest of the world, maybe? As he becomes more curious about the contents of the paper, he senses that the woman is beginning to regret having said anything, though he does persuade her to describe part of the paper's contents before stonewalling him completely.

"Well," she says. "There's the art competition opening later this year: Glorious Izvalta Under His um... she searches her mind for a translation 'his Goodness Majesty'."

"Okay – and what's this?"

"Oh that? It's just a tithe notice."

"A tithe? You mean a tax?"

"Well, yes – it won't affect me because I'm in a tourist industry, but it's traditional for the farmers to give money to the church."

"In January?"

"Well, it comes at all times of the year."

"It seems unreasonable to demand a tax from farmers in the middle of winter."

"Oh, they make enough money logging during the winter. His Highness knows all about the economy: he studied at Oxford," she adds proudly.

"But – well, excuse me for asking, but I thought you said it was a church tax. Why is the king involved?"

The woman looks a little confused. "You see? It is complicated – you don't know how it works here. Like I say, it is not for the tourists." She shuffles off back to her counter. Terry is left staring at the paper and wondering what else is hiding behind the heavy Cyrillic foliage.

When evening comes, Terry gravitates back to the bar almost without thinking. He's not expecting to see the woman, not after yesterday. But to his surprise, when he opens the door, there she is, sitting in what he's started to think of as his spot in front of the fire.

The barman catches him looking over at her, and with a paternal hand on his shoulder, he points Terry to a different seat. Terry nods as if to say he understands, but after he gets his mug of tzuica he turns back toward the fire. Pretending not to notice the remonstrations of the barman, he sits just apart from the woman in the big woollen coat.

She glances up. "Ah! The soldier boy is here again. What do

you want?" Her eyes try to pierce him, but they have a fogginess and a vagueness that suggest she's been drinking for a while. She doesn't appear nearly as fearsome today, and Terry can't help but see his opportunity to quiz her while her guard is lowered.

"Oh, I just thought we could talk. I've been told to apologise on behalf of the soldiers."

"Ha! Can't apologise with a gun in your hand."

"Right. Absolutely right. That's why I don't have a gun. I was trying to tell you before – I'm not a soldier."

"What are you then? Oh no, I remember – you're a child. A child. The world is all a blur for you; the lines are indistinct; each thing merges with its neighbour. Children, you see, have not yet leaned to put lines in between things. You understand what I'm saying?"

"No, I-"

"Of course you don't – that's my point!" She seems pleased with herself. "But you see the world almost as it really is. Very nearly. As it really is..." She trails off and Terry senses her attention wandering.

"Are you a witch?" he asks quickly, keen to say anything to keep her engaged. She looks at him for a second before laughing with genuine mirth.

"Is that what they think? The British Army thinks I'm a witch? With magical powers and... and a hat! Ha!" She chuckles to herself some more. "Fulcanelli, the witch. Ha!"

Hearing her name again, he thinks there's something familiar about it, though he can't say why.

"So, what are all the experiments for? The beakers and things?"

"Look, child. Look around you. Do you see any high technology industries around here? Do you? Industrial machinery? Factories? Life is simple – or it was before we started importing everything. People took wool from a sheep, they made it into clothes. But what if they want a bit of colour? Just a little colour? Well then they need to extract it – from the rocks and plants and insects."

"And for that you need..."

"Beakers and things," she interrupts. "There is no magic to that. There's no magic to anything I do."

He's disappointed, of course, but the rational part of his mind is ready and waiting with an 'I told you so'. One with Lucy's intonation. At the same moment, however, he makes a connection.

"Your name – Fulcanelli?"

"What about it, mister witch-hunter?"

"It doesn't sound very Izvaltan. But I've heard it before. Or seen it. I know – on the side of the church. That's where I've seen it! It's etched into a black stone on the side of the church."

"Yes." She seems suddenly subdued.

"Is it... did your family build the church or something?"

"No."

He waits for elucidation that never comes. "But it is your name, right?"

"Yes and no." She looks up at him with eyes that are only half seeing what's in front of them, half seeing an image from the past. "I knew a man once, with that name. But he did not build the church."

"So the name on the outside – was he famous or...?" He stops himself abruptly as he sees a tear well in the corner of her eye. She wipes it away quickly with a sleeve before it reaches her cheek.

"No. Not famous. I don't know why they haven't ripped that stone out yet. Monterek should have ripped out that fucking stone. It's not his." She realises that she's rambling, looks up at

Terry again. She seems to be trying to figure something out – to stare into his soul, looking for hints of his motives, his values, his true nature.

"Tell me, child," And this time when she says the word it is softer, no longer an accusing label. "Have you seen Jesus?"

He instantly knows what she's talking about. And yes, he has. "In the church. The golden statue – that's Fulcanelli's work?"

She nods.

"It's beautiful," he says. "Like it's alive. I... I stood there in front of it and I felt his pain almost, but also something else – like a warmth. It was... amazing."

The corners of her mouth smile, though her eyes are still sad. They flicker with the firelight.

"That is the power of alchemy."

His heart begins to race. "Beakers and things?" he echoes, dumbly.

She nods.

In the following silence, Terry contemplates his options. On the one hand, this might be an attempt staged by the locals of Svart to prove exactly how gullible a tourist can be. On the other he could be at the edge of an incredible revelation that might change his entire world, or *the* entire world. It's almost an instinct that guides his hand to his inside pocket, where there is an old-fashioned dictaphone which records onto a mini-cassette.

He brought it along to record some native Izvaltese for study. It's a little memento of his father that he fished out of a cardboard box in his parents' old attic. At the time he didn't know what possible use it could have – he just felt drawn to it somehow. But at this moment he can almost touch the prickly aura of destiny around the device. It feels as if it were meant to record this conversation so that one day, far from the craggy slopes and snow-clad fields of Izvalta, he will be able to share one of the world's oldest secrets – the secret of turning base metals into gold – and who knows what else?

He presses the record button and feels it whir quietly into action. Perhaps, far above him, moons and planets are also coming into perfect alignment, a giant piece of clockwork mimicking the miniature tape-winding gears of the dictaphone. As above, so below. Where has he heard that before?

"Will you teach me about alchemy?"

"No."

"But you are an alchemist, right?" He says it in a whisper though the background noise is ample protection against overhearing ears.

"I've already said too much. You are the last person I should talk to."

"It's not for them – the soldiers I mean – I... I want to know. About alchemy." And he does.

More than anything he wants to believe in something extraordinary: something outside the narrow span of possibilities he can see for himself and his future. If the world could be just a shade more magical, perhaps he could escape into it. And perhaps it's these thoughts that the woman reads in his tone and his face, mirroring thoughts that were once her own, that keep her talking.

"Alchemy is not what you think it is." she says.

"Oh? And what do I think it is?"

"You think it's magic."

"And what is it really?"

"Sacrifice."

He waits for her to continue, but she doesn't. "So you're saying that I can turn things into gold as long as I sacrifice something? Like what? Like time? An animal? Myself?"

She sighs. "You may never understand this, child, because you have things too easily. Your water comes from a tap. Your food comes from a shop. You have no capacity for sacrifice and that means that there can be no balance. You want to know about alchemy? All you must do is look at yourself. What in the world would you change and which part of yourself are you prepared to sacrifice?"

From almost anybody else it would sound stupid, like a fairground con, but from this particular stranger the words make sense. There's a simple truth to them: people are removed from the world; they can complain bitterly and yet lack the conviction to do anything; they aren't prepared to give up on small luxuries to make a change. And that goes for him too. But that's a cultural reality rather than a law of nature.

"You're not telling me that I can jump to the moon if I'm just willing to sacrifice something?"

"Hasn't it already been done?"

"But that's not alchemy – that's science."

"And what, do you think, is the difference?"

"Well, you can't really turn lead into gold with science – I mean, not easily."

"If alchemy were easy, don't you think more people would be turning lead into gold?" She takes a gulp of tzuica and bares her teeth as it hits the back of her throat. "The difference between science and alchemy is sacrifice – is bearing the consequences. It's why I'm here drinking this cheap shit."

There's something in her smile that makes him look at her again – her intensity, the dark look in her eyes. She hides it well, extremely well, but the woman is definitely drunk. He feels suddenly uncomfortable, realising for the first time that this may be neither a con nor a hint of some hidden truth, but the sad delusion of an alcoholic who thinks she's an alchemist. It's not a comfortable realisation. He almost gets up then and there, almost says, 'Well it's been nice talking to you', almost steps out into the cold night never to come back to this little place with the weird sign by the door.

"Would you tell me about it? Alchemy?" he says, his curiosity winning out over his doubts.

"I will tell you a story," she says. "A story that I have told to no other human." And she smiles to herself. "It may do me some good."

"My life has been hard, and when life is hard, sometimes I had to... obscure... reality. You pick your drug and the days blur. Like a child you see them – the hard lines are gone. It's more manageable that way. And then I had a child of my own. For his sake I wanted to give up the drink. I hated myself, but I couldn't stop. So I tried to make it less painful. I made a cure."

"What? A hangover cure?"

"In a sense. But the cure, you see, was total. The spirit you're drinking right now won't just pass through you – it will stay in your gut: it becomes part of you, and where one substance can perfect you, so can another cast you away from God."

"From God?"

She ignores him. "So your system needs to become more perfect to counter the evil in the gut. The body is a distiller – a separator. It is an alchemical component: it takes materials and it changes them. The most perfect body can drink all the poisons in the world and feel nothing – it will simply distil the good from the bad. The bad will pass straight through. So the true cure for poisoning oneself with drink is to make your body more perfect – a better distiller."

He lets her continue – it sounds suspiciously like pseudo-science, but then he was the one who asked her about alchemy – she's not trying to foist it on him along with an expensive dieting plan.

"I worked for months on the cure – the thing that would cure my body – rid it of the effects of alcohol so that I could take care of my child. I put the finished bottle on my workbench, ready for consumption, then I bought as much alcohol as I could carry, as strong as I could find it – the quality was not important. I started to drink. I drank for four days, before I came to the terrible realisation that if I drank this medicine, I would feel better, but I would never be able to lose myself again. My drinking would be entirely without consequence. My body would resist all poisons and I would be condemned to feel the full weight of the world at all times. Whenever tragedy struck I would have no recourse to alcohol; I would be fully aware of every minute – every second. It would be an end to my escape, and I wanted that escape so badly. I wanted to be drunk and lost, so I drank more and more. More days passed. I couldn't do it – I couldn't be without alcohol's release. I needed to know that I could abandon control. I needed the drink. So I kept on drinking. For ten days."

"Ten days straight? You mean without stopping. But that isn't possible. You'd kill yourself."

Then Terry is taken completely by surprise as she quickly digs beneath her coat, rolling up her shirt to reveal a strip of belly. It's flat and looks somehow leathery. He's shocked and disgusted – even more so when she grabs his hand and, before he can protest, presses his fingers against her exposed stomach. It's leathery, but soft. He feels like he's touching some animal, like a rhinoceros, with armour beneath the surface. He pulls his hand away, feeling an intense urge to wash it.

"That is only the outside – inside is even stronger. The alchemist arms herself against life, the ravages of time, and even poisons – especially poisons. I don't easily succumb to drink."

Terry starts to speak. "But, well, you seem quite drunk now..." And then realises that perhaps she hasn't stopped drinking since she left the bar yesterday.

The woman continues her story.

"So I drank for ten days and nights and then fell asleep. When I woke up I was blind. I couldn't see anything at all, just colours, and these I saw with my eyes closed. My head was not my head any more – it was like a nest of slugs covered in salt, all being sick and dying and turning themselves inside out. I wanted to remove my head and burn it. I don't know how long it took before I could see where I was.

"I saw the preparation – the proof against all poison. It was just waiting for me to drink it. I had no power any more – no will but the desperate need to make the pain go away. In that moment I hated the alcohol I had swallowed – it was the devil, pure and simple, and in front of me was a holy grail that would destroy the devil's power. I thought I was saved, but I was not in control of my body. I slipped. The preparation fell slowly, so slowly, to the floor. Where it smashed into pieces. Bits of glass and puddles of liquid with tiny mineral lumps in it. I cried. I thought that my pain and illness would go on and on – in that moment I thought it would never end. Every stab of sickness seemed to last an infinity. I thought seriously about killing myself.

"But nature is a balance. I had already made my sacrifice – I had laboured on the cure and the cure was still there, even though I couldn't possibly drink it.

"I returned to the broken glass bottle and, very slowly, I gathered it. Somehow, with stars in front of my eyes and the devil clawing at my insides, I collected it all into a crucible, then I fuelled the furnace."

Terry listens open-mouthed, imagining a hangover stretching for days and days. He surreptitiously looks towards the bar table, hoping to find a jug of water perched on the counter for customers to help themselves to. No such luck.

She continues.

"I watched the melting glass in wonder – it was so mesmerising that it very nearly helped with the pain. Those beautiful shades of red and orange – it was a beauty that would not last. I took up my blowpipe and half-blew, half-vomited into the centre of the glass. The shattered beaker of liquid still had power, you see? It caged my sick breath – I could feel it drawing the devil out of my stomach. In alchemy there is a thing called the nigredo – the essence of corruption and dirt and shit and sickness. It has many forms, but it often originates from within the alchemist herself. Inside that glass was refined nigredo. I trapped it in there, then withdrew the pipe, buried the pipe for its taint of death, but the glass ball I made still remains."

The woman's hands describe the object: the empty area of space between them becoming a source of fascinating revulsion, with an almost physical presence.

"So uh... did you feel better afterwards?"

"The illness was gone, but I still carry something of the curse of it. I still have that thing – the ball of nigredo. Sometimes I feel the devil inside it watching me, looking back at me always, wanting to break out and get inside me again. I've tried covering it up, but it does no good – I can feel it trying to escape its prison. I have thought to bury it, but..." She pauses. "It won't let me."

Terry puts his glass down. She sits back and raises the bottle to her lips.

"You're still drinking." asks Terry.

"I can't face the world without it. That is alchemy – a balance of nature and above all, sacrifice."

"So it's a kind of philosophy?"

"If by that you mean that it has no power over the world of the senses, then no, it is not a philosophy."

He sits back in his chair. How much does he believe? That she's an alcoholic? Certainly. That she drank for ten days? Well that's less likely. That she trapped – what? A hangover in a ball? He wants to re-translate her words for her – make them more appropriate for a West European audience. *She threw up, then she felt better*, but that isn't it – that's not what she's saying. What she's saying is that she did something like magic, and he really, really wants to believe that she did.

She leaves soon afterwards, perhaps feeling, because of his silence, that she has said too much.

"What's your name, boy?" she asks before heading out into the night.

"Terry."

"Petra Fulcanelli. I..." then she thinks better of continuing, turns and is gone.

It's late by the time he finally tumbles up the creaky wooden steps and out of the bar, into the cold. He's glad to be outside. For the first time he sees the stars. At this hour even the dogs are quiet and, despite himself, he begins to feel a certain affection for this country – if he can call it that. It might just be the booze of course. He wishes Lucy were here to share the warm fuzziness with him – although she probably wouldn't approve of the company he's been keeping, or the fantasies he's indulging. Home seems a very long way away from here. A place of bricks and mortar, of families and responsibilities, of banks and jobs and lawyers and choices. Nowhere at home is there a secret art buried in age and obscurity, and his girlfriend hasn't the same air of mystery as Petra Fulcanelli.

CHAPTER 3
HUNT

"Fucking... turn it off."

It's a daily ritual. Neil wakes up and turns his music up to the volume of a teenage boy's custom-made car stereo and lets it blare for a while.

"Can't hear you, mate," shouts Neil over the din.

"Bastard."

Terry has never been good at mornings. He's used to an alarm clock he can set to snooze, submitting his daylight hours to deferral after deferral like some zealous bureaucrat yawningly turning down petitions from the sun. Now he's on military time and everybody apart from him is on a strict routine. Finally, Neil takes the satanic noise-maker with him to the shower and Terry is allowed to burrow once more into his sleeping bag.

He can half-remember a dream that came to him in the early hours. He dreamt of Petra Fulcanelli. Clearly something of her aura remained lodged in his mind, whether he believed her story or not. He thinks of plucking the dictaphone out of his coat pocket and listening back to the conversation of last night, but he feels a reluctance to subject his hands to the morning chill that lurks outside the sleeping bag. Much easier to succumb to drowsiness.

"Come on, civvy."

Neil is out of the shower now, towel wrapped around his

waist, doing pull-ups in the doorway by wrapping his fingers around the top of the frame.

"Rise and shine – time for another day of uh... whatever it is you do." The phrases are punctuated by exhalations each time his naturally hairless chin reaches the top of the door.

The 18-year-old Londoner is a constant source of amazement for Terry, as well as his polar opposite. While Terry is racked with doubt about every little decision, Neil is certain about his entire life. He's simply signed that decision over to the military. He may complain about his commanding officers, but if a lieutenant ordered him to swim through quicksand, he wouldn't hesitate. Only a couple of nights ago Terry asked Neil whether he would shoot someone if he was told to. His unblinking answer was – 'Sure'.

"Have you ever?"

"Not yet."

"What if you were ordered to shoot me?"

"Sure." Neil answered with a crocodile grin.

Terry watches the soldier's exertions.

"You should do some of these – build yourself up a bit," says Neil.

"The brain is also a muscle, my friend. And I can exercise it perfectly well from my bed."

"Only one kind of exercise I like in bed and it ain't something I do alone, you get me?"

"Uh-huh. Rather too clearly."

"Oh yeah. Unn!" Neil thrusts his towel-swaddled groin at the air, there's a flurry of clothes, and then he's gone, leaving Terry to pick himself up out of bed in a manner not unlike road-kill trying to separate itself from tarmac.

There's a parade going on. Twenty soldiers lined up for inspection with a formality that's at odds with their ramshackle surroundings. Terry heaps teaspoons high with rabbit-shit brown granules, adds lukewarm water and sits down to watch through the window of the ad-hoc cafeteria. It's a dull start to the morning, but at least he doesn't have to join in.

He looks at last week's *Valta*. Turning the page, he becomes aware of a noise. At first, it sounds like a wasp, then it takes on a bassier note, like a large hornet. At first, he examines the corners of the room, then he approaches the low window, dipping his neck to see through, and frowns into the outside world looking for the source.

As the noise grows louder the soldiers appear confused as well. One or two even look like they're ready to break formation, before Rogers gives an order that sends every soldier charging for cover. Within twenty seconds there is a gun barrel poking out from every conceivable crack in the old walls of the camp and an unearthly hush has descended on the place – just like in the Westerns when the bandits are in hiding, waiting to take a pop at a nameless gunslinger from out of town.

Should he be doing something? Calling somebody? Maybe getting away from the window, where he remains, nose pressed to the icy glass with an undignified oval of condensation covering his mouth? It's not a clever place to be standing if there's an actual threat in the yard. Nevertheless, he stays there, frozen with indecision.

And then it appears – a thing so outlandish that it would be impossible to deny its reality. The thing that emerges from the chilly greys and browns is like a space-age dragon, fire-engine red with two enormous chrome pipes blasting out of the back – almost a caricature of a vehicle. The trike grinds to a halt just in front of the camp, its engine whirring down and down, dwindling to a gritty hum before finally stopping altogether. The silence crashes in as if the dam keeping it back has suddenly collapsed.

The rider deftly swings off the saddle and plants a pair of heavy boots in the snow. Their provenance, like that of the trike, is clearly a long way from Izvalta. They aren't made from a sheep, and they haven't been patched once. The rider briefly turns to inspect his thick tyres, apparently unaware of the twenty-odd pairs of eyes currently fixed on him. Finally, he removes his helmet, revealing an unexpectedly elderly man with a thick black beard.

In a split-second, soldiers are everywhere and for perhaps the first time, Terry feels truly afraid of the people whose company he has shared for the last week. Here then, is the long, precise reach of a global power; a scalpel with its tip penetrating the heart of this remote enclave, a dissecting blade made up of men. The window doesn't feel like it would offer much protection if they turned against him. The visitor is not nearly as impressed. He regards them coolly, with an expression that suggests that he knows whose hand grips the other end of that scalpel.

"At ease, gentlemen."

Rogers steps forward with a jovial handshake. "Your Highness! Gentlemen, this is King Monterek – our host – and our guest", he says. "You had us going there – not your standard Kawasaki is it?"

"I like my vehicles massive and powerful. I want a tank driver to shit himself looking at it. No, it's not a fucking Kawasaki."

"Coffee?"

"Thanks," says King Monterek.

Monterek is stoutly athletic, speaks with the Oxbridge eloquence of a Tory politician and clearly has the lack of morals to go with it. Terry pictures him dressed as Henry the eighth. He's full of bravado, of drunken stories, of bawdy tales about women he's slept with and people he's punched in the face with his dull, meaty fists. The guys love him, he's a man's man. Exactly the kind of person to make Terry feel uncomfortable.

Eventually the king works his way around to the matter at hand. "I'm glad you gentlemen are in the neighbourhood" he says, standing full upright, gesturing with his coffee mug. "Because I have *un petit projet* for you. My castle, you see, overlooks a patch of woodland we call the 'bear forest'. For the most part that's a local joke: the biggest beast I ever saw in there was a chipmunk – and not an uncommonly large one. But just last night I was watching the sun setting from my balcony – a truly formidable sight – blood red and almost pulsing like the beating heart of God. Basking in this ominous glory I glanced down at the land below. At the edge of the forest, was a big, fat, juicy bear. Fully 300 kilos of muscle – the biggest I've seen in ten years.

"He saw me looking at him, he looks up at me and I say to him, mouthing the words, 'I am going to eat you,' and I swear he must have understood because he stood there. Stock still. And shat himself."

Cue laughter, while the king pauses to take a swig of coffee. "Well, I did think to take a pop at him with the Dragunov – quality rifle, by the way – sometimes it does pay to shop locally – but he could see what was coming; scurried back into the woods.

"So I intend to track him down and shoot him as promised. I see it as my duty to impose something of a natural order – the supremacy of man over beast, and what better way to do that than to kill and consume? I was just wondering if there might be one or two hearty men who could be spared for the hunt."

Rogers' eyes light up like great whirling Catherine wheels, while the body of soldiers stirs in an excited murmur. The king, however, isn't looking towards them. His steady eyes under their wiry brows are aimed directly at Terry, who has long since emerged from the cafeteria.

"This young fellow. Yes, you my boy. What's your name and function? I note your lack of military regalia, so what are you? An embedded journalist documenting our fine country? Or a chef? Or perhaps your uniform is in the wash." He chuckles to himself while Rogers tries to cover his irritation at Terry's continued presence on the face of the planet.

"Uh. This... This is our translator, Morton," he says, and the king's smile is replaced by a frown.

"Vrasj unok Izvaltej?"

"Um. I'm not a very good translator." Terry's cheeks go the colour of beetroot.

"He's working on it," says Rogers.

"Why in God's name do you have a translator? Izvaltese is practically a dead language – of historical interest only."

"But what about the part of the population that doesn't speak English?" asks Terry.

In the military you keep your mouth shut. In front of royalty you keep your mouth shut. When standing in between military and royalty, with no more reason to be there than a goldfish has to be in the middle of the ocean, it's best to shut the fuck up. If Rogers' glare and Monterek's silence could have spoken, that's exactly what they would have said. After several loud heartbeats, the king generously puts Terry out of his misery.

"The more retrogressive commoners of Svart are hardly worth talking to. If they cling to their idiotic language that's their business, but one should expect nothing from them but ludicrous folk tales. Even from the fifties I saw quite clearly that the future was global, that we had to attract international interest, that we had to promote tourism and Western values in our beautiful homeland. We had to escape the narrow-minded communist dystopia that had taken hold around us, so I built schools and authored a programme of education for the poor, stupid people of

Izvalta.

"In that single move, I gave them a real future, although I freely admit that many struggle to understand it. By all means you may try to speak to some of the old peasants, but you might as well try talking to a pig."

Rogers clears his throat. "Yes – well to be honest he's a temporary addition. Could be called back at any moment."

Terry can't mistake the threatening note in his voice.

"You were saying about this hunt?" Rogers says.

Monterek is adjusting his gloves, and answers almost absent-mindedly. "Yes I'll take the boy."

"I'm sorry?"

"The boy. Mister Moron, did you say? No sorry – forgive *mon petit blague*. Mister Morton. If he doesn't manage to alert the bear with his wagging tongue, we may just catch the bugger."

"Are you quite sure? I mean..."

"Good Lord, it must be spreading. This mania for questioning monarchs. And I thought you were true Brits."

Rogers is silent.

"Well I must get going – preparations for the hunt, you know." As he revs his noisy trike to leave, the king yells to Terry. "You will be at the entrance to the bear forest in exactly four hours." And then the world is swallowed by the trike's din.

Only Neil grins at Terry as the soldiers file past.

"Lucky dipshit," he says. "Best scarper 'fore Rogers cuts off yer trigger finger."

It's advice Terry is only too happy to take. In fact, he takes it even further than strictly necessary, heading out into the city and staying well away from any street where he might be seen by human eyes. It's down one of the less travelled passageways that he almost literally stumbles across what must be Izvalta's only museum.

The bony lady who ushers him in insists on giving him the full tour, first pulling aside the moth-eaten drapes that have preserved the artefacts from the sun, but which, once moved aside, shroud the whole room in dust. Between the woman's heavy accent and her coughing, the tour is rather incomprehensible.

Terry notes with a slight grin the irony of some exhibits: the entire agricultural section is actually full of tools the Izvaltans currently use out in the fields. As far as the farmers are concerned, scythes and horse-drawn carts are contemporary technology – it's rather bizarre to pay to see them hung on a wall when in three out of four seasons you could wander into the fields and see them demonstrated for free.

Between coughs, Terry's guide points out to him a set of boards written in passable English that explain the origins of Izvalta, which she then proceeds to describe, rendering the boards unnecessary.

"Izvalta, you see here, founded in sixteen century." She coughs. "Of course, Izvalta exists before, but was not called Izvalta – called something different no-one knows."

She moves to the next board. "This man Lazari. Turkish man in sixteen Century. His friends from the empire Ottomanizu, they attack other towns – towns sell wheat and barley and uh... beer!

"But this Lazari. He is get lost in the Carpaticu and he come to valley. He say 'what is this very nice place?'" Her proud smile is broken by a few more racking coughs, but she ploughs on.

"This valley is Izvalta, but not yet! Lazari, he meets old Kristianitz teacher who teaches him to see... uh... niceness in this valley and tell him 'convert to Kristianitz – Kristianitz is all about nice'. So he does this, and God tells this Lazari that Lazari is king of this place."

"An unintended consequence then?" asks Terry with a smile.

The woman looks back at him blankly until he asks her politely to continue.

"Lazari now called this place Izvalta. All kings of Izvalta until today are descend from this first Lazari."

"You mean they're all Turkish?"

"All Izvaltan."

Terry scans a string of miniature portraits of Izvalta's kings – a row of dour Turkish faces with perfectly groomed moustaches, none of them quite resembling the Moses-like Monterek with whom he is dreading spending the afternoon. Couldn't he hole up in this little museum for the rest of the day? Maybe even until everybody has forgotten about the bear and the hunting trip.

Terry kicks himself for having even made eye contact with Monterek. Why couldn't he just bow and scrape and get passed over – rather than get picked out of a crowd of guys that all clearly wanted to hunt a bear. Just so that the king can toy with him in his discomfort, and probably make him do something like lure this fucking monster bear out into the open. Maybe they'll tie him up and dangle him from a tree like bait. Maybe Monterek thought, 'he's thin – he'll make a good toothpick'.

Maybe he should have just done what everyone else does and grape-shat out CVs and applications to any employer willing to give him a start, no matter whether it was a start waiting tables or clipping OAP toenails. Or maybe he should have acted grateful in the two interviews he did get. Maybe that fawning attitude would have got him either of those shitty data-entry-data-aggregation jobs – and got him out of being noticed by the biggest prick in this entire country. Not that it's a big country, but still.

The guide is looking at him with concern, evidently wondering why her one customer has so suddenly glazed over.

"Is the Izvaltese language originally Turkish as well?" he

asks.

She laughs with rather more gusto than seems appropriate. "No! Not Turkish at all."

"But it's nothing like Romanian."

"Actually, they are originally same." She points to a painting of a huge gate spanning the narrow gap between two steep valley sides. "This is painting without date, but probably is two-hundred years old. It shows gate separate Izvalta from outside world. Our customs, culture, language are all um... treasured? Safe! Behind this wall. 1870 around – wall comes down, we see that Romania has completely different alphabet!"

And finally Terry is given his first real lesson on the language he's supposed to be learning, though he does have to piece it together a bit.

Romania switched from the Cyrillic to the Latin alphabet in the late 1800s. Izvalta kept Cyrillic, but local changes in speech had also added or changed words, making Izvaltese completely different from Romanian. For instance, Izvaltans started to use family names for many things: the word for bread came from the chief baker's family and the word for shepherd – 'Grujnod' – was the name of a famous shepherd who had once outwitted a persistent wolf by dressing up as a sheep and leading it into a trap.

Terry gazes around the walls, suddenly aware of the potential historical significance of each item. This museum is precisely the place to start studying this country. It's not a textbook, but it is a breakthrough. Finally, he has a direction.

And it's abruptly taken away from him as the guide quickly draws the dusty curtains and announces closing time.

"But it's barely eleven." Terry protests.

"Early closing today. There is party at the castle. But you know this."

"Um... Sorry? What party?"

"Monterek party. Party of the bear. Everyone is going. Especially foreigners – you are honour guests."

"I don't think I've been invited."

"Of course you are. Have a nice day. Have fun at party!" she says, ushering him out of the door and up the stairs that lead out of the museum.

Almost before he knows it, he's outside, the door has chunked shut behind him and he's pulling his coat tightly shut against the cold. An unnatural quiet has settled on the city of Svart. There's not a soul to be seen, let alone an open café. The eerie silence puts him on edge, his eyes shift restlessly between closed doors and shuttered windows, imagining at each one a veiled figure peering out at the lone wanderer on the street. According to the town clock he's still got about two hours before he has to be at the woods. He'd rather spend that time inside, but he's not going back to the camp. He'd rather brave the cold.

By the time the king and his retinue approach, Terry's arse is practically frozen to a rock. All of them, the king included, are clad in well-tailored camouflage gear with matching caps. In their hands, matt black rifles that manage to look far deadlier than the machine guns carried around by the soldiers in the camp. With a little difficulty he stands, increasingly nervous at being the only Brit on this trip. What if they don't have bears here at all? What if that's just a code for hunting tourists? His mother would miss him, and Lucy, but who else? *Oh Christ*, he thinks.

The king is not smiling, and Terry remembers at the last minute that he should perhaps bow. He does so, awkwardly, which elicits a small snort from the king. When Terry looks up, Monterek is shaking his head, and his fellow hunters, each of them well over six-feet-tall and built like bulldogs, are smirking.

"Get up, stand up, greenhorn. Welcome to the hunt." His tone is not as caustic as it was before. "At ease, my good translator. I note that you might have prepared a little better – for instance, you might have thought to wear a different colour."

Terry notices only now that his coat is blue. Not an aggressively light ski-slope shade, but certainly visible – especially against the trees. He's screwed up; his heart sticks in his throat. What will this mean? Some kind of punishment or forfeit? Or if he's implausibly lucky, maybe he'll just get to go back to the camp, where guns and despots are just a shade more predictable.

"No matter. Keep quiet and you should be fine. It will serve as excellent practice for you. The art of not being seen." He chuckles to himself, then turns to the other hunters and nods, and together they stride into the forest slipping through the dense wilderness with the elegance of dancers. Terry follows at Monterek's heels, somewhat less elegantly.

"So. Translator, eh?"

"Yes, sir. Your Majesty."

"Let us dispense with the formalities, shall we, boy? Please do call me Monty. And this is Savis, Yeven and Gorsk."

The tall men nod with smiles that seem genuine.

"Terry. I'm Terry."

"*Bien*, Terry. And how are you enjoying our fair little country so far?"

"Oh, it's lovely. You know – cold, but..."

"And your lodgings – your camp? Is that comfortable for you?"

"Well I wouldn't say comfortable as such."

"What would you say? Come on, my lad – we're hunting partners, and Gorsk loves to gossip."

"It's true," Gorsk admits, showing three gold teeth as he grins.

"Worse than your wife," chimes in Savis, amicably.

'Monty' looks at Terry expectantly.

"Um... Well it's a bit of a dump," he concedes, at which the king roars with guttural laughter guaranteed to scare off any bears in the vicinity, not that that seems to matter.

"Oh my boy. Yes. Yes, it's a dump. I'm glad you noticed. I mean, there are far lovelier places in Svart. The British could be at Gorsk's wife's hotel for example. Beautiful place. Never understood why soldiers would insist on camping. Ludicrous, *non*?"

The conversation continues in this vein as they tramp along the thin, winding paths through the wood. To his surprise, Terry actually begins to enjoy himself. The king's new relaxed alter ego is affable and encouraging, as if he genuinely wants to hear about Terry's troubles: the girl back in England, her overbearing father, 'the eternal buggery of the job market' (everyone laughs at this). After half an hour they don't seem to be any closer to finding a bear until in a mossy clearing, Yeven, the quietest of the three hunters, stops to examine something on the ground.

Silently he nods in the direction of the tree line and the other hunters become serious, readying their weapons. Monterek's hand is clamped around Terry's forearm – the hand is big enough to easily encircle it. He's close enough that Terry can smell sour coffee on his breath and feel his prickling beard against his skin as he whispers into Terry's ear.

"Stay here. Don't move. No questions. We handle the rest." And they're gone – all of them. Not one so much as turns around to see that he's understood.

Terry is relieved to be alone. He exhales, then taps his pockets for a cigarette that he doesn't have. He looks around, sees a fallen tree, not too rotten, kicks it first to drive out any hidden bugs, and sits. There's not so much snow here, but where there is, there are hundreds of tracks made by birds and – a deer, probably. No bear tracks though – he's sure he'd recognise those. And thank fuck, because the last thing he wants to see close up is a bear. He closes his eyes and forgets he's even part of this landscape.

Instead, he's at home on one of the rare winters when snow muffles the sound of the cars, and he can sit in his parents' back garden and be alone with the universe. He could go inside and sit with Lucy, put his arms around her and watch some old film with John Cusack in it. Snow, quiet, comfort.

There's a sound, muted like the hiss after the crash of a wave. It comes again and again in irregular patterns, and Terry's eyes drift open. On the far edge of the clearing is the bear.

It's big, Terry thinks – but of course it's big. He's never seen a bear before – not even at the zoo – so all he has to compare this to is a picture-book version of a bear, maybe one robbing honey from a beehive. The size is not the only departure from the picture-book bear though. This animal also looks frightened. Patches of its fur are worn through so that the skin beneath is exposed. They look more like marks of sickness than battle scars. But these observations are made by Terry after the fact, while reviewing his memories of the scene. His immediate reaction is simply to back slowly away, hoping the bear hasn't spotted him yet.

As soon as he moves, the bear's eyes fix on him. They don't look friendly. The bear takes a flurry of steps into the centre of the clearing, sending snow hissing across snow. It's maybe 15 feet away now, and Terry finds he can't move. Make himself big, climb a tree, run at it, run away from it, pick up a stick, don't pick up a stick, throw food towards it maybe – but he doesn't have any bloody food. He's had so much advice about what to do if a bear shows up, why doesn't he remember any of it? Why didn't sodding King-of-the-hunt Monterek tell him?

Just as he's deciding on the foetal position, a twig snaps on the other side of the clearing. The bear's head swivels, and then falls forward as its body is wrapped around a bullet. The sound of the shot appears to come later. The bear staggers away from Terry, towards the crunch of shoes emerging from the forest. Monterek is first, calmly returning his rifle to his back and pulling out a pistol, with which he shoots the bear in the head, practically without breaking stride.

When Monterek's hand comes to rest on Terry's shoulder, Terry's eyes are still fixed on the bear bloodying the snow.

"Good hunt, my lad. Were you scared?"

Terry looks up from his squat position, arse still suspended in the air just above the fallen tree, still preparing to run or curl up or climb something.

"Uh-huh." is all he can manage.

"Well," says the king, adjusting his gloves, "it's a frightening prospect, being almost eaten by a vicious animal. Especially one of that size, eh? Frightening." He repeats. "One might say you're lucky that someone was looking out for you."

"Oh. Yes. Yes," says Terry, realising that a response is expected. "I'm very grateful, Monty."

"Your Majesty would be more apt."

"I'm very grateful, um... Your Majesty."

The king nods meaningfully. "Remember that." He commands. Terry feels numb. Grateful, certainly, but also disorientated, confused. The bear lies in a heap of blood and fur on the snow. Seeing it coolly dispatched, it's clear to him what he really has to fear: not the local wildlife, but Monterek himself.

"Now, my boy. One or two *petit questions* for you." The king leads Terry away from the bear's gunned-down corpse as the other hunters busy themselves trussing and strapping it to long sticks. In a haze, he finds himself describing in detail the layout of the soldiers' camp: the bunks, the cafeteria, the few outbuildings whose real purpose he doesn't know, but which are always locked and guarded. In his mind they're still just full of potatoes. He describes Captain Rogers, embellishing the description with his own personal feelings towards the man. By the time they reach the edge of the woods, there is nothing left for Terry to tell. Later, when the shock is over, Terry will realise the extent to which he's been played, but with the powerful presence of a king walking with him, one proprietorial hand on Terry's shoulder, he's not really capable of much else.

He makes for an easy mark, but not a particularly useful one, and the king's follow-up questions are met with a blank, apologetic look, until, with a note of frustration, Monterek speaks.

"You don't seem to know anything, nor do you have a particular function. One might ask what the fuck you're doing here."

"I don't know."

"No. No you don't, do you?" And with that, the king's interest in Terry disappears, sculpted over as if it was never there at all.

When they reach the edge of the wood, they are greeted by a crowd of cheering locals – at least they look like locals, but they're wearing the kind of clothes Terry's only seen in Izvalta inside souvenir shops. Everybody, young and old, has ditched their synthetic coats and is clad in intricate black and red stitched tunics with white lace collars. They appear less like modern-day peasants and more like an organised cult.

The bear carcass is strapped to the back of the king's trike, but is so huge that the head hangs forward and trails on the ground where, as the king drives off, it is repeatedly bludgeoned by the road. In a daze, Terry follows the procession up to the high town, watching as the bear's head is gradually distorted. Looking behind him down the road he sees how the trail of blood and bits of bear meat have attracted the bony animals of the lower town to come and lick at the cobbles, digging eager tongues down between the cracks.

At the top of the street the castle stands waiting to receive the dead, its spike-topped gates flung wide as the gates of Hell.

Someone punches him in the shoulder. One of those matey punches he's never received from a real mate.

"Lucky twat," says Neil. "How was it? Who shot it? Bet it weren't you. I'da been like bambambam – sucka!"

"Fuck off, Neil."

"Ooh, pissed yer pants did ya? Fuckin' wuss."

They press through the castle gates between indomitable 30-foot walls, where they become part of a churning mass of bodies dancing to discordant music: trumpets, drums, and string instruments of various designs all join into a frenzy of noise that ricochets around the stout stone courtyard, while the patterned locals gyrate in a perplexing array of movements.

Terry and the soldiers are processed through the courtyard and ushered into an enormous chandelier-lit hall. From the walls peer a gallery of stern, bristly-browed old men, each with a perfectly groomed and identical moustache. Terry recognises them as Monterek's ancestors from their likenesses in the museum. The whole room is dominated by a vast gold throne at one end, but even at a distance Terry can tell it's not made from the same material as the church's uncanny golden sculpture.

The king isn't sitting on his throne – instead he's standing on a massive wood table running the length of the hall. The bear's carcass lies at the king's feet, its head on a bloodied board, with its tongue lolling out, grotesque and alien, like it doesn't belong. Monterek, grinning like the devil himself, hefts a great axe, swinging it easily upward with one hand and rests it on his shoulder. He appears to Terry like something between a medieval warlord and a living Paul Bunyan statue.

"Ladies and gentlemen," bawls the king, with a voice that spits like roasting fat. He proceeds to tell the tale of how this bear came to die. Despite himself, Terry listens attentively to the heroic tale, waiting for the king to mention his name, or at least to acknowledge his existence. He never does. The story is a fantasy out of the pages of a children's book. To hear it told, one might think this was no bear but a dragon, terrifying beyond mortal comprehension – a beast that had decimated the tiny country with its infernal cunning, lust for destruction and breath of poisonous fire. He can still see the patches of mangy fur on the dead bear, though nobody else seems to have noticed.

The king draws to a close. "And just as today I have slain this bear as I promised, so too shall I slay any enemy of Izvalta." With this he takes a mighty swing at the bear's thickly limp neck.

There is a sickening liquid crunch as the battered head leaves the battered body, followed by a whoop of primal animal joy from all around the great hall. Terry turns away as the Izvaltans break into song – not in English, because what English song is appropriate to the slaughter of a bear? The soldiers join in with their own words, but it's all too much for Terry – he pushes through the smiling crowd and busies himself with finding some strong alcohol while the butchery continues.

His eyes glaze over as he watches the bear being dissected and distributed across a number of spits. With a cry of joy, the spit-bearers charge out of the hall, coming dangerously close to spearing several locals in the rush, and into the courtyard, where a huge bonfire has been lit. Terry can feel its heat from the furthest corner of the courtyard. He finds himself something of a sanctuary there – a vantage point from which he can watch the mad dance, which grinds away like some hellish piece of clockwork, each component made of humanity.

From this slight remove, Terry styles himself an anthropologist observing a truly local custom. However, looking up from his imaginary notebook he sees a couple of oddities in this gathering – each one mundane in itself but potentially revealing when put together. The first: not all of the inhabitants of the city are here – if the king had invited everybody in Svart to his feast, a single bear, no matter how gargantuan, would never be enough to go around. The second: everybody here is speaking perfect English – there's no sign of the men from the pub, no toothless old geezers of the kind you see everywhere in the lower town and beyond – just the bright, healthy faces of what passes for privilege in Izvalta.

He begins a scholarly article in his head. *In Izvalta, language is all about class. The country is divided physically, culturally and linguistically, (much like any other country). Those who live in the high town work in privileged industries, make more money, look healthier and they are taught to speak English; while the peons of the low town and countryside are considered beneath culture, beneath teaching. They wallow in old words and old traditions. The irony is that at this party, everyone is wearing 'traditional' dress – a fanciful hearkening back to the way things used to be for simple peasants leading simple lives, but those old ways still exist not half a mile away.*

Monterek bursts into the crowd wearing the bear's skin. The frenzy increases immediately. There are pops and bangs and toasts and shouted songs. The music is deafening; it feels like there are a thousand trumpets and drums trying to effect a forcible entry into Terry's ears, and his attempt to distance himself from the world in front of him is shot. Before he realises it, he's being taken by the hand and led into the fray. The hand that grasps his belongs to a girl whose black hair swishes in front of him, scenting the air with a flowery perfume. He thinks of Lucy and wonders if he should be resisting the tug on his arm, and the thought doesn't disappear when the girl turns around, fixes him with her green eyes and begins to dance. A combination of music and alcohol and the girl compel him to forget almost everything: questions of social order, the soldiers and their unstated mission, Lucy and her father, the alchemist and her woes, Monterek's hand on Terry's shoulder.

As the party continues, wedges of unconsciousness crowd in behind his eyes. Whenever they re-open and the world rushes back, what he sees is horrifyingly vivid. The girl is gone and he's in a crowd of Izvaltans all singing and shouting in heavily accented English. The soldiers are teaching them to sing 'Rule Britannia'.

At some point he experiences a moment of real clarity and becomes very aware of himself, aware of his drunkenness, and his need to be away from the castle. He plunges through the bands and the dancers. Eyes follow him. Captain Rogers, Neil, an old man chewing on a monstrous bone.

In the open night beyond the castle wall, his mind calms itself a little. There are islets of people dotted around the castle square, cigarettes in their mouths, huddling around the tiny flames of lighters like desperate cavemen in the chill. Terry accepts a cigarette from one of the groups. It tastes like rolled cardboard, but it's comforting. Grounding. Once again, he feels time slow to a manageable speed and he finally begins a graceless downhill lollop towards his bed.

It's the sight of the grotesque sign for the bar that makes him pause in his stumbling route. The bar door squeaks open, a shaft of light opens up onto the street, and into it steps a figure clad in a heavy woollen coat. She quickly ascends the steps and disappears into an alley a few yards away without so much as a glance in Terry's direction. In the cold air he smells the wood-smoke scent she leaves behind her.

He's not sure what it is that makes him follow her, although the alcohol certainly plays its part. It starts out as a half-formed plan to at least see the place where she lives, to fill out a little more of the mystery of this woman.

He half-runs across the market square and crunches and slips down the snow-covered cobbles until he catches sight of her again. When he finally does, she's at the other end of a dark tunnel of houses. He hadn't appreciated before how dark a city can be when there are no street lamps. The hard angles swallow the light the way a desert swallows water. He steps carefully now, painfully aware that his most careful steps are still likely to land him on his backside.

Ahead of him the alchemist's shadow disappears around a corner. Worried that he might lose her, he breaks into a run, keeping to the sides of the road where the snow is less trodden and so less slick with ice. It's also the part of the road most hidden from sight and he very nearly trips over a sleeping dog, which sits up and issues a warning growl. By the time Terry reaches the point where the alchemist disappeared from view, she is nowhere to be seen, though there is only one path that clearly leads away from the city centre. He takes that path, feeling completely lost and wondering whether he could even find his way back to the bar at this point. He's filled with a false sense of relief as he reaches the end of the alley and is spat out into a bright blue snow-covered forest. There is no sign of Madame Fulcanelli, but the little path through the trees is the only route available from here, so he sets out, drunk and determined.

The snow is deep and Terry's boots sink straight through the thin surface crust, and he's soon wading shin-deep. A hundred yards or so from the alley's exit it finally occurs to him that she must have left tracks. He pans a weak pocket torch around the surroundings but can't see any indication that another person has passed this way – ever. While his footprints are obvious, the alchemist's are nowhere to be seen. Of course that doesn't mean that she didn't pass this way – she could have taken a route through the woods to the right or left. As if to answer his speculation, a twig snaps up ahead.

Terry's head swivels, and he illuminates the forest with the meagre torchlight, smudging the hard edges of the long black shadows cast by the moon.

"Okay – I'll try going through the forest." He says the words out loud as if to establish his own certainty. He wades to the tree line, where he does find shallower snow and a kind of path, although whether it's a regular thoroughfare for people coming and going to the alchemist's house or a well-used animal track is not clear. He carries on, only a vague recollection of a reason driving him now, swaddled as he is against the cold and against coherent thought, with a blanket of tzuica.

Time passes – he can't tell how much as he has no watch or phone, and before long another of the tzuica's side-effects makes itself known: he's desperate for the toilet. Transferring his torch to his mouth, he walks a little way off the track, leans against a tree and unzips.

He is midstream when he hears a noise behind him. A growl. Not dissimilar to that of the sleeping dog, but far more unnerving – especially out here in the dark, far from any possible owner. He jerks his head around and the torch in his mouth illuminates a pair of animal eyes that contract in the light, narrowing into thin, evil-looking slits.

Terry suddenly finds himself very sober and utterly helpless. Behind him is the first wolf he's ever seen and it may well be the last. In some recess of his mind, one that's less afflicted with primal terror, he wonders if perhaps King Monterek is in the bushes, ready to dispatch another wild animal at Terry's feet. His right hand is still directing a stream of urine that thudders into the snow far too loudly. In yet another corner of his mind, he wonders whether he'll be allowed to finish peeing before the wolf attacks.

The animal bares its teeth, which shine ghostly white in the moonlight, then leaps at Terry's throat.

CHAPTER 4
ELZE

Elze is eight years old when, on a beautifully clear September day, she sees the stranger crossing the fields. The first thing she notices about the stranger are his drab grey clothes. The high collar looks out of place in the sunshine. He's tall and thin, with hair that tumbles a long way down his back the way Elze's mother's does, though his hair is white and hers is brown. It looks odd on a man, especially alongside his pointed white beard, which is a bit like a goat's.

Elze watches him as he strides across the fields, jumping a stream and weaving through a patch of walnut trees, where he briefly stops to gather a pocketful of the fallen nuts. He seems so confident in a wondering way, like a child – in an old man's body – out exploring. He passes out of view, but Elze keeps hold of his picture in her mind.

And then, because the stranger is a stranger, and she is a child, she enters him into her own mythology. There is a story her mother used to read to her and her sister every night before bedtime. It was a simple story about a girl who was captured by an evil wizard. Most of the story was actually about a handsome farm boy who came to rescue the girl, fighting his way through a forest of monsters to get to the high tower where she was locked away. In the book he defeated the wizard by dropping a chandelier on his head, then took the girl back home. Supposedly she was happy about it.

After perhaps the fifth time she heard the story, Elze stopped listening to the bit about the farm boy. In her version of the story, the girl had no interest in him. When she was abducted and brought to the wizard's tower, so dark and full of intrigue, she was really very grateful. She learned all kinds of spells from the wizard with which she could go amongst the common people, helping them and solving their problems. She explored the dark forest and discovered hundreds of new species of animals and other creatures, wondrous in their diversity. If Elze remembered the boy at all in her version, he would appear as a dim-witted idiot who invariably crushed the smaller creatures underfoot or killed them carelessly with his sword without even trying to talk to them. In her version, the girl dropped the chandelier on the boy, and she and the wizard lived happily ever after.

Once she learned to read, Elze got hold of the book and, with a thick black pencil, crossed out most of the words. Her sister complained to their mother and Elze was locked in the cupboard for three hours as punishment. She never picked up the book again, but she didn't need to: the story had rooted itself inside her head instead.

Something about the stranger crossing the fields makes her think of the wizard from that story: *her* wizard, surrounded by the aura of infinite possibility.

As she explores the woods, she imagines that he's there helping her. She's hunting for creatures – the kind that the casual observer might miss. They may be very small – so small that she almost has to cross her eyes to see them; or they may be easily visible, but only once they move. She lifts up every dead leaf, every mushroom cup and every patch of flaking tree bark to subject their undersides to close scrutiny.

She isn't allowed to take her pencils out into the forest where, according to her mother, she would certainly lose them. So when she finds new creatures, she remembers them, noting their shapes and the number of legs and feelers and armoured scales and colour, so that later she can draw a picture for her grandfather and he can tell her what it is.

She's careful not to try to remember too many shapes at once. She recalls the time she tried to memorise seven in one go, and when she drew them several ended up confused, with pincers in the wrong place and armour plates where long hairs should have been.

She has three in her head, nice and clear. A blue beetle about the length of her finger with patches of black and long antennae; a very furry butterfly almost like a moth but with orange wings with lots of little circles on the tips; and lastly a fat black beetle about as big as her fingernail, with spindly legs and two bronze patches on the shell. She sets off back home at a run.

The village boys are still where they were when she set out, playing soldiers in the yard. Their clothes are scuffed with dirty greens and browns, their faces lit up with satisfaction at the 'klop' noises made by their wooden swords as they come together. The boys are silly, though Elze's younger sister seems to like them. Sometimes she'll even try to offer herself up as a maiden to be rescued. Usually they tell her to go away and sew something, which she usually does.

As Elze approaches her house, the carefree day is brought to a sudden end. The birdsong is broken by a strangled wail emanating from the high town. Elze stops and stares up in the direction of the castle. The noise doesn't abate – instead another voice joins it, then another. The cry sweeps slowly down through the valley until it can be heard just across the field. She sees the women there clutching their hands to their breasts, bringing forth streams of tears as if they've been putting them aside for this very occasion. She jumps out of her skin when behind her, her mother too howls with a sorrow so instantaneous it seems ghostly. Elze is confused and disturbed. What is happening? Is it magic? It seems such a lovely day that to her all this weeping is quite intolerable and with all the certainty that a little girl can muster, she frowns at her bawling mother, only to be clipped sternly behind the ear by her father. He stands above her, casting a forbidding shadow over her.

"Cry," he says.

"But Daddy, I don't want to." She receives another clip around the ear. That does the trick. She starts with a sniffle, then as she realises that the adult world just doesn't want her to be happy and her daddy doesn't really love her – he just wants to make her sad – she lets loose a waterfall, wrenches at her hair and howls at the sky like a wolf. Her father turns to look at the castle in the distance, where the cries echo off the surrounding mountains and double back into the valley. The weeping carries on into the night.

When she is allowed to stop, she goes to find the only adult she trusts.

"Grandfather?"

The room is mostly dark, with only a small window illuminating his carved wooden trinkets and his faded map of the world. He's in his chair, but she can't see whether he's asleep or not.

"Come in, my dear," he says. He doesn't sound in the least bit sleepy.

"Grandpa, I had some insects to draw for you, but then everyone started crying and now I can't remember them."

"Not to worry, my dear. You'll find them again. Did I not teach you the best tracking skills?"

"You did. But why did I have to cry and the boys didn't? That's not fair." She doesn't tell him that not only did they not cry, but her neighbour Ivan even pointed and laughed at her while continuing to play his game, which actually made crying feel a little more natural.

"You're right. I think those boys should have wept with the rest of the country. The king is dead, after all."

"Oh."

"Did nobody tell you?"

"No."

"He was a great man. It's important to mark his passing. I hope his son will be as wise."

"I'm sure he will."

"You have such faith, my girl. I should warn you: people aren't always clever and good. In the forest it's much simpler. Everything behaves as it should. In the human world it's hard to tell who's really a wolf and who's a deer."

"Or a pink grasshopper?"

The old man laughs. "Oh, they're much easier to identify. But I've only ever met the one."

A few days later Elze's father is carrying her on his back as they walk up the slope to the high town. He seems to have forgiven her for not crying on cue and once more everything is right with the world. Elze likes the high town – she likes seeing all the people there with their nice brightly-coloured clothes and the stone buildings and spires, though she knows she'll never live amongst them as this part of Izvalta is only for kings and rich people and her family is not rich.

There are more people in the high town than she's ever seen in her life. It looks like the whole country is here, packed into a very small area. She sees an angry-looking man – he must be a foreigner – a merchant or something – because he's dressed differently and he's the only one here who's angry. His horse and cart are stuck in the crowd, and he's furiously gesticulating at the people to get out of the way. The people are just smiling back at him, trying to fling garlands of wild flowers over his head like a hoop-throw. Some are feeding his horse with treats from their pockets. He's not getting anywhere. She wonders if this man has anything to do with the stranger from the field.

When the castle gates open there is a cheer that's so loud that Elze has to put her fingers in her ears. From the stone walls spills a procession of people wearing dazzling clothes, all picked out in gold, and ceremonial hats. They carry intricately carved wooden pole things and long-stemmed gold crosses, chanting words that she can't make out. They walk very slowly and, in contrast to the rest of the crowd, they look very serious. Behind them, four strong men are carrying a big gold chair and this seems to be the main attraction. Everyone goes crazy when it appears, but the person sitting on the chair is just a kid about the same age as Elze.

She looks very carefully at the boy being carried on the chair. He doesn't look that different from any of the boys in her village, apart from the fact that he's cleaner and better dressed. He has the same thick black mop of hair as practically everyone else in Svart; the same puffy cheeks. She's confused: why does he get a golden chair? This must be a game they play in the high town, like the games the village boys play, except in the high town the grown-ups join in. This is exactly like the game where one of them shouts 'I'm the king' and everybody else pretends to be his servants or his soldiers and they go away to slay dragons in his name. But everyone seems to be taking this game very seriously.

Elze looks down at her father and sees that he is cheering with the rest of the crowd. If she's learnt anything from the other day it's that she's expected to do the same as everybody else – all the other girls at least – so she overcomes her misgivings and joins in, although a little half-heartedly, as the new king passes by on his way to the church and his coronation.

When she and her father return home they go straight back to their old routine. The harvest continues as it did the previous year and Elze helps her mother in the kitchen just as she always has since she was old enough. Having a new king doesn't seem to have changed anything, so it's hard to see what all the fuss was about.

For Elze the real news reaches her a few nights later. Her father has just returned from the local tavern, and is talking loudly, as he often does when he comes back from there, about a foreigner 'who claims to be able to cure all illnesses and make people live forever!'. Elze and her sister listen from their beds upstairs, where they can hear most of the conversation below.

"But of course," her father is saying, "that doesn't apply to us – he's only interested in keeping certain people alive, isn't he? The rich ones specifically!"

"It's a shame he couldn't have been here in time to cure King Marek." Elze's mother says, in a rather quieter tone that Elze has to strain to hear.

"Ha! Well, that's who he came here for – so he says. Convenient that he arrived too late though, isn't it?"

"How is that convenient?"

"It's not convenient for us – it's convenient for him. Now he says he *would* have cured King Marek, but if anyone else gets ill, tough luck."

"But he is a doctor, yes?"

"Well, no." Her father sounds a little less certain. "I think he's something else – now what was it? An alchemist! That was what they were calling him."

"Sounds suspicious to me. If he's a doctor, why doesn't he call himself a doctor, and what kind of a doctor doesn't treat anyone but royalty anyway? Sounds more like a politician."

"He won't share his secrets with anybody. Won't even demonstrate them to the king. It's a tell-tale sign."

"A sign of what?"

"Well it just proves that he's a fake. He doesn't want to tell anybody his secrets because he doesn't have any! He's a fraud! Not that he'll get away with it for long – I mean the man has no respect. Even Monterek – the king for God's sake – is supposed to 'prove himself'. If he turns out to be a good king, this 'alchemist' *may* help to prolong his life. I mean, it's... I mean, who's he to judge? Eh? One day soon you'll see. Someone's going to make him cough up his potions whether he wants to or not. Then we'll see what he can do. Not much I expect. Not much."

"Well that's politics for you, husband. A lot of stupid people bragging about what they can do, but do they do anything? No. When Monterek is older, he'll know better than to stand for it."

Elze is certain they are talking about the man she saw striding across the fields with his long white hair and curious clothes.

She clutches onto the word 'alchemist'. Unlike her parents, the word suggests to her only magic and mystery, as if the word itself has a special glow around it. That night she dreams that she's a bored maiden in the high town and the alchemist is the wizard who comes to rescue her from the doldrums of her life.

CHAPTER 5
HARVEST TIME

Thanks to its dense network of gossip and intrigue, word travels fast in Izvalta. The old shepherds that wander the valley with their flocks seeking out the best forage have little need of a newspaper: the news comes to them in sometimes complimentary and sometimes contradictory layers. It comes from farmers passing on the road, their carts laden with grain or wood; from hunters with rifles slung over-shoulder, on their way to the woods where the wild boar are ripening; from the lads in the fields who are happy to break from their planting or scything to stop and chat. And yet these are still just the outlying satellites swapping simple stories. It is only when they come home that they hear the true Fact of The Matter as they draw up their rough wooden chairs and sit down to supper.

Over steaming bowls of polenta and cheese they nod as their wives tell them how things really stand. 'That alchemist is still working up at the high town church'. They nod. 'And I dare say it'll be a lifetime before he's done.' They nod. 'Of course he's an old devil-worshipper.' They nod. 'Elena, Zapata's daughter, saw him pass in the street – swears blind he doesn't have a shadow.' 'What was Elena doing in the high town?' 'Back selling flowers to the rich folk.' They nod.

But everyday concerns are far more pressing than fools and

liars chasing gold – even more so when they involve marriage. Elze is thirteen years old and already she is starting to feel the pressure of a clucking flock of aunts and grandmothers all pulling at her curls and forever pointing her in the direction of various young boys who are still playing at soldiers in the mud. They all look the same to Elze – same clothes; same hair; same grass stains. She can see that they are going to live in the same place all of their lives, doing the same things as their parents – and she'll end up right alongside them.

Sometimes she feels that there can be no escape from this cycle of life which follows the same pattern every year, following the same seasons with the same celebrations and the same rituals. She sees the older girls married to identical boys, settling into identical lives. At these times she goes to a place in her mind where she keeps an increasingly fantastical picture of the Alchemist of Izvalta. The fact that she hasn't seen him for nearly five years doesn't impede her efforts – in fact it helps: she has absolute freedom to attribute to him incredible powers, like flight and invisibility, without ever having to bring his attributes in line with reality. Sometimes she imagines that he is watching over her unseen, until one day Ivan says something that brings the real world into sharp focus.

"We're going to get married."

"Who's getting married?" she asks.

"We are: you and me." It's summer, and they have been working together in the fields, the boy scything and Elze gathering the rye together in sheaves. The declaration comes out of nowhere and Elze looks up at him in surprise, then laughs at his joke. Ivan stops scything and looks at her, hurt.

"It's not a joke," he says. "Our fathers have been talking – I overheard them. They say it would be a good idea."

Elze looks at the grubby boy seriously, squinting into a

possible future where such a thing could be even remotely possible. She can't do it. She pictures Ivan with a moustache and a house and a horse and then puts herself into the picture beside him. It's a horrid image – so much less distinct and wonderful than the one where she and the alchemist ride away on a magical bird made of leafy tree branches.

"Are you sure you heard right, Ivan?"

"Oh I'm sure, because they talked about how you had pretty hair – and you do." Ivan is now blushing uncontrollably, and he turns back to the scything to avoid Elze's eye. The pair fall silent. They say nothing until the end of the day, when Ivan awkwardly tries to kiss Elze's cheek. She suffers herself to be kissed – after all, she doesn't dislike Ivan and it's clear to her that rejecting him would only upset the poor boy. Nevertheless, when he is out of sight, she runs as fast as she can back to the room she shares with her younger sister, flings herself down on her bed and weeps into her pillow.

She hasn't been able to talk to her grandfather since he got ill. His door is permanently closed and often guarded by a fearsome old woman – a relative from the other side of the family, who's never had time for Elze or her sister. He probably hasn't got much longer. That's what they said. And the last time she saw him, he didn't even recognise her. He kept getting her confused with Elze's great aunt – his sister – who's already dead.

So she'll have to face this decision alone.

That night, Elze grabs a few bread rolls and a piece of ham from the larder. She wraps it in a cloth and sneaks out of the house, heading in a straight line across the fields. In her mind is a picture of the tall, white-haired stranger striding across the same fields years earlier. She tries to follow the same path, but the thin light of a crescent moon doesn't help her much, and rather than leaping the ditches and streams, she falls into several of them. By the time she arrives at the lower town she's bedraggled and wretched.

There is a chill in the air despite the season, which makes her think of where she could be, snuggled up at home under a warm eiderdown. She steels herself as she picks her way through the mad crush of houses, sleepy and only vaguely aware of where she's going, until she is completely lost. Eventually tiredness overpowers her and she curls up in a doorway where she shivers herself to sleep.

The morning comes as an unpleasant surprise. A woman forcibly sweeps her off the doorstep with a broom like so much rubbish, and she finds herself face down in the chilly mud of the street. During the night her knapsack was pulled apart and the edible contents eaten by the dogs that roam the street. She is only glad that they left her alone. Coughing and bleary, she takes stock of where she is.

The route to the high town is clearer in the morning light and she feels silly for getting so lost the previous night – it's just a matter of walking up the hill, and from there, well – how hard can it be? He will be there amongst all the important people and close to the king, whom he can advise on important matters of state. She imagines him standing tall in majestic robes, next to the throne, where he can keep an eye on the future; an ear bent to the needs of the people. After all, he knows and understands even the concerns of the birds in the trees and the animals that scurry around their roots. He might even know that she's coming.

Elze hasn't ever seen much of the high town and she's never been here at all without her father. The buildings around her are taller than she remembers. As a child they were always presented with a friendly adult in the foreground to lend them some idea of perspective, but now she's alone and the grandeur of the streets makes her feel tiny and insignificant. She's accustomed to seeing mountains from any point in Svart, but here the houses crowd in and seem to leer over her on both sides, an aisle of judging façades through which she must walk in her muddy clothes. The rich people of the high town aren't yet awake, but somehow the houses themselves register their disapproval with their hooded slit-eyed windows. Closing her eyes to block out their gaze, Elze tries to imagine again what the alchemist's house would look like. A tower: that's important, but there are several buildings with round turrets and no single one of them looks quite right.

For an hour Elze wanders the high town fixing each house with a probing stare until her eyes and her body begin to droop with tiredness and she is forced to accept the hopelessness of finding her alchemist. She comes to rest outside a church, which she recognises as the location of the king's coronation three years ago. It looks older than her local church and very grand, but not in the same way – the walls aren't tiled and where there would usually be a dome of bright polished copper there are simple bricks that look tattered and worn. It's a grandfather of a church – elderly and welcoming and, like her own grandfather, always ready to forgive. Perhaps even ready to forgive her for running away from home.

A wave of relief washes over Elze as she finds the door unlocked. Inside the cool stone walls, she feels safe. An open circle in the ceiling admits the shallow rays of the early morning sun, and it is to this aperture that her eyes naturally drift, as if toward a divine arbiter that will answer her many questions. She treads quietly, slowly, the path to the iconostasis, but it's the alcove on the north side of the church that arrests her attention. It's like nothing she's ever seen before: a gold-lined cavern intricately sculpted into a hundred different scenes, each with characters fixed in dramatic attitudes: pleading, crying, denouncing and fighting. Elze is in awe. It is an emotion so absolute that she can feel nothing else; for a moment all of her other senses seem dull and blunt – her eyes have never been so overwhelmed. Almost without noticing what she is doing, she kneels and begins to pray open-eyed and open-mouthed to the incredible spiritual force that so clearly inhabits this sculpture.

"What are you doing?" The voice is sharp. Elze is so dazed that she only stares dumbly at the speaker and fails to answer. Eventually she identifies the man as a priest – someone who might help her – but it still takes her a full minute to answer.

"Oh – um," she says, standing and re-arranging her dress so as to achieve a mote of respectability, "I... I was looking for an... alchemist. Do you know – ah, do you know where he lives?"

The priest pushes a pair of round spectacles up onto the bridge of his nose in a gesture that belies his age, and examines the girl, initially with an expression of plain disgust and then with a grin that threatens to engulf his whole face.

"An alchemist you say? *The* alchemist? What could a little peasant girl want with a madman? Oh yes – he's quite mad, you know." He glances briefly at the sculpture, then steps in between it and the girl, so that he's practically haloed in gold. Doubtless this is his intention – it makes Elze feel that much smaller.

"If you're determined to find him, I believe he has a hut out in the woods. That's where he conducts his communion with the devil."

"The devil?"

"Oh yes. Don't you know that alchemy is the work of the devil? Or perhaps you think it right that someone other than God should be able to perform miracles?"

"Oh – oh no. No, that would be wrong," she replies, though she can't help but add a question in defence of her hero. "But what if he did miracles because God let him? Like Jesus. He did miracles, didn't he?"

"That's completely different," says the priest, suddenly sour. "Your impudence is astounding, little girl. I should talk to your parents and see that you're rightly disciplined." A smile crosses his face – one she doesn't trust at all.

"I don't have time for that of course. Perhaps a stroll to the alchemist's hut will be discipline enough... You can find your devil-worshipper in the wolf woods. Just follow the stream out of town. Don't get eaten on the way. Now get out, little girl – there are important people coming to pray soon and last thing they want to see is a peasant spoiling the carpet." With this he turns and ducks through the door to the diaconicon, leaving Elze dumbstruck in the presence of the golden sculpture. Wasn't the priest supposed to be nice to her? To guide her when she's as lost as she is right now?

Perhaps, if she's entirely honest with herself, she had secretly hoped that he would take her back to her parents, but he didn't. He allowed her to go off into the wolf woods on her own, despite the fact that everyone knows the wolf woods are dangerous, deadly even.

Just as Elze's doubts threaten to overcome her and the certainties of home begin to tug her like cord bound around her racing heart, she catches sight of that pair of intricately turned golden feet. Slowly she lifts her head to take in the full scope of the face above her. On the surface the figure looks just like the crucified man in her local church in the valley. But his expression is different; his mouth is not contorted into an expression of anguish, but a quiet, knowing smile. She stands and looks into that face – studying the smile as if to try to decipher the emotion that caused it – for what feels like an hour, and during that time her doubts break down, liquefy and finally evaporate. When she hears footsteps again in the back of the church, she quickly turns and leaves.

Back out in the morning sun, she finds her confidence restored. She feels the beautiful internal glow of a blessing that nobody can supersede or take away – not even an uncaring priest. With renewed conviction she strikes out again in search for the alchemist.

The priest might not have taken her intention seriously, but his warning about the wolf wood is best heeded and Elze knows it. The few people from her village that ever go this way are sure to take a dog, and sometimes even that isn't enough. Normally wolves wouldn't attack people; they keep a safe distance from humans, preferring to target sheep by keeping to the shadows until they see an opportunity to pick off one of the flock, but the pack in the wolf wood is different. After a particularly harsh winter, the wolves have been known to face down a dog and tear it to pieces in front of its helpless owner before turning on him too. Of course if you have a gun you can at least scare them off, but few Izvaltans do and Elze certainly doesn't.

She does know a trick her grandfather once taught her though. She takes her knife and cuts a long, narrow strip of bark about the width of a rope from one of the trees at the entrance to the wood. It's young, fresh and tough. She cleans off the sap on a patch of grass. Next she finds a place just away from the path where the mountain rock has broken off in flat planes, leaving a patch of rubble at the base. She picks a longish flat stone and one that's sturdier and pointed. Using the point, she chips away two notches, one either side of the flat piece, then lashes the bark around it and fastens it so that she has a length of cord with a flat weight at the end.

She gives it a practice swing and the weight feels good. If she swings a little faster, she can cut the air to make a low whooshing sound. Her grandfather told her that if you keep doing that as you walk, any ferocious animals in the vicinity will think there's something big coming through the forest and get out of the way. *Unless they're hungry that is,* he told her, *in which case you have to make sure to get in the first hit – with any luck it'll put them off.* She remembers practising in the woods, swinging her weighted string at imaginary targets. *Easier to hit them when they're only in your head of course.* Her grandfather said. She misses her grandfather. Maybe if she'd been able to talk to him she wouldn't even be doing this – not alone at least.

"Well," says Elze, twirling the stone above her head. "Here goes."

CHAPTER 6
THE BLACK HOUSE

If she had to imagine the kind of place a devil worshipper would live, this would be it. The house is pitch black, and the stone wall connects directly with the face of the mountain that enfolds the wolf woods, so that at first it appears to be an extension of the rock. Another peculiar thing: there are no doors – or at least there don't appear to be any doors, but on either side of the building are two piles of huge stones which, Elze realises, must be blocking the entrances. The stones are stacked high – about double her height. The larger ones have simply been rolled from their places on the banks of the nearby stream – she can see the shallow trenches they've pressed into the soft ground.

Elze wanders back and forth around the house, stopping to listen to the odd noises coming from inside. Perhaps, she thinks, her wizard managed to summon some kind of demon and maybe someone stacked the stones against the doors to keep the demon inside. Something tells her this can't be it – after all, moving all of those stones must have taken time. Surely if it was a real demon, it would have escaped before all the stones were in place – and could a demon be imprisoned with just stones anyway? She imagines a fiery red creature made of hot coals with the strength of a team of oxen and the speed of a swooping eagle. There's no way such a demon could be kept behind this loose barricade, so she reasons that if there is a demon inside, it must be considerably less scary than the one in her head. The thought isn't as comforting as it should be.

But the alchemist. Is he still in there, trapped behind all that rubble? She peers in at the windows, but they are made of a thick dirty glass that she can't see through – there's no light coming from the other side. She knocks lightly on the glass. No response. She knocks louder. Still nothing.

"Hello?" she calls out, hands cupped around her mouth, directing the sound straight through the glass. She waits for a few breathless seconds, then something moves inside the house and she hears a groan.

Perhaps he's dying – or maybe he's accidentally turned himself into some kind of monster. Not a demon perhaps, but something dangerous nevertheless.

"Hello – mister, um – mister alchemist! Are you alright in there?" The only effect is to produce stranger and stranger sounds from inside – the crash of breaking things followed by mad chuckles and snorts, so alarming that she feels compelled to pick up one of the stones from the pile that's blocking the door and hurl it at the glass. It makes no impact – even when she repeats the experiment several times.

Elze sits on the ground cross-legged for a little while, trying to think what she should do next. Of course, what she *should* do is turn right around and go back to her family; she should stay away from things that priests tell you are bad or evil, and if her father wants her to marry Ivan, she should respect his wishes. But, despite all of the shoulds, she can't convince herself to just walk away. And so she sits there, in a slight clearing in the mountain hollow, next to an innocently gurgling stream, facing the black house.

With a start, she realises she's been sleeping. The light has changed; night is falling fast and Elze suddenly starts to feel very cold and alone. Even if she starts walking the long road back to Svart now, she'll soon be walking through the forest in the dark, which is not a good idea. It seems miraculous to her that she's woken up alive and intact as it is. It makes her wonder whether there's something else at work here, keeping away the wolves. Perhaps the golden Jesus gave her a silent blessing back in the church. She hopes so, because now the choice is simple: she either faces the wolves or a demon. The wolves are definitely real, and if demons are too, she'll need protection.

She stands up and takes another look at the exterior, checking for gaps that she could squeeze through. She tries to shift a few of the rocks, but soon realises that she's just not strong enough. There's always the chimney of course. She looks up at it. A thin wisp of smoke is rising from it, which gives her pause, but it looks big enough for her to fit down. She's seen older children climbing the rock cliffs along the river before, wedging themselves into a gap with their backs to the rock and climbing up with their feet, and it never looked that difficult. She feels a twinge of fear as she imagines plunging into a cauldron of boiling water, though she reasons that she can always check down the chimney before descending.

Her mind is made up. She sets a foot on one of the larger stones and begins to climb. On her third movement, the pile shifts suddenly beneath her, and her knee strikes the jagged wall – drawing blood. But she clings in place and is finally able to get her arms and then her torso over the edge of the overhanging roof. She gradually makes her way on knees and palms along the tiles and reaches the chimney. It has a large covering to prevent rain from getting in. The gap between the cover and the chimney is just big enough to allow her access, as long as she breathes in and puts her head through sideways. Looking down, her eyes take a moment to adjust to the gloom, where the peculiar human noises have been joined by other less human ones – dripping, bubbling and hissing. She hopes that she isn't about to crawl down into a cavern of snakes. Looking down, all she can see is a scattering of embers from a mostly dead fire – the way looks clear.

Edging in feet-first, she begins her descent. The bricks at her back are warm, and they grow warmer as she gets lower. The chimney itself is only about ten feet tall, and after five feet the heat starts to roast her back and hands. She realises she's going to have to climb back up again, but she can't – she doesn't have the strength.

She stays wedged in that position, hands scalding, for almost a minute before the decision is made for her – her foot slips and she falls feet-first into the fire. She rolls away from the hot embers, frantically brushing them from her clothes. The pain of the fall quickly catches up with her. Her feet are okay, though her shoes are singed and she's covered in little burns and scratches, but she's all in one piece. She looks around for something to cool her hands – maybe a pail of water somewhere.

The room is dark and dusty. Precariously balanced lines of glass vessels tip hither and thither, threatening to spill their curious contents at the merest nudge. Several containers seem to have done so already, which might account for the caustic quality of the air, and there's a constant background noise – a microcosmic symphony of sounds – little drips, regular gurgles and a recurring 'tap-tap' 'tap-tap'. Despite the chaos of the place, it seems perfectly still. Elze doesn't move. It occurs to her that she can no longer hear the chuckles and groans that she heard from outside – instead she hears breathing.

Then she sees him standing at the other end of the room; her alchemist, but not as she remembers him. The solid, indomitable figure in her memory has been reduced to skeletal proportions. His hair, once white, is like so much spider's web hanging practically translucent in the candle-light; his stance is almost animal, bent and cowering like a dog fearful of being kicked; his eyes are wide, red-veined and sickly – they stare at her with an expression of abject horror.

"Sir?" she says.

And the alchemist begins a slow scream that builds to a roar of terror and anger and confusion. Elze is dumbstruck – she even looks behind her for what might be the source of his fear, but it's all too clear that she herself is the cause. As the scream builds, she begins to cry. What has this man been reduced to? This isn't the great wizard for whom she's abandoned a loving family. He *has* turned himself into a monster – a thing that she can't look at without feeling sick and afraid.

The alchemist now begins a mad dance, thrusting his head to the left and right as if his neck is trying to hurl it from his body, his hands tracing complex patterns in the air, while his feet stay weirdly still. It's as if he's trying to exorcise her, this little girl who's just fallen down his chimney and who now stands quietly sobbing and nursing her burns.

Elze now realises her mistake. She remembers her father calling this man a fraud; she remembers the words of the priest. She's in the house of a madman – a devil-worshipper who's been forcibly barricaded inside his house for the good of all Izvalta – and now she's barricaded in here with him. She plugs her fingers in her ears to block out the alchemist's obscene howling, and runs for the door.

The massive door bolt is stiff – it's not moving at all, so she puts all her strength into it. The alchemist's scream stops and Elze looks around. He is walking towards her. Desperately, she struggles with the door and finally, with the towering madman only inches away, the bolt gives. The door swings inwards with incredible force and something bowls her off her feet.

CHAPTER 7
THE POSSESSED

The candles don't serve to illuminate a great deal in the black house, which appears to be constructed of shadow made solid. At the edge of the light she's aware of the alchemist watching her as she rubs the sore spot on her right arm – the place where he threw himself against her. Of course a bit of a bruised arm is far better than being crushed by the pile of stones stacked against the door and she's at least grateful that he saved her from that.

"Qu'est-ce que tu fais ici p'tite fille?" he says – the first thing that's sounded like a sentence. "T'veux quoi, hein? D'or?"

She doesn't recognise the language – she's never heard it before and the alchemist can't, or won't, speak Izvaltese. At least he's calm now – the sound of his words are far less alarming than the sight of his mad dance. She tries to answer him, to explain why she's come, but she has problems even articulating it in Izvaltese.

Eventually the alchemist gives up on communication and goes to sit in a heavy wooden chair where he folds his thin arms and closes his eyes. Before long he's asleep, snoring like a skeleton full of loose and rattling bones. Elze takes the opportunity, candle in hand, to examine her surroundings. There is a low fog of dust and fumes about the place that makes the small hut seem a lot smaller than it looks from outside. She peers at the glass vessels hanging around the walls, the shelves of bottles with their lumpy green or red or grey contents, stones and powders of different colours in dishes. She can't make sense of anything she sees – it's all so alien to her that it doesn't even have the power to fascinate, unlike the parchment-skinned alchemist dressed in his strange grey clothes.

He's not scary as such, but despite the fact that he's just saved her from being crushed, she can't bring herself to trust him – not after his insane howling and dancing. Instead of sleeping, she stares at him for hours, long into the evening – a vigil borne both of fascination and a fear that he might wake up and do something horrible to her. Sometimes, when he wakes, he stares back, but there's no sense of recognition, like he's looking at a tree in the distance rather than at another person. Occasionally he opens his eyes wide again, as they were when she fell down the chimney, and he mutters under his breath in languages she's never heard before. Sometimes his body shakes, goes rigid and then relaxes. Over time, these attacks become less alarming to the young girl as she begins to believe that he's just sick. It's not that he didn't want to greet her, set her down by the fireplace and give her a cup of hot broth, as he would always do in her dreams, it's just that he can't because there's something wrong with him. It's not like any sickness she has a frame of reference for either. She's seen fevers and swelling and people breaking out in spots; she's even seen people with decaying hands and feet, but every sickness she's ever seen was clearly physical. This is madness – or perhaps possession.

Possession is something she's heard of – something that gets talked about sometimes in church, and it seems like a probable fate for a devil-worshipper, if that's what he is. It would also explain why he's in this house out here all alone. She wonders whether she should get a priest, but when she recalls the sneering man at the high town church, she thinks better of it: there's another way to tell. She knows it might be risky, but she's come this far – and he's *her* wizard, after all. Maybe he needs saving from the confines of his illness as much as she needed to escape the inevitability of her life.

One of the hut's walls is covered in books, their spines worn and tarnished. Slowly, she gets up out of her chair, taking care to make no sudden movements that might disturb the sleeping alchemist. She goes to the bookshelf and checks up and down, but runs into a problem: all of the books have titles in other languages. One after another she pulls them out at random and flicks through. Most of them contain a script of baffling characters alongside insane pictures depicting all kinds of scenes: dragons and snakes and forest animals cavorting and contorting themselves into odd positions, their landscapes filled with stars and symbols. Whatever these books may be, they certainly aren't what she's looking for.

Disappointed, she turns away from the shelf and there on the workbench, she sees it. It may not be in Izvaltese, but the ornate golden cross on the front cover is title enough. She picks it up and takes it over to the sleeping alchemist. She swallows a breath as if to try to swallow the fear itself, then she holds out the Bible at arm's length in both hands, pointing the cross forward. If she knew some magical incantation to ward off the devil, now would be the time to recite it, but she knows nothing of that sort. This is a gamble. If the alchemist is possessed by the devil, he shouldn't be able to bear the presence of the holy book. She tries not to think beyond that point. Step by tiny step she moves forward, until the book is only a couple of inches from his nose, then she stamps her foot.

"Aak!" he shouts, jumping out of his slumber. There is a moment where she thinks it's all gone wrong – that he is indeed possessed and that she's unmasked the devil with no hope of escaping him, as the alchemist's head jerks back and away from the book, almost tipping his chair over backwards. She advances, pushing the book into his face.

"See this, devil?" she shouts. "Go back to Hell, devil!"

The alchemist quickly grabs her wrists and forces them away. She struggles, but her strength is no match for his, no matter how bony he may look. He focuses his blinking eyes on the book in front of him and lets out a peal of laughter, bright and clear as a church bell on a crisp morning. It's a wonderful sound, brimming with life – a sound to dispel all doubt. He grabs the book and opens it up.

Elze sighs with relief: there's no need to go for the priest. Whatever can be the explanation for the alchemist's delirium, it's not the work of the devil. He smiles an enchanted smile, leafing through the massive Bible. Watching him is like watching a child rediscovering a once familiar toy. He opens up a page and begins to read, taking in every letter with one finger carefully tracing the lines. He runs his hand along the binding to feel its texture; he even stops to smell the pages. The whole process seems to comfort him. She can't tell what part he's reading, but she thinks that maybe it's the bit about Moses doing magic. It's so hard to tell how old the alchemist is – maybe he knew Moses a long time ago. Maybe he *is* Moses. No – that's ridiculous. Or maybe it isn't.

She watches the old man, but now with a feeling of comparative comfort – after all he is finally displaying something like rational behaviour, and she can let her guard down just a little. And Elze realises quite suddenly that she's tired – more tired than she can remember being. There's one bed in the corner behind the central workbench, but she doesn't want to use it if the alchemist is planning to sleep there. Eventually she lies down on the fur rug, then rolls it into a cocoon around her shivering body.

Like a play in which everything happens in reverse, a thick curtain of sleep descends, followed by a cavalcade of dreams from which she's relieved to wake. Just before she opens her eyes, she sees her father emerging from a fire. Rather than scolding her for running away, he opens his mouth wide, screaming in abject fear, then burns to cinders in front of her.

She can't tell if she screamed as well. It takes a moment for her to realise where she is, and when she does, she wonders whether she's actually still dreaming. Her surroundings, though unfamiliar, are not alarming – they have that indistinct silhouetted quality, as though they've been glimpsed out of the corner of her eye. The alchemist is still in his chair, the Bible open on his lap, so still that she has to watch closely to see that he's breathing.

Sunlight breaks in a wave over the rubble in the doorway. It pools on the dark stone floor, leaving a puddle of warmth – just enough to alleviate the feeling of being trapped in a crypt. Particles of dust hover, wobble and dance on slim currents of air and light. It's stuffy in here, with a rank undertone that makes her wonder how long the alchemist has been living like this. Perhaps this was the way it was even before people stacked boulders against the door. They need to get out. She could maybe get out the way she came in, but the alchemist certainly couldn't, so that means she's going to have to move the huge stones that have filled the doorway.

Taking a poker from the fireplace, she begins to lever them up one by one, tipping them back down the pile and into the outside world. Progress is slow. Her efforts gradually arouse the interest of the alchemist, but curiously, rather than coming to her aid he stands and watches, uncomprehending. Elze looks at him, panting with the effort of the work.

"You aren't going to help?"

He looks blankly at her.

"You had no problem understanding the book last night. How is this so hard?" She summons her strength for a push, putting all her weight behind the poker in front of a large boulder. The poker slips and for an alarming moment the boulder threatens to roll back towards Elze, causing her to run backwards to avoid it crushing her feet.

The alchemist laughs. Not the same laugh as she heard on the previous day, but instead a childish gurgle of amusement. As the boulder settles back into place she looks accusingly at the alchemist.

"Oh was that funny? You... You..." she shouts, exasperated before making herself calm down – she must remember how fragile he is. "Don't you understand what I'm doing? If we don't get out of here, we'll have no food and you might be used to that but I'm not – I'm not prepared to die – not for some incurable madman. Look." She demonstrates what she's doing, tucking one end of the poker under a rock, then using it to lever another one away. "Now you have a go." She hands over the poker, which the alchemist takes. It's a long shot, but he must understand. Gazing at it intently, he seems to grasp something, but it's not the thing that Elze was hoping for. With a manic look, he raises the poker above his head ready to strike her.

"No! No!" She curls up into a ball, expecting at any moment to feel the pain of the metal on her back. When she hears his laughter again, she stands and wipes the tears from her eyes.

"That was mean. Don't do that. Okay?" She tries to snatch the poker back from the alchemist, but he whips it away behind his back.

"Non." he says.

It's like battling with her four-year-old cousin, but a considerably larger and stronger version.

Finally, she finds another poker and sets back to work while the alchemist chuckles to himself. "You're just a sick man. Just ill – you need a doctor, but all you've got is me. I hope you'll understand that soon."

Some hours later, Elze breaks through the barrier of rocks. Outside in the fresh afternoon air, she begins to feel like herself again and with that feeling comes hunger and thirst. She plunges her whole head into the clear stream, then drinks her fill and looks around her. Her grandfather said that there was always food in the forest for anyone willing to look – when she was a young girl he taught her which mushrooms to eat and which ones to avoid, which grasses you could chew and which to put in a soup. She loved these lessons, although she never imagined actually needing the knowledge as she does now.

Back in the hut, she makes a cone of kindling, just the way she was taught, then steps back from her handiwork, looking for something to light it with. As she looks around, the alchemist moves silently to the fireplace. Elze keeps her guard up, just in case he tries to attack her again, but he seems not to notice her. She watches as the ghostly presence shakes a little powder from a clay dish over the wood, then takes two flints and claps them together, making a spark that sets the powder and the wood ablaze. The alchemist stands watching the flames.

"You don't have matches?" asks Elze.

He looks back at her blankly as if she were an ordinary fixture of the house.

Over the next few days, Elze tries to understand the man's sickness. It's bewildering: the madness just isn't consistent, coming in fits and starts without reason. Sometimes he's perfectly lucid; he smiles at her and says things that sound so pleasant to Elze that she imagines he's casting a beautiful spell on her. He watches as she gathers wood and drives away the spiders from their dusty nooks with a broom, and sometimes he will even help, nodding at her and mimicking her movements. But then he will be suddenly childish, upending a bowl of soup she's made for him or suddenly breaking out in screams and wails and beating the table with his fists.

All she can do when this happens is to run or find something to defend herself. At one point she almost gives up and leaves him to die on his own, after he forcibly tries to kiss her. When she resists he hits her with the back of his hand. She tries not to think of what might have happened had she not swung a heavy mortar at his head. Later, while he is asleep in his chair, she dresses the wound she inflicted, with tears in her eyes.

She's also getting used to one-sided conversations.

"How did this happen?" she asks the sleeping man. "When I saw you at first I thought you were a great wizard. I thought you were coming here to do great things and help people. Look at you now – you're the one who needs help. Without me you'd have starved by now. Maybe that would have been better – I'm only making you suffer more." If you see a bird that's wounded and can't move properly, it's best to kill it. To put it out of its misery. Her grandfather taught her that. Would he also counsel her to abandon a wretched human with nobody else to turn to?

Elze's new lot is sad: there is barely a day that goes by without her crying copious tears, while the alchemist seems to feel nothing and care for nothing. She has a kind of faith, though, that it won't always be this way – one day he will wake up and know himself again. Elze would be hard pressed to pinpoint the source of this faith. Perhaps it springs simply from the forest around them that provides their food and protects them in isolation from the rest of the world. Every enterprising sprout, shoot, beetle and bird is thriving here, and this forms the cornerstone of her faith, reinforced by the fact that the wood's natural guardians, the wolves, seem to let her be. She hasn't so much as heard one in the vicinity of the hut.

One day after countless others, she returns from an expedition into the forest. She's foraged several handfuls of berries and some hogweed, which is a bit old but she knows she can use it to make a soup. The alchemist is sitting on the bare floor, utterly engrossed in a book that he has open on his lap, and when Elze approaches he jumps up in excitement.

The book is leather-bound and simply made, with incredibly thin pages. Inside, in a close neat hand, are tightly packed inscriptions in a peculiar alphabet. She looks up at him and shakes her head, and his eyes lock with hers. They try to communicate something, though she does not know what. He points to passage after passage, jabbing frantically at the text, talking in a stream of gibberish that bubbles over in frustration. Then one of his jabbing fingers pokes a hole through one of the pages. His eyes fall to the floor, his body slumps and he returns to his chair. On his way, he lets the book drop from his limp hand.

Elze picks it up. "Is it a recipe book for spells? Potions?" she asks in vain, then, looking more carefully at the format of the inscriptions, "It's your diary isn't it? It looks like a diary. In code." The symbols look like no writing she's ever seen. She leafs through the book sadly, her eyes flicking across the mass of symbols. She hasn't a hope of understanding what it says – even if she could crack this code, she'd still have to speak his language to make sense of it.

The evening passes slowly, the girl studying the old man as one might study an ancient stone, trying to decipher the messages and secrets carved into his face; an attempt to circumvent the bonds of language that imprison them. Those lines speak of times of incredible happiness and terrible sorrow – things that she desperately wants to ask him about, but can't. When the fire dwindles into a heap of spent embers, she curls up in front of the fireplace, covering herself with the rug and as she drifts off to sleep, she resolves to crack the alchemist's code – even if it takes a lifetime. After all, she's not going back home.

CHAPTER 8
MAGIC

The chamois is still alive, whining sadly in a puddle of blood. It's a lucky find – usually the wolves would have taken it to pieces leaving nothing left, but the wolves of these woods seem to kill for reasons other than just for food. When the animal sees Elze approach it tries to get up and limp away, but the pain of the vicious bite just below its neck is too much for it and it falls back to the ground, helpless.

She doesn't have a knife or a gun or anything she can use to kill the poor creature. She looks down at her hands, wondering if they might be capable of strangling it. There is only one way to answer that question and, desperately trying not to think about what she's doing, she runs towards the wounded animal, grabs its neck and with her soft fingers, tries to twist its head around. But the touch of the warm skin under her hands is too much. The sinews underneath the fur twitch and recoil. It kicks at her, making a large painful bruise on her right arm, and another hoof narrowly misses her head.

She retreats a little way and watches. It's hard to watch the chamois trying so desperately to cling to its life. She closes her eyes and wishes now that she were at home – her real home – embroidering a picture of a brightly coloured harvest scene whilst sitting in front of the fire, as she used to do when she was a little girl, with her mother singing to herself quietly in the kitchen. But the only sound she can hear is the plaintive whine of this dying animal.

She knows she has to kill it. Not for herself – not to appease the groaning in her stomach, but for the sick man who's depending on her, whether he knows it or not, to get food. Something in her surroundings suggests itself: a chunk of jagged flint. She tries not to think about how she should use it, and before she can back out she forces herself to smash it down on the animal's head. It shrieks in pain and she continues beating the rock down and down and down. Finally, it is still.

Elze stores as much meat as she can fit into the alchemist's terracotta pots and jars then stocks them away at the back of the hut against the cool dark rock face. It should last them a while. Foraging is fine, of course, but they need to eat more than just soup if they're going to survive for any length of time. At some point she's going to have to go to Svart. That brings up a lot of questions that she's been avoiding. What if someone recognises her and tells her to go back home because her family is worried about her? What would it take for her to turn back and rejoin the world she grew up in? Surely by now they've assumed that she's dead – or maybe that she's run away to Romania – the country that surrounds and encloses Izvalta. It happens often enough, although many come back a few months later, retreating to the comparative sanity and safety of the valley, protected as it is by the world's disinterest. She recalls a cousin who did this. When he ventured outside the walls of the valley he struggled to communicate. Nobody spoke his language, and he lost his sense of identity. It was early spring, so he managed to get some work in the fields, but by summer he was back in the valley.

There are different questions if she stays here, like what to use for money and how to avoid the wolves on the path. Those questions must be faced soon. She's begun to lose track of time in this place. Every day is the same – even more so than it was at home. She wonders, as she wakes up once more in the fuggy hut, whether she has really escaped anything at all. Every morning she gets up, forages for whatever scraps she can find, dips a bucket into the stream and brings it back full of fresh water, then stokes the fire and makes a soup, which, like her, seems to get thinner by the day. All the while the alchemist sits in his corner, barely stirring until she tries to force a little food between his lips, at which point he will either look up at her adoringly or propel the bowl across the room and howl like a baby.

Then, one chilly morning, the pattern is interrupted. After she returns from filling the water bucket, she sets it to boil, and while she waits she picks a book at random from the shelf and opens it up. Like most of his books, it's full of pictures; a menagerie gone mad – she can't make head nor tail of them (despite the proliferation of both), but as she sits studying the pictures, the old man stirs and approaches. He seizes the book from her and practically jumps up and down with excitement, jabbering his gibberish all the while.

"What are you saying?" she asks hopelessly.

The alchemist lays down the book and rummages amongst the containers scattered over his workbenches, then triumphantly withdraws some receptacles from the mess: two dishes of white powder and a jar of liquid. Gesturing to the pictures in the book he explains in dumb-show that each figure corresponds to a substance. He stokes the fire, blends the two powders in a ceramic dish, picks up the dish with a pair of metal tongs and holds it over the flame. Finally he adds the liquid, which sputters when it meets the powder. Elze watches as the stuff dissolves, fizzes and turns a green-brown colour, giving off a vinegary smell with an undertone of sulphur, before turning completely solid. The alchemist then upends the chunk of stuff into a mortar and grinds it down with a pestle, sprinkles a pinch of the powder into a cup of water and is about to drink it, when Elze stops him.

"Wait!" she shouts. "Is it safe?"

The alchemist looks at her as if to say 'trust me' and swallows. He closes his eyes briefly, clearly enjoying the effect of the liquid, then he offers the glass to her. She sips at it nervously – it's like drinking rusty water at first and her body reacts badly to it, making her cough. When she finally manages to swallow some, she can feel it grating down her throat. For a horrible moment she thinks he's poisoned her, but then comes a rush of something indescribable – calm and wonder and beauty somehow fill her veins all at once. It's Elze's first taste of the elixir.

Over the coming weeks, Elze begins to see wonderful changes in the alchemist. After showing her the first alchemical preparation, he goes straight to his bookshelf and there he stays working long into the night until his candle is nothing more than a guttering stub.

Like a child confronted for the first time with the enormity of the ocean, the books command his full attention. Elze watches his fascination, his finger resting underneath each line for an age, positioned like a diving bell while his eyes dive down into the depths of the text. Resurfacing finally at the end of a sentence, an expression of bliss crosses his face and he nods slowly to himself before turning to the next. Elze has never seen anyone so rapt by anything. It makes her wonder whether she's missed something.

"What do they mean?" she asks the alchemist, not really hoping for an answer. "Aren't they just words? Are they very old words? Do they work differently to regular ones? Like spells?" Certainly they look older. Some of the letters look familiar – others like tiny drawings. Like the old man reading them, each one seems to carry the weight of its history on its form – in the way it has faded and seems to lean into its neighbour for support – and yet their shape, their essence, remains.

For weeks the alchemist is so intent on his work that she practically has to force food and water into his mouth to keep him alive. Then he turns to his equipment. For hours at a time, he mashes stone into powder, sets glass vessels bubbling with variously noxious-smelling liquids; beakers fill with distilled drips and drops. On occasion he will smile with delight; on other occasions he will yell incomprehensible words at the substances produced. Elze is never sure whether these are magical incantations or just him swearing.

Elze, meanwhile, fills her days learning how to survive in the forest. The chamois lasted a while, but they simply have no capacity for long-term storage in their home. When the carcass started to become rancid there was nothing for it but to take it away from the house and throw it where it could decompose. As it was, she only managed to drag the carcass a few dozen yards into the trees before she realised that some unseen thing had scented the meat. It had broken the invisible cordon of the alchemist's hut and was so close that she could hear it breathing even though she couldn't see it. As she ran back to the house she heard horrifying sounds behind her. The wolves still haven't attacked her yet, although she sees them from time to time.

"If you see them it means they've let you see them. Maybe next time you won't be so lucky." her grandfather would say. She's started carrying sharpened sticks with her alongside her noise-making rock – not that she's ever likely to be able to use one, but they make her feel safer.

To keep the food supply going she has been making traps of various kinds – mostly ones that rely on a heavy stone held up by an arrangement of sticks, which, when triggered will bring the weight crashing down. She's had limited success, but a couple of squirrels go a long way if used sparingly.

One day in early autumn, while the alchemist is studying one of his books, Elze looks over his shoulder. She still can't see what he sees.

"Maybe it's like an illusion," she thinks out loud. "Do I just stare at it until it means something?" She tries to copy the look in the alchemist's eyes, but ends looking down her nose, so that the characters blur into each other even more incomprehensibly than they did before. She tries just looking – for similarities and differences, but the symbols remain mysterious. It's while she's peering intensely over the alchemist's shoulder that he finally notices her studying his manuscript. He watches her for several seconds, then smiles. And with that smile she has her first brief glimpse into the man's soul. It confirms for her, rightly or wrongly, that there's still part of him living in his body – a person trapped inside a cage of madness.

He grins. She smiles back, then he leaps to his feet and charges for the door, snatching up the wood axe from its place among the logs.

"Don't!" she says. "What do you want with that?" But by the time the words reach his ears, he is plunging head first into the forest. Elze rushes after him, but finds him harmlessly employed in chopping down a tree. This is not worrying in itself, but given that they have plenty of wood already, she wonders at his urgency. Some hours later his motivation becomes clear: he's stoking the furnace.

The furnace sits like a squatting ogre at the very back of the hut, set against the mountain itself – a forbidding black iron and stone construction with a great bellows to one side, as tall as Elze herself, operated by pumping a footboard. Of all the oddities in the alchemist's hut, which include several jars of unidentifiable organic specimens, it is the furnace that scares her. At night she sometimes dreams that the furnace has torn up its foundations and is leaning ravenously over her makeshift bed, opening up its iron door to swallow her whole.

Right now the solid square of door is fastened shut with a heavy metal latch. As the alchemist lifts the latch the door swings open with a creak, revealing a chamber thick with soot as black as the rest of the furnace. Elze peers in, perhaps looking for the desiccated bones of the furnace's past victims, but there's nothing to see beyond the depths of the darkness.

The alchemist cleans it out with a stiff brush and, with great care, kindles a fire, which he stokes with progressively larger pieces of wood, feeding in log after log in a seemingly endless stream. It's a wonder that the logs can be consumed as fast as he's stuffing them in. Elze is happy to see this change in him, but this new rabid intensity worries her almost as much as the furnace itself, and as the heat in the little hut rises, she retreats back to a corner of cool stone and watches warily as the crazed old man is intermittently lit up in flickering orange.

"What are you doing?" she whispers quietly – a question intended for both the old man and herself.

It's early morning when he wakes her. Outside the windows the sun has yet to rise over the mountains and even the birds are still, but the house is hot and the alchemist's sweat has stained his grey shirt with fat patches of black. Beneath his bristling eyebrows, his eyes sparkle like diamonds.

"Petra. Come... with me," he says in broken Izvaltese. "I have... something... show... important."

She wonders what he means, but she lets him take her by the hand and lead her to the closed furnace. Taking a long metal rod with a hooked end, he unhitches the latch and deftly swings the door open. A wall of heat hits Elze and she takes a step back. Her eyes struggle against the glare of the flames, which gradually seem to resolve themselves into complex images – fiery birds, dragons, lions, eagles, all cavorting in a cavalcade of blinding energy. They fly and tumble and consume each other, running riot with a ferocity that shares nothing in common with the flames of a normal fire. It hypnotises her.

The old man watches Elze with a smile, then, taking the hooked rod, he fishes in the furnace until it comes into contact with something. He drags it forward. The edge of a black stone block appears by the side of the furnace, but it's so hot that Elze can't make it out clearly. The alchemist takes two rods of a similar material to the hook and positions them either side of the block. Tucking the ends of the rods under his arms, he lifts out the stone, depositing it on the floor at her feet, then slams the furnace shut.

The black stone sits and glows like a star that by some incredible chance has fallen straight from the sky and down the chimney. It radiates a furious heat, far too hot for Elze to endure, but while she backs away, the alchemist takes a pair of heavy leather gloves and moves forward to stand over it, basking in it. She watches him nervously – he looks so frail and flammable that she worries he might just catch light himself, but the heat only seems to lend energy to his lean body. He pulls upward on the block, splitting the hazy black surface a couple of inches from the top. The crack turns into a gape and the gape reveals something even more mesmerising than the fire of the furnace – a perfect well of molten gold.

"Gold," the young girl mutters in wonder. It's faultless. The unbroken surface, the rich depth of colour, the almost tangible sense of weight. She doesn't need to pick it up to know that this substance has mass – it seems to have its own gravity. It's not like a thing; more like a force. It invites her to dip in a finger the way one might dip a biscuit into molten chocolate.

"It's beautiful," she says.

There's a clunk. The alchemist drops the lid of the block and Elze briefly glimpses his face contorted with sadness before he turns away from her. With difficulty, she pulls herself away from the golden pool and touches the alchemist lightly on the shoulder.

"What's wrong?"

He winces, then turns to her with tears in his eyes. "I fear... soon... forget," he mutters. "I forget, Petra. The Work is done." He indicates the books scattered around his workbench. "These – they help." He taps his head.

"You mean... this – making the gold – it makes you feel better? You read the books and you remember things, right?"

He nods. "The books, yes. But... it is over. Forget. Finished."

The alchemist was once a tall man, elderly and imposing, but here in this hut with tears in his eyes, grubby and shrunken, he seems more like a little boy. She puts a hand out to stroke his hair.

"Why can't you just... well – carry on?"

His eyes open, but he looks at her confusedly.

"Keep doing alchemy. Keep reading the books. Make more."

He shakes his head and gets up, his worn frame suddenly bereft of the demonic energy of the fire, and he creaks back to his chair. The girl runs after him and blocks his path.

"Teach me," she says.

He smiles. "The Work. Not easy." Again he taps his head. "Need brain." And he clutches one hand to his chest. "Need Soul," he says, and finally he brings his two palms together in an attitude of prayer. "Need God," he adds sadly.

"I can do it. I can."

"You are... small. You need grow. Run. Outside. Air. Life."

"I don't need any of that, sir."

"Alchemy. You are bored. Slow."

"I don't care. You don't understand what it means to grow

here – I would grow into my mother and my children would grow into me; into my neighbours. There is no change, nothing to become but a copy of what's gone before. I want something different. Anything."

"Okay." He nods. "Petra." The suggestion of a smile drifts across the man's face, then he turns back to the puddle of gold, closing his weary eyes.

"Sir, what does 'petra' mean? You said it before."

"Petra – you. Petra. Rock. Like the mountain."

She starts to correct him – to introduce herself – and then she realises that the life of the little girl called Elze is one that even after this short time she no longer recognises as her own. She would much rather be part of the mountain – it seems to fit her better.

"Petra. Then that will be my name. What's yours? Your name?" She points to him.

"Fulcanelli... Jean. Jean Fulcanelli."

"Well, Jean Fulcanelli, I'm pleased to finally meet you."

It's many weeks later before she finally asks the question that burns on her lips at that moment. By this time, his Izvaltese has improved a great deal – so much so that she realises that he must have been completely fluent at one stage before his madness.

"Monsieur Fulcanelli," she says. "What is alchemy?"

The alchemist's serious face breaks into a wonderful smile. "It's a good question. An important question that few alchemists ever think to ask. There are many answers, but I will tell you mine. Alchemy is the work of God undertaken by mortal men. At the beginning of recorded history, you see, a group of strange figures appeared. They were first seen in Kemia on the banks of the Nile river in Egypt. Egypt is probably not a place you know of, but it's not so very far away really.

"The strange figures that appeared there were angels sent by God. They taught humans about the structure of the spheres – those above us and the sphere upon which we live. They spoke of incredible sciences: how to take a thing – a solid, unchangeable thing – and make it into something very different. The angels could change anything around them into whatever suited their purpose, but they were not magicians – they simply applied the right kind of process to the right kinds of material. All they needed to know were the properties of the things around them, and using their knowledge they could shape the world and they could even shape themselves, perfecting their minds and bodies with preparations drawn from the Earth.

"Their teachings are the basis of alchemy. For a while, mankind heard the strangers' teachings and used them to shape a better world, structured not by violence but by equality. It did not last. We made God regret sending his envoys to humanity and in return he sent floods, famine, confusion, and scattered the teachings of alchemy to all corners of the Earth. Over the centuries, much knowledge has been lost and even obfuscated by nonsense. Alchemists were plagued and shunned, but alchemy was never the source of mankind's corruption – it was the hope for mankind's redemption. Of the scraps of knowledge that remain, I have but a few and they are contained in the books that surround us."

The girl is wide-eyed. "But what can it do? You showed me the gold, and the special drink..."

"The elixir," corrects the old man.

"Yes. The elixir – but what else can alchemy do? Can you fly? How about talk to animals?"

"I have never flown. I have no wings and God never meant me to. I told you that alchemy is God's work, but mankind cannot presume to change God's plans or alter His structures. A man is a man and a bird is a bird. Their bodies are distinct. Each can be made more perfect, but the manner of perfection is different for each."

"But..."

"...And that is enough for today I think." He smiles gently at his new student. "We have time."

Petra, the newly-christened, the wide-eyed and curious, fails to mask a sigh. Fulcanelli plucks one of the thinner books from the shelf and hands it to her.

"Here," he says. "Diagrams of the spheres and their inhabitants. There is some fanciful imagery, but it may open your mind a little."

The first page opens to a complex line drawing with stars and suns and moons and figures in among them. She tries to frown the image into some kind of order.

"I've had most of these books for over a century," says the old man, more to himself than to the girl. "And they have lived lives far longer than mine, passed down from generation to generation. It seems fitting that they help me to remember myself – after all, these books know me. They're like old friends – in some ways they're the only friends an alchemist is allowed."

CHAPTER 9
THE ALCHEMIST

The boy takes the dog-eared book from her hand. When he opens it, he sees shapes. At the moment they don't mean anything – "but they will", she reassures him as she bends down to stroke his muddy blond hair.

She takes the book and carefully tears out two pages. He winces as she does so: he hates to see the book hurt like that, but he trusts her. He likes the touch of her hand on his head – just as it is now. Rhythmic movements and a gentle song, followed by... words. Not shapes but words. Things that rise out of the fog of his mind. Things he's never experienced. Things he will never know. Words.

11 July 1939, Buchenbach, Black Forest

A low rumble in the distance. That sound. That scent on the air. I fear the time to depart approaches.

It is five years now since I came to the Schwarzwald. Here I have found stories; folk tales of dealings with the devil and of strange happenings. I have been immersed in the deep waters of alchemy. Faust, or an individual who has come to be called by that name, passed here before me – it was nearby in Staufen where he first undertook the Work. The locals still talk of it and more besides. I am still convinced that many of the folk tales are allegorical, as is the preferred form of communication amongst fellow practitioners. Hansel and Gretel, for instance, could be that embodiment of the masculine and feminine, of the frater and soror mystica; their trail of breadcrumbs, the prima materia. The other figures in the story are more ambiguous – if I could get my hands on an early woodcut it might give me clues that would escape the notice of a more casual observer.

But this is all academic speculation: more important by far is the safe haven that I have found here – a sylvan island removed from the petty concerns of the Paris fraternity and the artful bourgeois.

In Buchenbach, I have found seclusion and have escaped nearly all human interaction. But the world, it seems, grows smaller daily both physically and ideologically. Ideas, I have observed, condense into single streams of accepted thought while 'civilised' cities, like parasites, insinuate themselves into nature's bosom, burrow under her skin, and suck dry her blood. It grows harder and harder to find a corner of the world where she hasn't been burned back in swathes and filled in with concrete, the mark of uniformity and ignorance.

And now I feel conflict threatening – it hangs in the air like a cloud heavy with rain. I hadn't fully realised that I was leaving until this morning, when I found myself letting the fire dwindle and the furnace cool. It seems that I've even stocked my pantry with tins and dried fruits that will not perish on a long journey. It comes as some surprise to me that I am preparing to move even without having made a conscious decision. But I suppose that just as a hand learns to key a flute when the eye sees a sheet of music, so a body may recognise the stimuli for flight even before the conscious mind. It makes me think that our common sense picture of the mind's relationship to a body is certainly incomplete, for we believe in a nexus of control rooted in a brain – a single organ – while in reality my hands and feet have an agency all their own.

I hope to complete my preparations tomorrow. My equipment will have to come with me as it will be hard to source elsewhere. Also a quantity of gold – minted, I think. I have a handful of Roman forgeries, which were a tiresome business, but at least their original provenance won't be questioned and God willing, neither will the story of an unhappy archaeologist selling his final few artefacts for food. I think one of the villagers might have a pony and an old cart they would be willing to sell to me – but this is turning into a list of tasks I must complete. Enough!

16 July 1939, Donaueschingen.

The roads are a constant stream of military traffic. One can hear it from miles away – the steady crunching of heavy boots. As they pass, each face turns toward the curious old man with the horse and cart going in the opposite direction. From underneath my broad hat I see the lines of young men all ready for the fight. Not enough of them looked scared – they must have very little idea of what they are doing. And yet to see their faith makes me reflect on myself.

I once had high ideals. I sought to do God's work; I believed I could improve the organism that is the world. Over time those ideals have faded and I am left with just the deed. My hands create perfection through alchemy, but I have ceased to believe in its importance. Perhaps this is why I have started to fail. It's been seven months since my last successful transmutation and I have no reason to believe that my abilities will return. At least those young fools have belief.

Tomorrow I take to the river. I have, with some difficulty, secured a small rowing boat. It will suffice to convey me and my personal effects and equipment. My books will have to be well protected against the spray from the water. In the knowledge that the boat may be inspected, I don't think I will try to disguise my cargo – the bulk of it is unlikely to be of interest to anybody. Curious officials may try in vain to find a tome written in a language that they understand! I have provisions to last maybe a fortnight, after which I will have to restock. My small measure of gold I will keep upon my person at all times. It will be wise to take precautions there.

I confess to being a little excited by the coming voyage; it is too easy for an alchemist to become set in his ways – the Work is in essence a routine – but there is no reason that life should follow the same pattern. Life must, I suppose, evolve – a curious sentiment for a man of God, but not untenable, for who drew that first sketch of man if not God? We must evolve and develop, otherwise what is it to be human at all?

20 July 1939, Upper Danube

It's hard to find the opportunity to write. The journey is tough on an old man who isn't accustomed to rowing or handling the currents. As yet the river is only slim. As it widens I will have to be particularly cautious lest I overturn the boat on the rapids, but I'm learning fast. I'm also enjoying the wondrous effect of transit on the mind of the traveller. I had forgotten the joys of letting one's thoughts drift along the river channel and over the gentle contours of the land. It seems that only when we physically move can we really step outside of ourselves and ask those questions that are so fundamental to our being.

The question I've been pondering is simple, but the answers to it have such implications! I must have buried it deep, for it has not surfaced before. Out here, however, it seems there is no escaping it: it's running with me, matching my pace as I drift down the river.

The question is: why? What do I hope to achieve by following this discipline? I have developed the work of de Montluisant; I have taken it to its conclusion. What comes after a conclusion? Ordinary men are blessed that they do not live long enough to see how little their impact has been, but God has chosen a different fate for me. I have unlocked the secrets of the world, but the world remains inscrutable and indomitable, and I must ask myself why.

When I began to learn, the Work itself was enough: I learned to distil the elements required, to process them in the correct manner, to attend to the heat of the flame and the consistency of the substances. I gave myself fully to the Work, but now I wonder what purpose it serves.

I know and accept that the alchemical process speeds God's work. Making something more perfect is in itself good, but surely there is a greater good?

I worry that I have become a mere slave to the Work, yet on its own, the Work is nothing; it influences nothing; it makes nothing better. There, it is said now – a denial of all of the alchemical teachings since Hermes Trismegistus himself. I do not wish to spend the rest of my days a lonely alchemist on my own in some desolate wood, doing God's work in such a way that only He and I will know the benefits.

My thoughts have taken a curious path, but resolved themselves into the following: What if I were to take this art of perfection, which is valued by my fellow man, and employ it in certain ways? What if I could increase the perfection in the world by a factor that exceeds the efficacy of the Work itself? Put another way, if I lend my abilities to the support of a worthy cause, could I perhaps effect a greater perfection in the world – a perfection of societies? A philosophic perfection to be sure, but a perfection with real applications.

I could follow the example of the Flamels and use my wealth to build hospitals, but how long can that continue? When the hospitals fall into disrepair after I am dead, what will I have achieved? Daily I see lines of men marching intently towards destruction. What do I hope to achieve by erecting hospitals so that they can be blasted to nothingness, or worse, so that they can heal the wounded, allowing them to return to the fight? No – the only way to effect change must be to influence thought and culture through government.

But how to give money and support to a political entity without it having some undesired effect? I can make a perfect metal, but I cannot create a gold that will never corrupt the heart of the recipient. I can make a panacea that will cure all ills but I cannot lace it with knowledge, to touch the soul or the understanding of the imbiber. The successes of alchemy are all too often curtailed by greed and ignorance.

I must sleep. Succumb to the siren song of a pile of blankets. What nonsense – I must truly be tired.

CHAPTER 10
SCARS

Terry's first thought is that he's on a mortuary slab, although the pain in his joints suggests that he isn't actually dead yet. But then there's the smell – a toxic, sulphurous smell that crawls in through his nostrils and attacks the back of his throat with sandpaper and poisoned needles. In his half-dreaming state, he becomes convinced that what he's smelling are the pits of Hell. His pulse races as he desperately tries to confirm that he is still alive and in the real world, but he can't see properly, let alone move.

He rubs his eyes open with a barely responsive left hand – the right is inexplicably inactive, like he's been sleeping on it, but without the reassurance of pins and needles to signify that the blood might return. Blinking away his bleariness he sees only wood beams set against black stone walls. He tries in vain to move his head. It feels like there's something tying it down, although exploring with his one functioning hand this apparently isn't the case. So he tries to pick up his own head using his hand like a grabber on the end of a crane. It's heavy, but he manages to lift it maybe a half inch off the bench to peer into the deep black shadow that surrounds him.

"Ovst! Ovst! You're not finished yet. Stay." Forceful hands return Terry's arm to his side and his head clocks down painfully onto the hard surface. He doesn't see who those hands belong to.

"Where am I?" he asks. "Hello?" Nothing. As consciousness fully returns, so does panic. "Hello? Hello?" His mind races, but it finds no footing – it runs on air like a cartoon character suspended in the empty space over a cliff edge. He remembers a party. He remembers a foreign country. Odd costumes. Alcohol. A bear? Was that a dream? He remembers a woman with a cure for the ultimate hangover and wonders if he should go to see her – if she might have anything to help him. Then he recalls following her through the snow and into the woods. What was he thinking? And how did he get here? Where is he in fact? His eyes roll shut.

Some time later, Terry wakes up again with a splitting headache. The noxious smell is still in the air and he still can't move, but his body feels slightly better.

"Hello?" he tries. "Hello – is anyone there? I feel terrible. Headache. Is this a hospital? Do you have headache pills? Ibuprofen? Aspirin? Paracetamol? Um – Tylenol? Alka..."

And then she walks in. She looks smaller without her coat on, and more fragile. It's not just the lack of a coat that makes her look older; it's the streaks of grey that he sees in her hair; the creeping crow's feet around her eyes. She looks like she's been up all night.

"Madame Fulcanelli?"

She's silent. He can see her inspecting a bloody bandage wrapped around his torso, although he can't feel either the bandage or the wound beneath – he can't really feel anything apart from his joints – and they could be attached to sticks of wood for all he knows. It takes a great effort of imagination to connect his own body with the red bandage, and when he does so, he feels suddenly afraid. He makes a monumental effort to survey his own body, but it's like someone has snipped the strings to his personal marionette.

"Is that my blood? What happened to me? Am I going to die? I can't feel my body."

She looks at him with cold grey eyes – eyes in which a fire has burned out leaving just ash behind. "You will not die," she says. "Sleep if you can."

Tears leak unbidden from his eyes as his fear redoubles. "What happened?"

She says nothing and moves beyond his field of vision – he can hear her doing something. A grinding noise and a bubbling.

Some minutes later she asks him to open his mouth – one of the only things he seems to be able to do at the moment – and she pours a brown liquid down his throat. It tastes slightly metallic. She gets him to swallow it, then turns and leaves the room. The headache begins to disappear. Soon Terry nods back off to sleep.

He dreams he's being chased by a bearded madman who wants to chop off his head and limbs, eat him bit by bit and then suck dry his bones. The madman is most of the way through one of his arms when he finally wakes up in a cold sweat.

Madame Fulcanelli is standing above him. She tells him he's been here three days, and he has to take her word for it – he's drifted in and out of consciousness so often that days have lost meaning. All he knows is that he's grateful – she's certainly taking care of him. Life has returned to one arm and he's using it to eat like never before, as if there's a ravenous parasite inside him. He finds meat and bread by the bedside and ploughs through them with this insatiable appetite.

He's recalling fragments now: a pagan feast with fire and dancing and music. Then snow and forest. Then something attacked him. Is that why he keeps thinking of bears? While he tries to piece together his memories, there's a movement in the hut – a change in the shadows that he catches out of the corner of his eye. He has the unnerving feeling that somebody is watching him, and he twists his eyes into sides of their sockets in an effort to scan the room – his head is still practically immovable, as if it were set in concrete.

"Madame Fulcanelli?" Nothing.

There's just enough light to make out a clutter of disused glass, earthenware and knick-knacks, but he sees nothing peculiar, until he notices the whites of a pair of eyes stock still in the gloom. He waits in vain for them to blink, finally deciding that it's just his imagination.

Then they move.

"Who's there?" Terry shouts. The shadow shifts in response. Finally, after an intense minute or so there is a reply.

"My name is Hávulk."

The voice is that of a small boy, soft-spoken and slightly nervous. Her son – he's been forgetting all this time that she had a son. She told Terry about him that night in the bar.

"Hello, Hávulk. You startled me."

The boy says nothing so Terry tries to fill the silence. "I'm Terry. You speak English?"

"Yes," says the boy from the shadows. "You're from English aren't you?"

"Uh. I'm from England, where they speak English."

"Oh."

"Where did you learn it?"

"I learn everything from Petra. She teaches me lots of things – soon I'll know enough to help her properly."

"Help her do what?"

"I'm not supposed to say because alchemists must be very secretive."

"So you're going to help her with alchemy then?"

Hávulk is quiet for a moment. "I suppose I can tell you that.

I'm going to be an alchemist like Petra. Why are you lying there?"

"I don't know, Hávulk – I think I'm getting better."

"Yes, I think you are too – when I first saw you, you looked really terrible. There was a lot of blood."

"Do you know what happened to me?" he asks, but the boy has already moved on.

"Are you a soldier like the ones in the books? That would explain the blood – they're always getting shot – apart from the good ones. You must be a bad soldier. I probably shouldn't be talking to you."

"It's okay – I'm not a soldier. I'm just a translator, but I – well I'm working on it. I'm sure your mum wouldn't mind you talking to me."

"Who?"

"Your mum – your mother. You know, Petra."

"Oh – Petra's not my mum. I don't have a mum. I'm a golem."

"You're a what?"

"I'm a golem – I was made from clay."

"Like in the story?"

"What story?" he asks.

Terry remembers it – an old Jewish story about a Rabbi who made a clay man to protect the Jewish people from their oppressors. It was brought to life with magic words, which were either carved into his skin or somehow put inside its head. It was presumably supposed to be some kind of allegory for spiritual awakening – except didn't the golem go mad and start killing people?

Whatever he's talking to certainly sounds like a boy – a little peculiar in his intonation perhaps, though not beyond the standard distribution of odd accents in the region. The boy must just be using the wrong word, but there should be an easy way to find out. "Step into the light, Hávulk."

The child defensively shuffles backwards further into the darkness. "Why?"

"I just want to know what a... golem... looks like. Don't be shy. I won't hurt you – I don't think I can even get up."

From what he can see, there is nothing curious about the creature that reluctantly steps forward out of the shadows: Hávulk appears to be a boy of about nine or ten years old. He's lean and intelligent-looking. The only thing of mild curiosity is his light yellow-tan hair, which is an oddity compared to the mostly dark-haired population. His is the colour of – well, it's not quite clay, but it's not brown or blond either. It's almost indeterminate, like it could change to blend in with its surroundings. His eyes are golden brown and steady under bristly brows, his ears slightly curled at the tips. Nothing out of the ordinary.

"Well, I think you look like a boy, Hávulk. Did the children at school tell you that you were a golem?"

"I don't go to school," he says.

Petra walks back in, doubtless having heard the whole conversation. "Hávulk," she says, "vra smi ett nage?"

He nods. "Tyk," he says, then turns, grabs a towel off a hook and bounds outside with all the energy of a gazelle. Petra watches him go, smiling a small satisfied smile that goes some way to dissolving her aura of mystery. In that moment, she seems a lot like Terry's own mother as he remembers her when he was little – proud and loving.

Her smile persists as she props a pillow under Terry's head. His body is grateful for the shift in position: he's finally beginning to feel his blood circulating again.

"Where's he going?" asks Terry.

"To swim."

"To swim?"

"There's a mountain stream not far from the house."

"What? In winter? Won't it be freezing?"

She turns to him with something like impatience and once again he notices how tired she looks. "Mr. Terry, why are you here?"

He's taken aback by the question – he doesn't really have an answer. "I – I don't really know. I remember the king's party. Then I think I... uh... followed you from the bar."

"You followed me?"

"I think so," he says, reddening.

"Why?"

"I think I wanted to talk to you – I..."

"Did you think I might tell you how to turn lead into gold? Was that it?"

"No – look, I mean... I was drunk. I do silly things when I'm drunk." He adds feebly, "Everyone does."

She looks as if she's about to say something, but just nods her head slowly.

"I remember being in the forest after the party. I think I was attacked by something."

"A wolf, Mr. Terry – that's what you find if you wander around these woods on your own at night. The Izvaltans call this Karkvitz – the wolf wood."

"But I thought wolves never attacked humans."

"You must have looked at it funny." She smiles "Is that the right phrase?"

With some difficulty he nods, happy to see her light-hearted side.

"The wolves in this area are different from others. Like Izvalta itself, they are enclosed by mountains and have been apart from the rest of their species for centuries: they have their own habits."

"I'd already had a close encounter with a bear. I can't believe I was attacked by a wolf as well."

"This is not the city, Mr. Terry. There are living things. Dangerous things. But you are lucky in a way."

Terry lifts up a corner of his bandage. Where his arm should be is a limb so covered in scars that he barely recognises it. His legs too are covered in scar tissue: his entire body seems to be made up of vicious tears of flesh that have miraculously bonded back together. He covers the arm again and looks away, then looks back. "Jesus Christ. What – what... will... I'm a mess. Is this me? What about my face? Can I see?"

Silently she hands him a makeshift mirror – a polished piece of metal, in which he sees a face that looks familiar but, like the rest of him, is marked with criss-crossed lines of purple-pink scar tissue. He starts to sob. Looking again at the mirror, he wonders if he can end it now – break off a shard and stab himself through the heart. He's never been vain, but at this moment he doesn't know how can he carry on with such a face. He thinks of Lucy back home. Could she accept him like this? Really? Could anyone be so selfless? It's certainly not a trait that runs in her family.

"Mr. Terry. Look at me."

He turns red watery eyes to her.

"The scars will heal. There are some cures known to the ancients but unknown to modern science. You're lucky."

"Really? Lucky? I'm not sure that's the right word."

"You'll look like you once did."

"But how?"

"That I cannot say. But trust me."

And somehow he does. Somehow he knows that she isn't lying – isn't just trying to make him feel better. He really will heal and that is almost as alarming as the scars themselves. He rubs his damp eyes with his one working hand.

"I suppose I owe you my life."

"No – you owe me your silence. There are people who want this knowledge – some people in Izvalta – maybe your soldiers too. It has been protected for a reason. The man who taught me about these things died protecting it. Perhaps I too should have protected it by simply letting you die. But what is done is done. You will just have to be silent."

"But if you can do these things, save people from the brink of death, why wouldn't you want to share the secret? I mean, I could post it on the internet tomorrow and – well, I don't know what would happen."

She closes her eyes and smiles unhappily. "I have some idea what would happen. It's one of those rules that seems to be written into the fabric of this world. The lot of an alchemist who tries to share her knowledge is an unhappy one. It is also not an easy knowledge to share. Some say the true prima materia, the first ingredient for the Work, is simply an open mind. There are few enough of those."

"I'm sorry, Petra," he says "I've put you in danger."

Her smile is a reassuring lie. "You might have sped up the process – I had hoped to avoid another visit from the soldiers for a little while at least. How long do you think it will be before they look for you here?"

He doesn't know – doesn't know how long, what they'll do if they find him here – or even if they've noticed he's gone. All he knows is that he doesn't want to be found. He's part of something now, a truth far beyond his comprehension, and to be yanked back into the real world is unthinkable.

"You will have to leave tomorrow," she says, and tells him to rest, but he can't. Sleep feels like an impossibility: he keeps running his fingers over his scars, willing them away, hoping on each touch to notice a slight smoothing and a return to his old skin texture. Every time Petra catches him doing this she swats his hand away. "Let them heal." Just like his mother did when he had chicken pox as a boy.

After an hour of this, Madame Fulcanelli gives up on settling her patient to sleep. Instead, she stokes the fire and they talk. Mostly they talk about the world outside the valley – a world she's never seen before. Terry's accounts, however, never quite satisfy the alchemist.

"To know what a city is like," she says, "you have to breathe the air and listen to its heartbeat. Not that I don't appreciate your descriptions, but I know about the Paris that can be described by a book – I even know its language. What I want is to feel its soul."

It occurs to Terry that anyone might feel the need to see the world after living in this cramped space. "How long have you been in this place? Here in the woods I mean?"

"A long time." She sighs.

"And Izvalta? Did you always live here?"

"Always."

There's a little whimpering noise from beyond the light of the fire: Hávulk is sleeping softly there. Petra smiles over at him.

"He was telling me something about himself." Terry clears his throat – he can't help asking the question. "He seems to think you're not his mother."

She considers before answering. "There is a sense in which that is true."

"What sense?"

The woman laughs freely. "If I give you an answer, you'll ask and ask for more answers. Each answer will lead to a new question and you'll end up grasping at thin air. It will be much simpler for you to understand that I am his mother. Don't I act that way?"

"But he said he was a golem – I mean, he's not literally made out of clay, right?"

"You think he's maybe been carried away by a metaphor? If I told you that yes, that boy sleeping by the fire was made of clay, it wouldn't help you to make sense of who or what he is. You need to understand this – the first premise of alchemy: there is no 'you' and 'me'; 'the rock' and 'the mountain'; heaven, earth, trees and dirt – all of these are *human* labels, and they define things by their differences rather than the things they have in common."

"But what does that mean?"

"Viewed correctly, there is not so much difference between lead and gold, or between a little boy and a lump of clay. How much difference is there between a man and a corpse? You, for now, are a man."

"A grateful one."

"Ha! Gratitude. You'll be well enough to leave tomorrow and that is what you will do. For now, please try to sleep."

She plumps the pillow underneath his head and quietly snuffs the candles with a little brass cup.

"It's been good to talk to you, Terry. Goodnight."

He's aware of some commotion. People moving around. Hurried whispers. Strange sounding words with an overtone of panic. Then he's literally jerked into full consciousness. Hávulk is there tugging frantically at his arm – the one that until quite recently felt like dead flesh that was still attached. Pins and needles shudder up it now, insistently reminding him that he's alive.

Petra marches in. "You must leave," she says.

"But I..." he says, gesturing to his legs.

"Get up! Get up!"

He leans forward to test his legs, but there is no time: she lifts him with unexpected strength from his recumbent position, landing him painfully on two feet. Now she's throwing clothes at him – not his, but those of someone roughly his size.

There is a knock at the door – firm, verging on violent. "They mustn't find you here." says Petra, looking into Terry's eyes. "You did not come here – you got lost after the king's party, understand? Silence. Complete silence. Your wounds will heal. Show nobody."

Terry dumbly nods assent. He's almost dressed as the knocking comes again.

"Hávulk." She gives him a barrage of instructions in that strange language, whereupon the boy takes Terry's hand and with the force of a small locomotive, pulls him towards a very low door at the back of the house – something the size of a large cat-flap. Before squeezing through, Terry looks back at Petra, who has covered the blood-stained bench that's been serving as his bed with a half-butchered goat carcass. Hopefully that will be enough to fool any visitors, and he can take a pretty accurate guess as to who they might be – after all, he's been away from the camp for over three days now.

Hávulk knows the area well. Terry is dragged and jostled through a dark tunnel, through mountain tracks and undergrowth, over rock outcrops and back down into sheltered, snowless caves that thread their way under the surrounding peaks.

After what must be an hour of tumbling through the rough terrain, the pair finally emerge into the valley of Svart, with the Valta river shivering along its floor. Terry is exhilarated – it feels like the first time his body has ever been so alive and responsive – it feels brand new. He looks over the snowy landscape and an incredible thirst for adventure wells up in his chest. The feeling is quickly subdued when he remembers his situation, and he raises his hands to his face. Judging by touch alone, he must be a monstrous sight. He keeps his head down as they walk.

They are in an area of Svart that Terry doesn't know, covered in ramshackle farms constructed from tumbling stones and flaking plaster, as if the people that built these houses were only mildly concerned about whether they fell down within the year. Outside the buildings stand clusters of emaciated cattle and sheep cropping at clutches of damp grass that poke through the snow.

Hávulk trots in between the buildings, stopping at a tipsy wooden doorway. He knocks and waits for the occupant to undo a little knot of string that serves in lieu of a lock. The man behind the door is old, with crooked teeth and a head that appears to be gradually shrinking in proportion to his body. He smiles broadly at his visitors, though he stares openly at Terry's face for far longer than is comfortable. He shares a few words with Hávulk, then addresses Terry.

"You soldier, yes? Rat-at-at rat-at-at." He mimes a machine gun. "You fight, yes?" He points to Terry's face. The story makes sense, and at least the old man doesn't seem concerned – quite the opposite. He motions for Terry to come inside, where he leads him to a tatty bed and Hávulk instructs him in those serious tones peculiar to strong-minded children to stay until his scars are gone; that he should plead drunken insanity and a sudden fever in answer to any enquiries he may receive as to his whereabouts. About his host he learns nothing at all, apart from the fact that he's a farmer who speaks very little English, which should excuse him from interrogation by the military.

Terry holds out a hand to stop the boy as he turns to leave. "Hávulk."

"Yes?"

"Thank you. And tell your mo... tell Petra thanks too."

"That's okay. I'm happy that you came to visit. It's lonely out in the woods. Will I see you again?"

"Sure," says Terry, secretly thinking that it would be best for them both if he didn't.

Hávulk is gone and the farmer is making busy kitchen sounds in the next room. Terry looks down at the strange clothes Petra gave him to wear and spots a problem: these clothes are old and worn, but made of a woven grey material far too elegant to belong to this farmer. As he prepares to tackle the daunting task of miming a request for old clothes, he wonders what happened to his own. Presumably they were too ripped and bloody to salvage.

Taking off his gloves he uncovers the patterns of violent scars that spread across his hand. Perhaps it's down to sheer hopefulness on his part, but they seem less pronounced than they were before he started his journey. He unbuttons his shirt and looks down to see more of the same all over his body. It's taking a lot of faith for him to convince himself that they'll ever completely heal – in fact it's taking a lot of faith to believe he isn't dreaming or hallucinating. It's almost like he's blundered into some rumple in the fabric of reality – a rabbit-hole to an undiscovered territory beyond the edge of the map of science and conventional knowledge. In the universe he thought he belonged to, Terry should have been mauled and eaten. But somewhere in the margins of that universe he was saved. Petra brought him back from the brink of death somehow, but with what? Alchemy? Even if she had some kind of miracle medicine, how could it possibly re-grow flesh and even organs? If the scars are anything to go by, the wolf had a good meal – it didn't just attack then run away.

The farmer enters with a herbal tea in a dirty plastic cup, which he offers to Terry, grinning broadly. Terry chokes on the first sip – it tastes horrible.

"What is it?" he asks, but the old man just nods and gestures to the cup. Whatever it is, it puts him straight to sleep.

The next day the army finds him.

People keep looking at him oddly. He tries to will away his scars, but he can see from peoples' faces how obvious they are. As a gruff lieutenant jostles him through the camp to the captain's office, smiles drop, curiosity twitches at the corners of people's brows, and even Ethan Smith, who Terry thought couldn't be wrong-footed by anything short of apocalypse, stands there with a cigarette halfway to his mouth, just looking at him.

He catches sight of his reflection in a window. He's looking better – or is it his imagination? He holds his hands to his face, tracing the valleys and craters. His skin itches and he longs for a shower – perhaps he could wash away the scar tissue like so many loose fish-scales, revealing a fresh new skin underneath. But there's no time – he's being taken directly to the captain.

For the last fifty yards he's been trying to jumble together a story. Bear attack? Fever? Disease? Divine intervention? The lieutenant isn't asking any questions and somehow that makes Terry more nervous.

They reach Rogers' door, but the lieutenant shoves him on with an iron grip on his shoulder. They're not going to the captain's room. Perhaps he's being led behind the camp to be shot. *No, Terry*, he tells himself, *You've done nothing wrong. Not really*. Then he sees where he's being taken: the blockhouse. The only part of this makeshift encampment that's been fitted with a reasonably thick door – a door that looks considerably sturdier than the building itself. He doesn't recognise the man holding it open for them, nor the one in the lab coat who studies his face the way one might study an insect under glass, before guiding him into a room filled with beeps and clicks. Lots of computers; they outnumber the chairs by at least three to one.

"Stand there, Morton."

He's in the centre of the room. Rogers is there at the

entrance.

"Clothes off," he says.

"What?"

"What, sir."

"Uh. Ah – sorry. What, sir?"

"Your clothes, Morton. Off."

"Why?" It seems a magnificently silly question. The wolf's savage bite marks are there on his face and hands. It feels like the ones on his chest are glowing through his coat for all to see. The question is never dignified with a response and when the farmer's simple wrappings are removed, so is any question of lying about an illness. There's no way these scars are the result of a fever. But still – he must find some excuse. Anything to protect Petra and her secret. He folds his arms loosely over his belly; a token gesture to guard against the chill and complete loss of dignity, but even this is denied him.

"Arms down," commands the captain.

"No stitches," says the other, a small man in his early forties wearing a pair of neat spectacles that give him a studious look.

Terry forces himself to speak, fearing that his silence is making him appear guilty. "I... I haven't had stitches – I mean, I haven't been cut – this is just a rash isn't it? From sleeping on coarse wool or something – maybe I'm allergic, but there's nothing wrong with me."

"You're not well placed to make that judgement I'm afraid." The smaller man's voice is not unkind, but it's cold. "My name is Henry Mitchell. I'm a doctor." He smiles briefly. "Now Mr. Morton, I can tell you for a start that what you have there is no rash. These are atrophic scars." He points to several places on Terry's body with a latex-gloved hand. "You see where the fat and muscle has been removed below the surface of the skin. This results in the dimpled effect you see over the right hand side of the torso."

The lecture is mostly for Rogers, but Terry also examines his body, which now looks so unlike the one he remembers that he doubts his ownership. The patterns etched into it make it appear like a moonscape with wide purple craters.

"Now, what is remarkable," the doctor continues, "is the speed at which this scar tissue has formed – ordinarily I would say that we were looking at a wound inflicted over a year ago, but I suppose that this rapid healing is only the second of two miracles: the first is that this young man survived at all."

It's Rogers' cue. "So, Morton, you don't know what those marks are? Let's start with what you do know. What happened to you on the night of the king's feast?"

For a brief moment he considers telling Rogers about the events of the last few days, but it's dismissed as soon as it enters his mind. It's not just about owing Petra his life; he feels a connection that runs deeper even than that. He won't betray her trust. He tries to look innocent and perplexed.

"I was drunk, sir. I just remember waking up in that farmer's hut."

"And you're sure you remember nothing else? Well that's not entirely surprising. I suppose we'll just have to let science do the talking won't we? Over to you, doctor."

The doctor guides Terry to a chair with an arm-rest that angles his arm slightly downwards. It's a good deal softer than the alchemist's bench, and yet somehow far less comforting. The doctor finds a vein, swabs, and sticks in the needle. The feeling in his arm once more begins to fade away, a phantom limb phasing out of existence once again. Rogers is talking at him.

"In all honesty, it doesn't make a great deal of difference whether or not you tell me what happened while you were AWOL. Those marks of yours are as legible as 6-foot copperplate.

Wolf bites – you can tell by the size of the mouth. The teeth are shorter and sharper than a bear's. Unless you were savaged by a dog, which is unlikely even in Svart. And there's only one place you'd have run into wolves that would attack a human. My best guess? That patch of forest to the east of the city. Human population: one suspected alchemist."

Terry keeps his mouth shut.

"Of course, we looked for you there, but you'd already made your escape."

"What are you going to do with me?"

"We're going to see if we can use you to get some clues as to how this magic healing works. I trust you have no objections?"

"I didn't think it would make much difference if I did."

Before the captain can respond, Mitchell intercedes. "Mr. Morton, this is not a matter for argument. Just think on this: the treatment you received after your wolf bites, if we can find out how it works, could help millions if not billions of people. I'm not given to large pronouncements, but if this is what we think it is, then the world of medicine could be transformed in a matter of months. Who knows the full extent of this technique? Perhaps it can be brought to bear on our toughest cancers, our most lethal diseases, restore sight to the blind, mobility to the injured."

And finally Terry sees why the military is so excited. No more limbless veterans coming back from wars and jangling their collection cups on street corners. No more need to send them back to convalesce at all – just heal them up and put them back on the field a few days later. A zombie military kept alive by whatever dark arts have been applied to him.

"So this is going to be a new era of military medicine?"

Rogers sighs. "We don't need medicine today. We could put down the toughest opposition with a half dozen drones at a distance of thousands of miles away. Soon we won't be able to send a man in to do a soldier's job – it won't be politically viable to put our own boys in danger, but soldiers are what we need. We need men on the ground, not some adolescent with a joystick. I mean look at you, Morton – how you've comported yourself over the short time we've been here. The computer geeks are just as clueless. We need disciplined, trained soldiers to be a strong hand in Afghanistan and Syria, but people expect zero casualties. We need to do our work without sending bodies back to mummy and daddy.

"Something else to consider, Morton. It's not just you. Looking at the statistics, Izvalta is a hot-bed of miracle cures. No-one else has been stupid enough to get torn apart by the local wildlife, of course, but in the last five years there has been zero infant mortality in this country. A country with a single, pestilential pit of a hospital I wouldn't visit if I had tuberculosis for fear of catching something worse. You know what else? The only people to actually die in the last five years have been serious accidental deaths and a couple of little old ladies that froze to death in the winter. There has been no death by disease – no death by ageing even. Izvalta has the healthiest population on this entire God-forsaken planet. You've seen it – some of the poorest people here are practically wallowing in their own shit, there are stray dogs running around all over the place. It's a perfect breeding ground for diseases, but the people are impeccably healthy. Now that's interesting, isn't it?"

Rogers seems to sense Terry's doubt.

"The sources are good – this has been corroborated. We've talked to the local doctors, who seem to think it's down to some heavenly blessing, but the real proof is in the graveyards. Turns out the only undertaker in town got laid off three years ago. He hasn't been replaced."

"So what, you think my... scars are somehow related to the

general health of Izvalta?"

"Perhaps," says the doctor. "I've been studying the conditions here, but there's nothing chemically abnormal about the Izvaltans. Their diet is poor; high instance of vitamin deficiency; life expectancy should be in the early 60s. There must be some external factor keeping people alive, and you might have just stumbled across it."

"Wait – does that mean I'm going to live forever?"

"That's what we're going to find out," says Rogers.

It took only three days to recover from near death, but it looks like the same stretch of time in the hands of doc Mitchell might undo all of that. Whatever he's been infected with has brought on a deep fever and he feels like he's swimming in porridge. He has been relocated to a bed in the centre of a plain room. Running around the bed is a curtain, which occasionally parts to admit blurry figures wearing face-masks. They speak to him only to ask how he feels, and his response never seems to alter their demeanour.

His mind doesn't so much wander as drown. Characters loom up from the depths. Lucy is there in a pretty summer dress. They're at a party where she dances with a bear and a wolf that starts to tear chunks of flesh from her legs, and this seems to send her into a state of ecstasy. Terry is powerless.

Petra Fulcanelli appears often. Running. Sometimes with Hávulk. He hopes they haven't done anything to her – if they do it will be because of him.

In another foggy vision a stuffy Eton-bred politician speaks platitudes into a bank of media microphones. "Working with our friends the Izvaltans, we have developed a substance that could potentially lengthen the lives of the world's population – perhaps indefinitely. Sadly, due to certain restrictions, which I am not at liberty to discuss, the um... serum... cannot be made available to everyone. First in line, of course, will be Her Majesty, The Queen, followed by all of those men, and some women too, who have demonstrated their fitness for immortality by their performances on that most democratic of stages, capitalism.

"The people of Izvalta will be granted the full support of our peacekeeping program: this support will take the form of an enhanced military presence, which will be tasked with protecting the region from potential threats, including anyone that might wish to plunder Izvalta's valuable resources. It is our clear duty to protect this tiny, defenceless country against these would-be malevolent forces."

Through a gap in the curtain, Terry can see the doctor talking to a computer screen showing two images: one, a serious looking man, all jowls and wrinkles, and the other, a vague bluey-purple blob. Unlike the press conference, this scene has an aura of reality, but Terry can't be certain it's not another dream.

"Now this is a fresh sample of what we're calling 'Stone TX-1'," the doctor says, focusing a microscope so that the blobby image blurs and sharpens.

"It looks normal," says the man on the other side of the screen. "That's what we were expecting after all. What have you got on the CMP?"

"CMP is just coming up. Calcium is high, but that's about it. I'm running with the current theory and testing for sulphur and mercury..."

"Tell me he had a medical before shipping out."

"Standard procedure – had a blood pressure of a hundred and thirty-two over eighty-six, but probably just white coat syndrome. Mercury is coming up positive. Bloody hell, are you seeing that?"

"That's way too high. Are you sure that's right?"

"Certain."

"How long has it been?"

"Our best guess is five to six days."

"So that'll have halved or more since first ingestion. It's a miracle he survived this 'cure', whatever it was."

"Looks like we have sulphur in there too – not as pronounced, but significant."

"Have you weighed him?"

"No – why?"

"Just a thought. Put him on the scales."

Terry is assisted to his feet. "You feeling okay?" asks Mitchell, but not in a way that suggests that he cares. Terry balances on the scales with some difficulty.

"Good Lord," says Mitchell. "When was the last time you ate? You've put on nineteen and half kilograms since your last weigh-in." He steps back but can't see where Terry can have put it all – his gangly figure hasn't changed at all.

"That's impossible," comes the voice from the computer. "Unless he's eaten an iron bar or something. Henry, in all seriousness I think you need to do an x-ray. Look for metals, dense flesh, anything out of the ordinary – there must be an explanation."

"We're just getting one set up – had to get it sent from..." The doctor's sentence is interrupted by a bang – it sounds like a shot, followed by more shots and shouting.

"What was that?" asks the man on the screen.

"Something happening outside." The silence is barbed with anticipation, but nothing else happens. Then there are shouts in the corridor. The door bashes open.

"Doc, doc! We need you out here now!" It's Neil. For the first time Terry sees how young he is without his armour of bravado. He looks scared to death.

"What – what's going on? Private Spencer. Private! What is the situation?" Mitchell is also panicked. All Neil can do is point lamely and say "Jim – he's ah. Fuck. Fuck."

The doctor hurries out, leaving Terry leaning unsteadily against the desk where a face peers oddly out of the screen, trying to gauge what's going on. It takes a few moments for Terry to realise that he can walk without assistance, albeit not well. His head is still swimming. He goes to the window and peers through the blinds, ignoring the voice from the computer. There are bright white floodlights outlining the perimeter of the base, illuminating a few yards of cold, muddy terrain and the weather-worn brickwork of the outhouses. There are no tents on this side of the encampment; there's not much of anything in fact. Then something moves into the light. The figure stares right back at Terry's eye as it squints through the blind. And then it's gone.

"Hávulk." Terry murmurs to himself. Or something that could have been... it's hard to say with the room spinning. The only clear and distinct thing he's aware of is his pulse, which he can feel inside his skull, throbbing through his temples. Everything else is muted and confused.

Outside the doctor's room there is an occasional heavy footfall in the corridor, and once or twice men squelch swiftly past the window, pointing guns and torches into the night. Gradually the activity subsides. There are no more shots fired.

"Get him out of here. We need this room." Rogers is at the door, pointing to Terry. As he passes, Terry sees a man in bloody camo gear being supported between two soldiers like a drunk. His head is tilted right back as if he's singing at the stars. For a moment Terry thinks this is the root of the madness – one of the soldiers got pissed and started shooting the place up so they had to knock the poor idiot over the head. Then he sees that the man's head isn't thrown back: it's not there at all.

CHAPTER 11
IZVALTA

26 July 1939, approach to Ingolstadt

I sit at the side of the river, bread in one hand and a cup of purified water in the other. I have been here for hours, just staring at the water as it rushes by, the stones on the river bank, a heron watching patiently for passing fish.

I have been reflecting further on the nature of the Work. I look back on my time with the Fraternité d'Héliopolis; our 'alchemical miracles' and our '*savoir profond*'. Undoubtedly we created marvels through our understanding of alchemy, but for what? We safeguarded the Hermetic teachings, but have they done any good? Have they ensured that good people will prevail over petty minds? Not at all. I see now what I must have known all along: that we were only ever selfish fools, content to retrace the divine steps and prolong our own lives, but too scared to share this knowledge except through a thick veil of misdirection.

I remember the fevered nights and days I spent describing in full each and every step of the Work – it was to be a manual of alchemy unlike any ever written: advice for the novice, recommendations for sourcing materials, precise instructions for the correct use of equipment. Piece by piece it was laid out. Any person in the world, be they rich or poor, with access to this book and some basic equipment would be able to follow those self-same steps. Alchemy would be the great equaliser: wealth and longevity for all, irrespective of birth or social boundaries. And then I returned to the conclusion of my teachers: that this knowledge could not and should not be freely given, but controlled. And how to control it? Obfuscation by means of impenetrable cyphers that could only be cracked by the most devoted of the intellectual elite.

These cyphers were to be our shibboleth, but the ability to untangle them was proof of mania as much as of genius, and the brotherhood was thus populated by madmen. How many read My *Mystery of the Cathedrals* and understood its parallels between Christian carvings and alchemical teachings? Who could draw out their secret? Over-educated and over-stuffed aristocrats; the deranged of mind and spirit. If I had meant to share the Art with those to whom it might have made some beneficial difference, I would have published my manual, rather than instructing my readers to look back to a religious tradition so muddied and nonsensical that one could waste several lifetimes studying it.

As it was, I got what I deserved: full exposure to the arrogance of a bunch of self-selecting luminaries along with their bickering and backstabbing. How many lives have been lost in the attempt to de-mystify a set of natural laws that might have simply been taught? I think of all the poor fools drinking poisons they believed would preserve their bodies forever. Some charlatans, true, but who was I to decide? To choose how to disseminate divine knowledge like a priest for the elite.

I am a different man now: time and distance have shifted the contours of my soul as surely as the wind and waves alter the landscape over many centuries. I will not say I am closer to perfection, but I am perhaps further from sin. I feel such a desire to share my knowledge – God's knowledge – and why should I fear discovery?

Perhaps the people who value so highly the gold that I produce would realise at last that its value is only relative: that if they really desired it, they could have it in infinite quantity and therefore it is valueless. Perhaps if they sampled the elixir they would not strive so for power in this short lifetime? Ah, to Hell with it. For all that I may understand the soul of nature I cannot comprehend the minds of men.

2 August 1939, just beyond Regensburg

As the channel broadens, my boat begins to feel more and more insignificant, like a coracle in the middle of a vast ocean. It's liberating. My years of hermitage slide away, the world unfolds before me, and behind every bend in the river it seems, is a new kingdom of possibility.

The border of Austria must be close at hand. I have passed Ingolstadt and Regensburg, the latter heavily industrialised and not as I had imagined. The larger cities are all building up to war – that much is clear, though thus far I have escaped too much scrutiny. Germany is preoccupied and the fishwives who sell me salted meat and bread at inflated prices are happy for the extra income as long as I hurry back out of sight. I have developed a practice of hiding the boat under some overhanging foliage at a distance outside the smaller settlements. I then seek out a market or a farm and I pay with the Deutschmarks I picked up from selling the gold. I have dropped my cover story, finding it far more expedient to pose as a mute wanderer. People still look at me oddly – my appearance is striking I suppose – but they are quick to forget what they wish to ignore.

As long as I remain a step ahead of the spread of war, God willing, I will come through this alive – although what end He has in store, I cannot know.

There seems to be a page missing here – a tear where a single thin sheet has been extracted. Although it puzzles her, she doesn't give it much thought and the boy continues his reading the next night.

12 September 1939, Breznitza Ocol, Romania

The Patchwork Man: that's what I'll call him. It occurs to me only now that I didn't ask his name, although I'm not sure he needs one beyond this title. I haven't met a great many people on this journey: the need for anonymity has precluded it, and yet had I met a thousand I suppose that he would still be the one that left the greatest impression.

From what I can gather I have been travelling the border between Serbia and Romania for some days now, through a set of sheer cliffs that seem to have been blasted out of the hills. Finally, after midday, the cliffs began to sink on the eastern side and I took my first opportunity to disembark.

Mooring my craft out of sight I travelled north-east with no particular goal in mind, until I came across the little town of Breznitza Ocol. It is one of the first places I have felt a little safe. Children were playing in the street and as I approached I heard the church bell chiming the time. Three beautiful peals. It seemed so pure and untainted that, for the first time in almost two months, I allowed myself a small comfort and turned to the local tavern – which is where I met the Patchwork Man.

His clothes were a collection of motley scraps: in every village he passes, he picks up a scrap of cloth to mend the rips in his clothes, or a piece of metal that he can hammer onto the tips of his boots. His costume is so ragged that it's a challenge to identify the original material of the coat, while his boots are so over-cobbled as to be completely impractical for anyone but him – they must weigh a kilo each and yet he lifts them with ease. Of course, he is built like a Viking, with a long thatch of beard to match.

It is the source of some wonder that after the terror of my journey I would so readily accept a drink from this complete stranger. However I put it down to three things: Firstly, I believe that one can judge from a face the temperament of a fellow's soul. Secondly, his wild costume bore no resemblance to the regimented uniforms that have dotted my route and haunted my nightmares, and thirdly, he hailed me in French!

This Belgian mountaineer has, over the last year, been hiking the full length of the Carpathians. He started in Poland in the summer and somehow weathered a fearsome winter under his incredible coat (he treats it with what he calls 'wool fat' to keep the rain off – it's just one of the inventions he's come up with to survive). It seemed like madness to me: I asked him, "Did you get advice from any locals before you went out?" He just laughed. "And have them tell me I'm an idiot and I'll die like one?" His philosophy is incredible to me: everything I ever learned was from someone else; by studying the words in a book or by listening to my instructors. I try to think now of an innovation of my own and I cannot, yet here is a man who is certainly not as well educated as I and possibly not even as intelligent, who is fearlessly relying on his wits and ingenuity to survive each and every day. There is a freedom to it that I admire very much.

The stories he told – of great chasms bridged by enormous fallen rocks, of almost falling to his death a dozen times – and why? He could not or would not say, but his words resonated with me – I shall recall them as best I can: "The mountain has a soul. This whole range has a soul – a big one. It seems to me that when I walk a mountain, it becomes like an old friend. When you approach the mountain in the right way, with the right kind of respect, it will protect you. All of those times I thought death might be catching up with me I was saved – pulled back from the edge by the mountain itself." I see parallels here with the Work: they are both solitary pursuits, both entail a kind of communion with the natural world and both yield a result that could be deemed supernatural by the casual onlooker who doesn't understand the technique. It is fascinating to find an art so close to my own and yet so different. Certainly it has made me look at the mountain in another light, although I am no mountaineer.

"On the mountain ridge I have no care for borders or one country's authority over another. Up there, there is no territory but nature in all her glory," he said. This too struck a chord, and so ready was I to exchange philosophies that before I knew it I had told this man of my great mission.

My purpose, it appears, has resolved itself into a clear objective: to find a benevolent ruler and to support that ruler – plainly speaking, to extend their reign through alchemy.

But oddly it seemed to me that my pronouncement fazed

him not at all. Instead, on hearing this, The Patchwork Man shook his head. "It's a thing peculiar to Westerners," he said, "that we must always concentrate on the smallest part of a system and look to it for answers. A single individual can't dictate the structure of the world – be he a pope or a prime minister." In this I disagree with him. We are not like stones on a beach with no single stone exerting more influence than another. We are more akin to setting honey: once a crystal forms, the rest of the honey begins to set in a crystalline structure. That first crystal can be introduced by an individual. It is an idea, the lines of which can be followed. Once the honey is set, of course, those ideas are set into it and the application of heat is required to return it to a fluid state. I know that the right kind of structure exists somewhere in human society and I am resolved to find and aid its propagation. I will create or grow that first crystal.

Though he disagreed with my aims, the Patchwork Man told me of a place he visited not so far away, not more than a week's hike – even for a man who hasn't yet found his mountain legs. He described a curious enclave where a king still reigns with the full support of his people, where this support is well earned through acts of kindness and far-sighted leadership. He described building programs for schools and churches and the most wondrous festivals in the area, where Romanian visitors from the foothills come together with the locals at certain times of the year in communal celebration. It makes me nervous to anticipate it, but perhaps I have found what I'm looking for: my Utopia – the crystal that I must nourish and grow.

It is late, but I can barely think of sleeping – the possibilities continue to dance around my head and in front of my eyes. I'll have to leave the boat and find myself a guide with a horse and cart. I expect it will be a hard road, as I am not so used to the terrain as my friend, but I am hopeful that my long journey is nearing its end.

19 September 1939

Izvalta. Somehow the name suggests freedom – an escape from earthly concerns. Perhaps it is the lure of hope that frames it so, but as I crossed the fields this morning the air seemed fresher and more pure than any I have ever breathed, the homesteads more idyllic than any I have seen, and the approach to the castle more utterly magnificent than the most spectacular vistas of Greece and Italy. I felt compelled to leave the horse and cart in the charge of the young lad whose services I engaged at Breznitza Ocol. I left the road to wander the fields and forests for a short while – an incredibly rewarding experience yielding the discovery of diverse flora, including some of the best walnuts I've ever tasted. The valley is long and broad, leading up to majestic mountains that seem to have been sculpted with particular attention by God's hands, such is their shapely precision. The castle is built into the foot of these mountains, with the city of Svart spread below alongside a great forest that must be as old as the planet itself.

I have lived over a hundred years now, but I have never seen the like of Izvalta. I hope that the Patchwork Man has not exaggerated the freedoms that may be enjoyed here at the hands of the country's notoriously enlightened ruler; that it is indeed a nation emancipated from the concerns of petty politics, tyrant landowners and violent men. Should my hopes be borne out in reality I look forward to passing my gifts into worthy hands, for they are a burden that I long to share.

For tonight I have secured myself a room above a tavern in the picturesque lower end of town, which was no small feat – their language is quite alien to me! Tomorrow I shall seek out the king.

20 September 1939

Disaster! I am too late: the king is dead. As I approached the castle I could see the anxious crowd. From what I could gather, the king lay dying, and as a foreigner and a complete stranger I was denied access. Seeing my hopes dashed, I became desperate and began to insist that I could cure him – such folly! Of course I was not understood initially as not one of the local people speaks French, but some common ground was found in Latin, which I was able to exchange with a clergyman. I was treated with some suspicion – I am sure that some of the old ladies thought I was the devil or death itself and were making signs with their hands to ward me away from their beloved ruler. Then one old woman came forward, her arms outstretched towards me shouting "Haralambie! Haralambie!" I later discovered that this is the name of a local saint said to cure people and drive away pestilence, to whom I bear some resemblance.

Would that I truly possessed Haralambie's powers! I was allowed to enter, perhaps because of this physical resemblance, but as I looked behind the curtain where the man lay I could see that I was too late. The king was breathing his last. He was not old – my diagnosis is that he succumbed to the sudden onset of cancer of the blood. I am not certain that I could have saved him even had I arrived some months earlier. Saint or no, I found it hard to raise my eyes to meet the expectant crowd as I quit the royal chamber.

There is a curious tradition here at the death of a king, whereupon the local women wail as if the day of judgement has arrived. The men simply go about their business while this goes on, and it continues for hours along the entire length of the valley. What began as a curious phenomenon quickly became a source of extreme annoyance as the noise hindered my communications while I was questioned by a group of those close to the king – supposed nobles of the land – about my presence at his deathbed.

Where had I come from and why had I come here of all places? Who and what was I? They did not seem so ready as the old woman to accept that I was Saint Haralambie in mortal form, though this was certainly not my claim. With a few priests translating, I confessed that I was no saint, but that it was my aim to give a gift of longevity to the liberal-hearted ruler of the country so that he might continue his enlightened rule even into the next century. Would that I had had the capacity for some innocent lie, but I was exhausted. I simply couldn't think of an alternative reason for being there: already I had disclosed the fact that I was capable of great medicine and I do wish to win the trust of these good people. That will not be achieved by lying to them from the start, but I fear I should have kept some details back.

For now, at least, I am spared from performing the miracle promised. The new king is just a boy of fourteen years and is as healthy as a tiger cub.

Perhaps there is something to be gained from this situation, for I can tutor the boy; steer him down a noble path – a path along his father's reputedly selfless lines. My fantasies will surely pick me up and carry over the nearest rainbow, but I can't help my optimism. God's plan must be that I should help to mould a new Utopian society from the base material of this community. It will be an island of peace in the turbulent ocean of European war. I just pray that the madness that seems to have overtaken so many of the towns I passed on my travels will not march to the foot of the valley and demand audience.

22 September 1939

I have seen gold devoured by aqua regia, the green lion, in a matter of seconds, but it is greed that is the swiftest agent in the mortal world. It insinuates itself into the heart of man as quickly as a thought, and there it remains, sucking in blood on the one side and pumping poison from the other.

My status as an alchemist having been disclosed to all, I was summoned by the nobles of the high town (the de facto governors of Izvalta until the boy Monterek comes of age) to perform acts of magic in court. I kept my head as far as was humanly possible, but the request infuriated me beyond all reason. I did go to the court, however, and I told them of the things that alchemy can and cannot achieve. "Magic," I said, "is a collection of parlour tricks performed by conmen, whereas alchemy is the science of the perfection of things. While magic is paganism pure and simple, alchemy seeks to do the work of God and cannot be achieved without His presence."

They were taken aback, and I am glad, for I refuse to be pushed around. But there is still an expectation that I must prove myself and somehow pay 'tribute' to His Majesty. Am I to bow down to a whelp? I have made it clear that my support is far from unconditional and that I will owe no allegiances. I will take nothing of their hospitality, preferring to pay my own way at the inn, and so I owe them nothing. Sadly, however, I have only a little money left and so my independence is threatened. Would that I could simply make some gold – I have my equipment here, after all, but I cannot start the Work in some common inn, where a maid might barge in and upset a delicate process. I require peace and space.

And then there is my other worry – that of failure. Before my departure from the Schwarzwald, I had been failing to transmute so much as a grain of base metal and I ascribed that failure to my wavering convictions. Now my convictions have returned, but my motives are mixed, and this troubles me.

Albertus Magnus's words have been well borne out by history: an alchemist should avoid the affairs of princes and noblemen. It is common that once a contract is made with such a figure, the alchemist will fail and be condemned to any one of a number of gruesome deaths. Certainly many 'alchemists' who followed this path and succumbed to it were simple fraudsters, but I wonder if even a true alchemist might fail in producing gold for a prince or even for a state. How, after all, is one supposed to fix on the holy principles of the Art if one has thoughts of secular gain in mind?

My hopes now rest largely with Gregor, the king's personal chaplain, selected as a companion for the boy by King Marek before he passed away. He is some ten years older than the king and is well versed in Latin. It is through him that I most often communicate with Monterek. I think he realises my predicament – the fact that I must stay here and yet will not offer up my talents to the mercy of the state as it stands.

Gregor has suggested an alternative course of action: that I create a devotional work for the church, for which the church would recompense me not in monetary terms, but with labour. The people of Izvalta, in return for this work, will gather to construct for me a home of my own design in a location far enough removed from the settlement of Svart that I shan't be disturbed. It appears to me to be an excellent solution – and one that I must confess inspires me greatly even in my desperation. It must be considered further.

27 September 1939

I have resolved to undertake the work at the church. After all, I have experience in church sculpture, though I have never tried my hand at it. I may even create something that hints at the alchemical: perhaps a firmament and an earth reflecting each other in the horizontal plane. 'As above, so below.'

Though my interviews with the noble blood of Izvalta continue to be frosty, I feel something of what the Patchwork Man must have felt here. Just taking in the landscape and breathing the air is so conducive to goodness that I can hardly imagine a false motive in the whole universe. Of course I should guard myself against this kind of idealism – I must remember that it is a political madness in the minds of men that has forced me to flee to this far-off region and that I am not beyond its clutches.

As part of my deal with Gregor, I have secured the post of tutor to the young king for a weekly lesson in politics based heavily on the beliefs of his pious and generous father, about whom I am learning a great deal. I hope that through this instruction the young king may find his way to becoming a ruler in his father's image. It is for this goal that I nightly pray.

3 June 1940

Thanks be to God for these thick walls. Now I understand why everybody in this country keeps a dog and why the labourers who are helping me with the building always travel through the woods together, never tarrying beyond the moment when the sun dips below the mountain's edge – which is of course, why the project is progressing so slowly. At first I thought that perhaps the legends of Dracula or Vlad the Impaler in ghostly form might be the source of their anxiety; some throwback that the locals still credit, for there is a quantity of local superstition. But that is not the cause of their reluctance – I don't even think they are aware of the myth. It's the wolves that scare them.

I had not appreciated the gravity of the problem until tonight, when I decided that I would stay in the house so that I could make an early start on it tomorrow. I have problems communicating with the labourers without the aid of Gregor, but I was able to read their expressions as if they were written in ink. 'On your head be it' they seemed to say. Nevertheless, they departed without me, leaving me in my as yet roofless house.

Now I hear several of the beasts sniffing and scuffling around the building. It certainly wouldn't be wise to leave the safety of the walls at this point, but I am at least confident that no wolf can jump the ten feet required to clear them.

2:46am

The howling is driving me crazy and the wretched beasts keep digging at the foundations of the walls – thank God I had them set deep, yet I am constantly on edge and I still can't sleep. A curse on Gregor for picking out this plot of land! I am now wondering if he didn't purposefully suggest this place so that I might be eaten up. But why? Surely the sculpture I am working on is God's work. It is the church and the people of Izvalta that benefit from my labour. If I die before the work is finished, what good will it do?

I see what it must be: Gregor doubts me. He thinks I'm just another con artist hanging around the court. One that must be disposed of quietly in an out of the way location. I must show him that he is indeed mistaken, but first I must survive to see tomorrow.

4:20am

There's nothing quite as terrifying as a wolf's eyes in the night. To see them one realises the difference between human and animal: one flash of those eyes was enough to show me the imminence of my death. It was certain. The wolf would feel precisely as much sorrow in devouring me as I would feel in eating a slice of ham. I thought I was dreaming, but there they were, fixed in the darkness – those eyes. I'm amazed that I managed to repress the scream that leapt to my throat once I'd realised that my own eyes were open and this was far from a dream.

The walls hadn't been high enough – it seems that a hungry wolf can jump ten feet – especially when he knows there is a meal on the other side. The hut was deep in shadow and I could barely see. I reached out slowly to pick up something – a stone or a piece of wood; anything I could throw or put between the creature and myself. I was rather surprised to see that the wolf's head did not exactly follow my actions: the eyes remained where they were. Had he not seen me? This was too much to hope for, I know, but given its lack of movement, I decided to try to fend it off. An agonising few seconds passed in which I scrabbled for a box of magnesium flares that I had prepared for the purpose of travelling by night and yet still the jaws of death had not clamped around my neck.

The instant the flare fizzed into light, I saw something very different in the wolf's eyes. They widened and became for a split-second almost human. I recognised in them that terror that is shared between all mortal things – the terror that I had experienced only a moment before.

In the illumination, I saw that the wolf hadn't quite managed the whole jump over the wall: it was stuck, its forelegs hooked over the stone and hind legs presumably dangling on the other side, scrabbling wildly at the air beneath the overhanging lip of the wall. I almost laughed – the thing looked so pitiful. I could see its gaze fixed on the light of the flare, which it withstood for only a few seconds before it twisted and launched itself backwards off the wall and fell to earth on the other side. I heard it stumble in the darkness, padding uncertainly away from the house – it seemed that the flare had momentarily blinded the poor creature.

I suspect that sleep will not come easily now. In the morning I will prepare more flares, but I think it would be unwise to stay out here again without a roof on the building.

29 September 1941

I have made as much time as the Work and my devotional sculpture allow to visit the young king, and yet even when I do speak to him, I feel that my tutelage falls on deaf ears. As I arrive I see Gregor sneaking away like a rat disturbed whilst feeding on carrion. He smiles a false smile at me when I pass. Would that I had not made any deal with him at all, for I no longer trust him.

It seems that I cannot interest the boy in any kind of political theory, nor can I make him follow any subject – even the most basic of sciences. It is with a heavy heart that I recognise exactly the form our relationship is to take: Monterek will not listen to me unless I am instructing him in alchemy. I have told him that he will not hear anything of alchemy until he has proved himself as a ruler, but this does not satisfy him: he will have it now. When I tell him that there is much preliminary learning to do before one can even think of attempting the Work, he accuses me of nothing less than treason! I fear I am no pedagogue, and I certainly cannot teach one who would not be taught, even though the well-being of this whole valley depends upon the few moral lessons I might manage to instil.

My greatest challenge with the boy is in his attitude to God. This whelp has a heretical notion that far from living to serve God, it is God that works for the king's ends, that it is God who appointed him; it was even God that arranged the death of his father so that he might accede to the throne. Would that wringing Monterek's neck might achieve something.

If morality does not come from on high, it must come from either the society that surrounds us or from the goodness in our hearts, but I fear that no king will ever feel the compunction of social pressures and this king will never understand what it is to have goodness in his heart. I am not hopeful of turning him.

I have not given up, however: I will allow myself the span of time required to complete the ornamentation of the high town church. If Monterek shows no moral improvement over this time, I will simply leave and continue my quest to find a prince of genuine worth elsewhere.

2 November 1943.

My work is turned against me.

The piece is completed. It is, though I say it myself, incredible. The characters of Christ and the host of angels are wrought in such a way that they seem ready to depart the piece and wander about the countryside spreading the word of God far from their confines. For the first time today I stood and looked up at it and felt quite in awe: I do not think that my own hands alone could have created such a thing and I take it as certain evidence that my hand was indeed guided by the divine. I hope that the people of Svart will be similarly moved, for this work differs so extraordinarily from their flat, two-dimensional renderings of the saints, that even the most nescient observer must see the elegance and the boldness of the contrast. I realise, however, that their understanding of it will be corrupted. This much was made clear at the unveiling ceremony.

Gregor was presiding as usual (he has remained as the king's favourite where others have fallen by the wayside). He gave a brief sermon that, while it extolled the greatness and virtues of the Lord, also stated directly that the child king – now approaching an unsavoury adolescence – had been appointed by god and that his every whim must be indulged. He proclaimed that the sculpture was indeed a tribute to God, but more importantly, it was a tribute to the boy, and at this my heart sank to its lowest. The project to which I have tirelessly devoted three years is to be seen as an homage to the brat! Would that I had the words and the fluency to protest, but such protests could only serve to alienate me more from the people I wish to free from these tyrannies.

I can see now that I misjudged Gregor. I had figured him for
a selfish opportunist, certainly, but I had not believed that
he would so betray his faith. It is now clear that he believes
in no glory greater than the king's, apart, perhaps, from his
own.

With every man and woman in the country bending over
backwards for him, the child will of course grow up to be a
self-serving fool – how could it be otherwise? He will never
be required to think but of his own temporary fancies.
Izvalta has already seen examples of his selfishness: he has
ordered a great display of fireworks and festivities to
celebrate his next birthday that will not be funded from the
capacious royal coffers, but by compulsory 'donations' from
the common people of Izvalta! Each will pay some two
hundred akches – a sum that amounts to a month's earnings
for a farmer, but will go completely unnoticed by the high
town.

I cannot help but feel that a large portion of the blame for
the child's misdirection is due to my own poor tutelage.
Every time the impudent boy asks what he stands to gain
from egalitarian rule I am so appalled that I sit and stutter
for a full minute before I can make an answer. When I find
my words and tell him that heaven awaits for the just and
good, he simply suggests that he need never see the next life
once I impart to him the gift of life eternal. Daily I come
closer to swearing to him that he shall receive no such gift
and now I do swear it. I see that I shall have to leave as soon
as I can. If I can.

14 June 1944

As my days draw to a close, I worry that my alchemical
achievements will have proved to be the cause of more

wasted human life than just my own. I cannot point to a single person who has benefited from this gift. I once believed that the Work could restore balance to the human race, but I am now convinced that this is not so: rather it reinforces and exacerbates existing divisions. I have finally refused to aid the brat king in his quest for immortality and I have made clear my intention to leave this place at the earliest convenience. I know that I will be denied freedom of passage.

I expect that very soon – possibly within the hour – my door will be broken down and I will be taken to the castle. There I will be tortured until I reveal to the whole court the secrets of transmutation and life eternal.

This is not, of course, the first time I have faced such a threat. However on this occasion, I have no recourse to flight – there can be no escape from this place that will not have me running straight into the hands of my aggressors or to certain death at the jaws of the wolf pack. More to the point, I am not willing to run again. It has become clear to me that I do no good on this earth and therefore if my enemies will take me, I shall let them – but they will not have the contents of my mind. They may steal my books, of course, but their teachings are opaque at best and written in several languages and cyphers. I have no fear that any man in Izvalta will discover the secrets of alchemy from them.

My mind, however, can be unlocked and this I must not allow to happen. To this end I have prepared a formula of Spirit of Salt and Mercury. It is my intention to inject myself with this formula on completing this diary entry. It is my belief that the mixture will not kill me, for such an act would be against God and I have an aversion to suicide, but it will deteriorate my mind to such an extent that my knowledge will be safe from King Monterek and his devilish court.

Being alone in the world, I say good-bye to nobody.

It's the end of the diary. She had wanted to hear it, but it makes her so sad. The boy too has tears in his clear, bright eyes. Wordlessly they rise and prepare for bed.

Just before she blows out the candle, the boy notices a scrap of paper, hidden from sight down at the foot of the table. He listens for the woman's breathing, waits for it to assume that calm rhythm, slow like the first long drips from the icicles in spring. Then he gets up and feels for the thin page, with its one ragged edge where it was once torn from the book. What is a page torn from a diary? A bad memory? Torn out but not destroyed – tucked into the back perhaps. A reminder? Even if he could decipher the bizarre code, it would be impossible in the dark. There's only one way to read the page, and this time he will do it on his own.

He reaches to the back of his head, page in hand. He feels the alchemist's hope and his fears. Word by word the story has become part of his life in a way that no other story could. He burrows into the words, crumbling the paper into thin veins of thought which root themselves in his mind. The words become part of him. He becomes the words.

CHAPTER 12
THE MARKET

It's 1951. Petra is 20.

Outwardly, she is rather like the rest of the young women of Svart – perhaps a little paler, a little leaner, but with the same dark hair and the same gently pointed features. There are subtle differences though: in the low town and agricultural communities of Izvalta, people have missing teeth and blotchy complexions caused by a variable diet and numerous nicks and scars from everyday wear and tear. Petra has none of these little defects and people occasionally assume that she is from the high town.

Today, as she makes her way to the central market, she catches a look of recognition on the face of a lady luxuriously clad in silks. The look fades quickly away as she takes in Petra's clothes, which are drab and ordinary at best, ragged at worst. This doesn't happen often; mostly people see the clothes first.

As always, Petra is bringing a few things to trade. She doesn't want to risk peddling alchemical cures or lumps of gold. She's made that mistake in the past: she tried to sell the very first lump of gold the alchemist produced for her, without realising the curiosity that a young girl in possession of a piece of pure gold would attract. At the time she hadn't seen that it was a dangerous business. Where had she found this piece of gold? Had she stolen it? Had she found a gold mine somewhere? Soon she was the focal point of a crowd that was far too interested in her. She claimed that she had found it in an attic. It was an heirloom, she said, at which the crowd laughed uproariously.

"Who are your parents, girl?" someone said.

She didn't dare mention them – she hadn't even seen them for months and although she'd thought about them often, she knew that she couldn't go back to them. The mention of her parents sent such a rush of fear through her that she simply snatched up her lump of gold and fled. Sounds of astonishment and laughter in equal measure followed behind her as she ran.

The next time she appeared at the market she was more cautious. The one or two people who recognised her warned her not to go telling tall tales like that again, and thankfully that was the only repercussion. After that, she would only bring a blanket or something equally innocuous to sell.

Now she maintains as low a profile as can be expected in a bustling marketplace where most people know each other. She still has a lurking fear of running into her mother or father. Often they appear in her dreams, asking what they did wrong, why she ran away and what kind of life she lives now. They never seem to blame her for running away, they just ask her endless questions; simple questions that if she was sure of herself, she would have simple answers to.

"I'm here for Jean," she whispers to herself half-asleep in the drowsy nook of the morning. "It's important that I'm here. The Work is valuable – it's useful."

"Why?" asks her father mildly. "Who is it useful to?"

"Why, it's useful to Jean. If we didn't continue the Work, he would die. He would forget everything again, Daddy. So we have to. We have to keep doing it. I have to keep learning."

"You should let him die," says her mother, rocking back and forth on a chair, eyes on her knitting. "Let him die and come back home."

"Mother! I can't. He's... I love him."

"Do you?" asks her father.

"Well – well I suppose so. I must."

Her father just smiles thinly. She sees doubt in that smile. It's her own doubt; it's her own dream and the characters in it are seven years too young. They could even be dead. She wouldn't know.

Petra is still careful about what she sells at the market. She mostly brings dyes she's made using minerals: red from calcining lead; blue from copper carbonate. They're not really an alchemical secret – more a by-product of the art that she's developed while learning about the Work. She is justifiably proud: sometimes she has the urge to run and show her mother – who taught her how to colour her own clothes using local flowers. She remembers a pretty blue dress that she used to have. It's probably her sister's now.

Petra approaches her usual trader – an old lady peddling woollen clothes, thick durable cloth and the occasional animal skin.

"Ovst, ovst." The old woman shakes her head as Petra approaches. "I cannot make use of your dyes, young lady."

"Why not?" asks Petra.

"Dye costs too much. My customers haven't any money for these things any more. They will pay only as much as it costs them to stay alive and a little colour doesn't make it any warmer."

Being well acquainted with the bargaining tactics of the stallholders, Petra is immediately suspicious. "Very well – a special deal for the new year – Only twenty akches this time, but you can expect the usual price again in the spring."

"I am sorry, young lady – I just can't make use of it. You

could try Madam Valk – she often sells to the high town. They seem to be doing alright." She sighs deeply and busies herself about the stall. Petra watches her, looking for traces of deception.

"Fine. Eighteen. That's my final offer."

The woman doesn't turn around. "Ovst," she says.

Petra is frustrated – the winter has been a long one and their stores are severely depleted. Dyes have been such a reliable source of income until now. She turns to leave, but stops to ask the woman one more thing. "Why is there no money?"

The stallholder looks at her curiously. "Surely you know about the collection?" Petra's face is blank. "The school collection? We're going to be taught English. It's for... uh – what was the word?"

"I haven't heard about it," says Petra, and the old woman looks at her curiously.

"A message went round all the houses. Collection. To pay for English teachers; some from abroad. Unless the collection hasn't reached you yet. Where do you live?"

"Oh, I expect it just hasn't got there yet – or maybe I was out. I expect it will get to me."

"Prosperity. That was the word. It's for the prosperity of the country. We need to learn English for prosperity. Or at least the young ones do. It's a national investment, which we're all making. And everybody's got to help pay for it, you know. That means you too. Because you know we'll all be better off soon – what with all the uh... the prosperity coming in. Then you'll have a market for your dyes and knick-knacks."

"Oh. Okay. Thanks." Petra turns away, her basket under one arm. Looking around the square she sees the ragged, colourless people of Svart and feels sorry for them. Prosperity seems a very long way away – probably some years beyond the horizon of their lives.

With a shrug she goes to conduct her business with the high town trader Madam Valk – a woman that she has instinctively avoided until now. She still has a feeling in her blood that she is poor and she doesn't belong amongst the pretty buildings, the spires and cobbles. The people in the fancy costumes are just that – people in fancy costumes. It's not like they're real – they wouldn't understand the harshness of real life.

From Madam Valk she gets much less money than she was expecting. It's curious to her why those who can so obviously afford more always seem to pay less – but she pays it little heed, gathers her provisions and sets off home.

The Work takes a lot of time and patience, but in this undisturbed corner of Izvalta, time is something that they have in abundance.

With time, Jean Fulcanelli has managed to wrest control of his body from his unthinking alter ego. As long as he can go through the motions of the Work, his mind remains focused; no longer does he rant and rave incomprehensibly or throw things around the hut. He and Petra are even learning to talk to each other.

Their language is in part a product of the books that lie scattered and open around them. His French and English have met her Izvaltese, losing themselves in the interaction and producing an eloquent offspring peppered with titbits of Latin and Greek. It would be impossible for anyone in the rest of Svart to understand even the length of a sentence between them, but within the womb-like black walls of the alchemist's hut, they share an almost perfect understanding.

The process of alchemy, on the other hand, is still unclear. Only now is she beginning to learn the philosophy behind the Work without which, Fulcanelli assures her, the Work cannot be completed.

"So if I did everything that you did without understanding what I'm doing – what? It just wouldn't work?"

The old man smiles at her. "Alchemy is not what you think it is."

"Oh, and what do I think it is?"

"You think it's magic."

"And what is it really?"

"Devotion. It requires the soul. Without God, the art of transmutation is meaningless. In order to understand any code, you must first understand the author and what he is trying to express – only then can you begin to take his words apart and reshape them. And so it is with alchemy. God has written a structure into the world and you cannot hope to change His world without understanding it. In order to learn the structure, you must devote yourself to God."

Petra, thinking back to the priest in the high town who would have happily let her die in these woods, says nothing of her doubts and her feeling of mistrust for holy teachings, yet the alchemist's slant on devotion is unlike any religious teaching she has ever experienced, unconcerned as it is with rituals and saints. Jean's belief is a passion that shines in his eyes and electrifies his body.

"Each substance," Fulcanelli tells her, "is striving for perfection. Given long enough, it will achieve that perfection. Of course you'll find a lot of things in the world that don't seem to be doing this – they seem to be moving away from perfection – but if you see the world as a whole; see the mountain rather than just the stones, maybe you will also see this process. We treat the world as a collection of separate objects, but it is humanity that creates the boundaries between one object and the next, not God."

"So when we make gold we're actually making something

more perfect? Speeding up the process?"

"Exactly."

"But what happens if you take that gold and then make it even better? Is that possible? Would it become... human or something?"

Fulcanelli smiles. "The first thing you must understand is that humans are far from perfect. Quite apart from that, it is God that decides the path something takes. The path of metals is different from the path of animals, you see?"

"But didn't you say that only humans make those distinctions? If God sees only the continuous and undivided world, then even inanimate objects must be related to animals, and... and somewhere on the scale of perfection must be thought and self-awareness." She's giddy with the enormity of the idea, but while her eyes brighten, a shadow crosses the alchemist's face.

"Such things are not to be toyed with, Petra."

"But I don't see why not. I want to know what a wolf might say if it could talk. What about a bear? What if they were given a more perfect voice? And what if a simple piece of clay could be motivated by wise words?"

"This is not a thought you should pursue," he says with a voice of quiet thunder. Then, in a more conciliatory tone, "It is true that there are degrees of perfection: I have told you several times that the alchemical débutante will create a gold of say fifteen carats, while the master can create a gold of almost a hundred percent purity. However, I would warn you against exceeding those parameters laid out by God Himself. Self-awareness is reserved for humanity; movement for the animals and to a lesser extent the sprawling roots and flowers that lift their heads to the sun."

She's not used to hearing anything but loving encouragement

from the alchemist and his mild admonition shocks her – it even annoys her. How can he presume to have all the answers? She tries to get him to tell her why he's so opposed, after all, isn't it just a question of distillation? A purer form of the philosopher's stone, perhaps made with purer materials; a different source for the nigredo, the first ingredient of the Work? But the alchemist remains strangely silent, refusing to answer her continued peppering of questions.

Even as the years pass, as Elze the girl grows into Petra the woman, and as the elixir restores, little by little, the reddish glow of vitality to the alchemist's once-hollow cheeks, there are certain topics about which he keeps a stoic silence. He will not speak of the past, though Petra begs to hear his stories, which must span centuries. 'There is no wisdom in my tales.' he is fond of saying, though it seems to Petra that he is never short on dire proclamations – warnings about the dangers of meddling in the business of princes and kings.

On several occasions, usually in the early spring, Petra will decide that she has had her fill of his rhetoric, and storms out, threatening to leave him and go back to Svart permanently. She never does, though she is never sure why not. Something keeps her here with the old man throughout these frustrations. Perhaps a feeling of responsibility for the life she once saved, or perhaps something more like love.

CHAPTER 13
STRANGERS

The alchemist is in a great hurry – it's the first time she has seen him so agitated. "Petra, quick! There are men in the woods – royal guards. They're coming to the hut!"

She looks at him stupidly, rubbing her eyes awake. "Why?"

"Why? Why? Petra, they will take everything. Including us!" He turns toward the cold furnace and lifts the latch that holds it closed. "We must hide – here." He holds open the door of the furnace. "I'm switching the catch – after we close it, it will only open from the inside."

She looks at the furnace doubtfully, suddenly remembering the fear she once had of the thing. "But what about the books? They won't take the books, will they?"

He looks at her sadly. "There's no time."

"Can't we save them? Not even one?" she pleads.

His hand travels automatically to his chest as if to reassure himself of something there. He shakes his head and grabs her hand. "There's no time."

They wait in the cold darkness, breathing thick grains of oily soot for what seems like hours, but must only be minutes. Petra puts the alchemist's thin arms around her. He isn't warm, but having him here is a comfort. She wonders to herself if this isn't just another manifestation of his madness; an echo of some earlier paranoia that's out of place in their quiet little home.

There is a knock at the door. She can just about hear it. It's soft – the friendly, mittened knock of a neighbour come to sit around and chat about the weather.

Then she hears the door crash open.

"We left boulders against the doors," says a male voice that sounds familiar to Petra.

"Well somebody removed them." A younger, smoother voice. "Looks like they removed the alchemist too."

"He was delirious, sire. Babbling like an idiot. We found the poison bottle right there. We tried it on one of the dogs – it tried to bite off its own tail and legs, then it dropped dead. The alchemist knew what was coming and he simply committed suicide. We walled him in as if he were already dead. Of course you were very young at the time."

"I remember it well, Gregor. You told me there would be no immortality and no gold and that was that. I almost had you executed."

There is a break in the conversation. Petra tries to keep her breathing slow and steady. She can't hear the alchemist at all – not even a heartbeat. For an alarming moment, she thinks he's actually stopped breathing, and her body tenses – she's reassured by a little press from his hand on hers.

"Well, he's not here," says the younger voice. "But it's inhabited. Look at these bottles and tubes all neat and tidy. Have you been harbouring an alchemist, Gregor?"

"King – this might be exactly how we left it – I honestly cannot recall – apart from the stones, and they were probably moved by curious locals or looters hoping to find something."

The younger voice has a bored, impatient tone. "Well there's one way to find out if anyone's living here – you two – you're staying here tonight. Anyone comes back, you tie them up. Keep them alive though – they might be able to tell us how these... contraptions work."

A clumpy, shuffling sound resonates through the wall. "The books seem to be intact," says the older man, whose voice Petra suddenly recognises: it's the voice of the priest who once directed her, with a lupine grin, to seek out the alchemist in a hovel in the woods. And this is the self-same man who had sealed Jean inside? She feels her skin bristle hot with hatred.

The younger answers. "Yes. Rather suggests that old Fulcanelli may still be alive and kicking, doesn't it? Tell me, Patriarch, if you had power over life and death don't you think you'd have mastered deception? Figured out how to make yourself look mad? Christ, you don't even need a potion for that."

"Indeed, King. But if he isn't here, where is he? How has nobody seen him? How has this man, mad or otherwise, survived in the middle of a forest full of hungry wolves?"

"You have no imagination, Gregor. You! Open this furnace will you? Might be an alchemist in there. Or gold perhaps."

Petra's heart suddenly feels sick with fear as she hears someone yank on the door to their sanctuary.

"It's stuck. Probably just old." There's the sound of multiple hands and tools being applied to their hiding place, but after several minutes the bored voice stops them.

"Alright. Don't care. Plenty still to see out here," he says and Petra feels the relief wash over her as the footsteps move to another part of the hut. Now he must be flicking through one of the books. "Can you read any of it? Let's have a look... The hell do all those pictures mean?"

"Symbols, King. They represent elements of the Work, but as I have told you many times, study without apprenticeship to a master of the art is near impossible."

"You have said that, Gregor, far too many times. This is a

puzzle you *will* solve. I know you are a man of linguistic talent and as for decoding symbols, well you're a priest aren't you? We'll take these books. And the equipment too, I suppose. Maybe leave the furnace – I'll install you in a suitable room in the castle. One with a chimney. God it stinks in here." He breaks off to give some commands, ushering in a small army of heavy-clomping boots that clink glass and thump together blocks of books. Close to their hiding place, Petra hears the priest talking quietly to himself.

"All these books. Spotless, well dusted and intact. Where are you, you old bastard?"

She barely hears his footsteps walking away over the pummelling of her own heartbeat.

They wait and listen to the sound of unknown people slowly piling up every item of worth in the small house and then carrying it away. After ten minutes, silence finally settles. Petra tries to move forward, but the alchemist's hands stay tight around her.

"Shh," he whispers very quietly.

Petra starts to sob silently: she is thinking of what will happen with the books gone, what will happen to Jean's mind. They wait while time, like a well-fed cat, yawns and stretches and settles to an unbearably slumberous pace; she feels every second.

It's the sound of a second band of home-wreckers that wakes her. People taking the last of the books and equipment – and later, the clanking and tearing of someone searching even more thoroughly. She listens to them dispassionately as they speculate about the equipment and its uses, their minds gravitating to crude perversions and pure nonsense.

Occasionally someone tugs at the furnace door, but she couldn't care less now. She's hungry and cold and confused and wishes that she could stop the procession of pictures that are entering unbidden into her mind, of faceless forms upending and ripping apart their meagre possessions as if they were taking her soul itself and tearing it in two.

Jean is shaking her gently awake again. He guides her out of the hiding place, triggering the door's catch somewhere in the sooty dark. They tumble out, blackened and bruised into what's left of their home.

It's been stripped bare. The furniture is in sorry disarray – the tiny straw bed in one corner with its blankets shaken and ruffled, and straw pulled out in heaps in search of hidden treasures; the old alchemist's chair overturned by the window; the few odds and ends of eating and cooking utensils pulled out and strewn around. It makes Petra feel like a ghost come back to haunt her own house long after passing on. But she settles her mind and tells herself it's not beyond repair, although what she really wants to do is scream, shout and cry at the feeling of violation – that a group of complete strangers could do this to her home. The bookshelves look naked, fleshless, supporting nothing at all.

Petra looks at the alchemist and she remembers what she has truly lost. In his eyes she sees the light of recognition – he knows her and loves her, but without his library there is nothing to support his mind. That recognition and that love will fade.

"What happens now?" she asks. The question betrays how little she has changed in seven years, how like a child she still is and how much she has come to depend on the alchemist for direction. It betrays her vulnerability, her passive compliance with fate, and it frustrates her even as she says the words.

"Now?" He tries to meet her eye, knowing that she is looking to him for guidance, but he can't – he's too old and has seen too much, and he knows what comes next. "You must go, Petra – go and live your life. I... I cannot survive without the books. My mind will disintegrate and I don't want you to be here when it does."

"No! We'll get the books back!"

"We cannot. Petra, I am an old man – I should have died long ago. I know the man who took the books. It was Monterek, the king, and Gregor, his lackey. If we reveal ourselves as alchemists, we will be tortured until we give up our secrets. The risk is too great."

"But Jean..."

"Hush now – it was by God's will that I came here; by His will that you found me, and He has decreed that my time is over. I'm grateful that he gave me the chance to know you, but it could never be forever."

She can't raise her head – her throat is choked with sobs. How can he be so selfish? To be prepared to just leave her, all the while proclaiming that God is somehow the reason. It seems so easy for Jean to give up his life, but he doesn't know how hard she fought for it – how many days of endless, miserable doubt she went through to keep him alive when she could have walked away and left him to his madness. She tries – and fails – to persuade him to try to retrieve the books or to travel the world in search of others. He is reconciled to his fate in a way that provokes in her anger and despair in equal measure – her faith, her beliefs, her connection to life and the world – all of it cries out against this wilful resignation.

"I'll stay here with you. You can't make me leave."

He smiles a weak smile that upsets her even more – it's so powerless, so defeated. "Very well," he says, and then he asks the impossible. "Just promise me one thing: promise that you will let me die. I will stop drinking the elixir and when my mind is gone, you must not try to keep me alive. That way both of our sufferings will be short-lived."

She mumbles something that could be a promise, but isn't.

She notices the first sign three weeks later, when she finds Jean nursing a badly burned hand. He tries to hide it from her, but his hasty bandage is obvious, as is the pain he's in. She re-dresses the burn, covering it first in ointment, saying nothing.

"Please leave," he begs her. She doesn't answer. Petra is beginning to realise how she feels about the alchemist, and with that knowledge, the impossibility of leaving him.

"Why did you do it, Jean? You did this to yourself, didn't you? Not just the burn, but the poison too. That was what those high town thieves said – you poisoned yourself. Why?"

"Petra, this will do no good – I cannot be saved – not like last time."

"But why not? You're not even trying."

"Look, I'm old – I'm ready to go. God made an imperfect world where He could have made a perfect one. Why? To test us! I have been tested and I was too weak to prevail. I destroyed my own mind because if I had not, it would have been taken from me forcibly – my knowledge would have fallen into the hands of that petty tyrant, Monterek, but I could not face death so I chose a death of the mind. No more tests from a God who inspires only doubt; no more devotion to an art that corrupts a great deal more than it heals. I could not bear more – and I cannot bear more.

"You don't know what an end is – you're still so young. When you contemplate a lifetime you imagine one of pure joy. You have no idea of the sadness and the regret. Truly an end is a blessing."

Petra struggles to hold back tears.

"We are not gods, Petra. We must have our entrances and our exits."

"Well I choose not to die. And I won't leave you." Her petulance recalls a foggy memory of the little girl waking him from madness, casting out his demons with gritted teeth. It makes him smile.

"And what will you do when you don't have me to live for?"

"Then I'll live for myself. For the mountains and the streams and the rocks." She has a thought. "Jean, you know a way, don't you? A way that you might be saved."

"No." It is a flat denial, but she detects in it a falsehood.

"You do. Your soul could live on somehow, as part of something else."

"Petra, I have warned you against such ideas. There is a path for animals, a path for humans, a path for the rocks. Only God-"

"Will you shut up about God!" she yells, suddenly angry with a fierce intensity she's never felt before. "Can't you see that it's all you – you're judging yourself – you're deciding to end your life – you're defining your own limitations. You have an incredible knowledge, but you're scared to use it without some permission from an invisible being. God's just an excuse."

They've fought before, but never like this. The alchemist rises to his feet, shaking with rage. "How dare you? How can you deny His existence – it's in everything we've worked on – it's all around us. It's... He's..."

"It doesn't matter whether He's real or not – the only one making decisions here is you. That's all. But there's nothing stopping me! I'll do it – I'll do what you refuse to do – I'll make a clay man and give it thoughts and dreams, and somehow I'll put your soul inside. Why not?"

"Because it's against my will!"

"Who's will? Yours? You have no will – you poisoned yourself – you chose to die rather than be tested by this God of yours. But I chose to make you live, and I'll choose that again. Look," she softens. "If God has a say in this, then He decided to put me here, and He will give me the means to keep you alive."

"No. It cannot be done."

"Jean, I've known you too long – I can see when you're lying.

Just tell me how – I will do anything, but you mustn't die."

"Would you kill?"

"What?"

The alchemist closes his mouth, then his eyes, getting himself back under control. He has said something he hadn't meant to say, and he will say nothing more.

"Would I kill?" she asks the silent man. "Is that's what's required?" To bring life to the inanimate – to create a... what did the philosopher Cornelius Agrippa call it... homunculus? – she must have to sacrifice another living thing – another human.

In the days and weeks that follow, Jean begins to exhibit further signs of mental decay. He will say nothing more about salvation. In his more lucid moments he is overwhelmed by sadness – a sadness in which she refuses to join him. Instead, Petra leaves the house to scout out the palace gate, making enquiries, probing for ways to get her hands on the books that may restore Jean to sanity, then when that seems hopeless, trying to fathom the alchemical process that might transplant his soul into a body free of poison. When this too begins to seem impossible, she turns to the man she has come to love and cries copious tears of regret that she has squandered these last precious days with him. Finally, she keeps watch over him as the light fades from his eyes.

CHAPTER 14
TZUICA

She drinks. It's about all she can do to assuage her guilt. When the alchemist finally died it was no shock. Over six long years she watched his mania return and then evolve, even while she painstakingly followed the twenty-one steps of the Work. He would watch, but his books had become such a necessary prop to his mind that when they were gone he no longer recognised Petra's movements, no longer understood the development of the Work, sometimes snatching up a beaker and smashing it on the floor or mixing wheat flour in with a preparation of sulphur. Slowly and painfully, Petra learned that he was completely gone and was replaced once more by an unreasoning madman, and that the more she fed him the elixir (when she was able to prepare it without interruption) the more this madman was able to do her harm.

She had to make new equipment for herself: she carved a pestle and mortar and even, after weeks of diligence and burns, managed to blow glass skilfully enough to recreate the vessels required for distillation – vessels that were constantly smashed by the man-sized child that was once Jean. When she began the Work again it was like meeting an old friend. Unlike Jean, she found that she didn't need the books anymore; she had internalised the processes of the Stone and somehow knew its changes and moods. She could recall methods and philosophies perfectly and would even turn them in new directions, applying them to other areas of nature, though the formula for the homunculus remained beyond her reach. For a while, the Work and its derivations were enough for her – they had to be, because she had to face the fact that her Jean was not coming back – and she could not somehow transfer his soul to a healthier vessel.

Daily life spent alone in Jean's company quickly led to depression and she looked for some kind of escape. She found it in books – quite different from the alchemist's books, these were more like the ones she'd read as a child, full of fantastical characters: rogues, wizards, and heroes of wars that might have happened or might not – recent history had largely escaped her. It happened that the few travellers and tourists who came to Svart would leave their reading material on shelves in the hotels and an enterprising hotelier was flogging them off at the market for a few extra akches. Petra was probably paying over the odds for them – especially as some were in languages even she couldn't understand – but it didn't matter; here was a new set of worlds to escape to, and escape was something that she needed badly. She would read to the alchemist, which seemed to soothe him although she could never get him to look at the pages.

She tried to save him. She tried. Then she let him die, and it's this that she can't face.

She remembers his frailty gradually overtaking him, and this is when the books turned stale. She couldn't read past the end of a line without being wrenched back to the sad figure that sat dribbling and dying right in front of her eyes. It took all the determination she had to withhold the elixir that would have kept his body going.

Now she drinks. It's new to her; she had never tried it until a few months ago. She drinks every day. Sometimes that's all she does. Sometimes she wakes up completely unaware of where she is. Momentarily, in those small hours of the morning, she believes that she is at her old family home on the outskirts of Svart – the one she ran away from some fifteen or so years ago. Her parents would still recognise her, she is sure. Physically she hasn't changed that much because of the elixir. Outwardly she appears to be barely twenty years old.

She's in the market square. The high town church bell has just chimed for the evening service so it must be approaching six o'clock. There is a refreshingly warm drizzle in the air and every nook of the valley is full of pure white edelweiss. She almost feels like she could just walk home, back to the hut in the woods, with a clear head unmuddied by the cheap home-made spirit they sell at the bar.

She looks down at the bloodily-drawn bar sign propping up the wall. 'Tirig og Kam': Tirig and the bear – characters drawn from a local tale that cautioned against gluttony and over-indulgence. She remembers her grandfather recounting the tale, replete with mad, comical gestures. Tirig, the fat, drunk landowner (a mime he particularly enjoyed), went hunting a bear, but his horse collapsed underneath his weight and he was too drunk to stand up and run away, so the bear ate him whole. Of course the moral of the sign never seems to make a difference to the drinkers inside, but on this occasion, perhaps at the memory of her grandfather, she almost turns away. Then she considers returning home, and what her home looks like now – a dusty, filthy mockery of the haven it once was. It's a long time since she cleaned and she's started to hear rats in amongst the thick stone walls. When the furnace was burning, the fumes were enough to keep them away, but it hasn't been lit for a long time – after all, what's the point of practising alchemy when it can only bring her misery? Complete oblivion would be so much better. She pushes open the door.

There is a fiddler in the corner playing an old song. The men at the bar stomp and clap in time. It seems that no matter how poor they are, the peasants of Izvalta always manage to be upbeat about something.

She gets a bottle of tzuica and sits. People try to talk to her – all men. It's not as if she's made an effort with her appearance, but the attention seems unavoidable for an unaccompanied young woman – especially one that seems so intent on getting drunk. One by one she deflects their advances, but as the tide of her thoughts drifts gradually towards the dismal, she becomes less tolerant of their chatter.

"Enough!" she declares out loud to the bar, and to the tanned young man with unruly mutton-chops who's just approached. "I am in mourning. I wish to be left alone."

The young man nods and turns back. There is at least a respect for death in this country.

Petra looks contemplatively at the tzuica in her cup. The young man wasn't unappealing. But would he have been capable of filling her head with wonders beyond her understanding? Would he have been wise or virtuous or well-travelled? No. He's just another farmer. The bottle of tzuica is soon finished.

She hears the door open behind her. The fiddler sends a note sailing in the wrong direction, then slows and finally stops. Petra doesn't look around.

"Don't worry about me," says a voice. It's familiar, but she can't place it in her current state. "Just you carry on." Then he says something in a whisper, which occasions a bout of laughter – knowing and vicious. She turns around to see a group of strangers – men in well-cut coats. They look out of place here. The locals aren't laughing

Nervously the musician starts again, but the foot-tapping has stopped, along with any conversation above a murmur. She turns back around and forgets the intrusion.

"Buy you a drink?" asks a stranger by her elbow. She looks up, red-eyed. "Wha?" she says.

"A drink?" He nods at the barman, who serves up a new bottle of brandy with some speed. He even deposits on the table two gleamingly polished glasses, before backing away respectfully.

The stranger casually sips his drink while Petra knocks hers back. She tries to focus on his face, its features doubled and bleary, and she doesn't give a damn. The questions and answers come and go in an inconsequential haze. Yes, she likes her tzuica; yes, it's good of him to buy her one; thank you for the compliment, but she's not here for the company; well if he insists on talking there's little she can do; her name is Petra, what's his? And he laughs.

"I don't often meet women who are young and unmarried," he's saying.

"Who says I'm either?" she slurs.

"Dear uh, 'lady', you are wearing no ring, and frankly I don't imagine that any husband would allow you to drink at a bar. He would keep you under better control."

"Oh yeah? I need a man to control me, do I?"

"Apparently so."

"Who the fuck do you think you are?"

His grin broadens across his face. Somewhere behind him the door bashes closed. It's suddenly very quiet in the bar – most of the patrons seem to have left, apart from the ones that came in with the stranger. "They know who the fuck I am."

"Well I don't – and I don't much care for your..." she searches for a word, "...your face. You're an ugly bastard with a stupid beard. Now piss off and leave me alone."

"Hmm. No. I don't think so. I think you should be taught some manners." He gestures to the people around him, and suddenly there are hands on her – all over her – dragging her out into the street.

They're yelling words at her and his face is there, right in front of hers, bulging red and suddenly in sharp focus like it's under an enormous magnifying glass. She knows that face – the same face on that idiotic equestrian statue in the high town – the same face that shows up in every issue of *Valta*. And although it's grown older, it's the same face she once saw at a parade, while she sat on her father's shoulder wondering what made this chubby boy so special. Monterek. King of Izvalta, the man who pulled apart her life.

She starts yelling at him, cursing him in every tongue she knows and spitting in his contemptuous face. The only effect is to bring down a rain of fists, which blunt her consciousness even further. She's dimly aware of being dragged into an alley, where behind narrow windows, densely woven wool curtains are twitched aside and then hurriedly twitched back into position.

She can see just above the buildings a corner of the crescent moon and finds herself wishing that it weren't alone in the sky. That it could be joined by the sun, to take comfort and strength from it. But the sun is gone and the moon is alone in her cold black sky. Petra's one comfort is the tzuica, which, although it doesn't entirely obscure what's happening to her, does make it bearable. Her clothes are being ripped apart now and she's pushed back against a cold brick building. She looks up at the moon and becomes it, looking down on herself, shedding her white light over the valley, the mountains and the world beyond. She takes solace in the knowledge that the moon cannot cry.

CHAPTER 15
CAMBION

The thing that has begun to grow inside her feels alien, like something lumpy she's swallowed, but it's stuck in her belly, not her throat. It's a parasite; she's been infected and she needs to be cured. She will not bear the hands of a doctor, however, probing at her young flesh with lecherous fingers, only to then prescribe something disgusting, like actually giving birth to the parasite. No, she will cure herself of this sickness.

The cures are of her own design and their common element is poison. The first dose is simply more alcohol. When she sets foot in the bar again, there's a silence – the sound of many eyes turning downward. The barman doesn't charge her for the three large bottles of tzuica she takes away. He clears his throat as if to clear his conscience.

Days later, she knows that her treatment has done nothing; she can feel the baby inside her, alive and well, doubtless nourished by the elixir that Petra still drinks, and capable of ingesting as much alcohol as she. So she turns to herbs: black hellebore, belladonna and hemlock. Then she tries arsenic. Over the course of the first three months, Petra brings herself perilously close to death, almost succumbing to its skeletal embrace, but she knows that the baby is still with her, still alive, and that she is destined to give it life. Jean would have said it was God's will, but she believes in a natural order more closely aligned with nature. For her, there is no moral figurehead – but there is a... a pattern to the world and some things are meant to be. It doesn't stop her from feeling scared or alone.

As her body starts to take over her will, sending her mad with hunger, thirst and sickness, Petra becomes terrified of what's inside her. Is the parasite controlling her? It's not yet born and yet she is already its puppet. What if she gives birth to the devil himself? What if it wants revenge for her mistreatment, her attempts to kill it in the womb? She fixates on the pain; she's heard that giving birth will be painful – what if the thing inside her makes it worse?

The only thing that gives her some comfort is her plan, which becomes clearer and clearer each horrible, belly-swelling day.

"Transmutation," she says to herself. "Everything has a soul. Me, a tree, a rock, a lake." She knows that the different forms can be brought closer to perfection: a stone may aspire to be part of a greater being; part of the mountain. A lump of lead might become gold.

"But," she mutters, "Something more is required for something to change beyond its path, and all the devotion Jean could muster would never suffice. This requires sacrifice."

Jean is dead, his soul is gone, but perhaps there is yet something of him that exists; an echo that retains a knowledge of his voice. She has an idea – a theory. If knowledge was once handed down to primitive humans, then maybe humans themselves were once little more than clay. Were they like animals themselves, transformed by knowledge, by words? It's this idea that gets her through the next six months.

She's not ready when the baby comes. She's spent the previous week awake, unable to sleep for fear that it might arrive at any moment, and then there will be the ordeal. But after a week of tension, the contractions finally surprise her and she throws herself down on the straw-covered floor, bathing herself periodically with water ladled from a nearby bucket.

"Soon," she tells herself out loud. "It will be gone. Soon." And that helps her get through the pain.

When the tiny bloody lump is finally ejected from her body, an immense tide of relief washes over her – until she realises that it's still attached. She's had no experience of this; nobody ever told her about giving birth and so the umbilical cord looks to her like an attempt by this demonic baby to attach itself to her for life – a sick, slippery tentacle reaching inside her, refusing to let go. She pictures the baby growing and growing even into full adulthood next to her as she shrinks and withers, her insides sucked out through this deathly white tube.

As she reaches out for the knife, the baby starts screaming – clear proof that it knows what she's going to do and that it wants to stop her, but she won't be a slave to this thing. She takes a loop of cord and cuts into it. It's tough and resistant, like a thick, sinuous vine, and she has to summon up all of her remaining energy to get through it, sawing hard, with teeth gritted.

It's done. Her eyes close, minutes pass, then a purple lump spills out onto the dusty floor. The thing's root inside her is gone. Sitting in a pool of blood she finally feels clean. After nine months of fear and sickness, her body has been returned to her. Half-way through a thankful prayer, she passes out.

When she wakes, she finds the bloody little thing breathing, closed-lidded, its demon tube flopped to the side in a puddle of blood. She recalls its father, drawing away from her, his violence dissipated; spent. There's a curious similarity between them; father and son.

Over these months, the figure of King Monterek has become twisted in her mind. Since that evening when she stared up at the moon, his grunts and snorts, his greedy pawing, his hair and his breath – all have become those of a demon, an incubus that planted in her a seed. Which makes the thing in front of her simply a cambion: half-demon, half-human, against the laws of both God and nature. The classification simplifies what she has to do now.

From outside the hut she hears a wolf not so far in the distance, howling a long low howl. It's joined by others; voices of the night – a fitting audience for this Work. Petra solemnly lays the baby down on a table and takes a lump of clay from the workbench. Ignoring her tiredness and the baby's incessant cries she starts to sculpt the clay, shaping it into an oval, which gradually takes on the appearance of a chubby body. She adds arms, hands, legs, feet – all fat and wrinkly like those of the sleeping child. The head is almost perfectly round, but slightly misshapen on one side and she copies even this detail. She omits the tube. This baby's belly will be perfectly even, unbroken by the evidence of man's corrupt intervention.

Then, with the same sharp knife that she used to cut the cord, she copies every part of the baby in front of her: every wrinkle and dimple. She makes strands of clay and rolls them gossamer thin, then positions them carefully on the clay head. Nights and days pass and the cambion wakes and sleeps and wails, but she remains undistracted. This is to be her baby – a beautiful and perfect counter to the corrupt spawn beside it.

Now her son is formed. He is ready to embrace the world. All that is required is a sacrifice.

The boy wakes, blinks at his new life, breathes. His birth is unlike that of the cambion; it is calm, silent, graceful. She thanks the world for her blessing, but there's an oddness about the clay boy as he crawls the mud and stone floor of the hut, wandering aimlessly back and forth from corner to corner. He pulls at the edges of tables; makes things crash down on top of him, but never cries or seems upset. When he eventually stops and sits still, it doesn't seem to be because he's bored; there seems to be no reason to his actions at all. Perhaps this is just what babies do – nevertheless, Petra regards the boy, uncertainly.

"Do you need food?" she asks the baby, and it looks back with its dust-coloured eyes. She instinctively holds the clay boy to her breast, where he does nothing at all. And she begins to understand that the thing in her arms is simply existing. It does not have such a thing as an instinct or even will. It exerts no energy on its surroundings, there's no resistance, no desire – nothing but animated clay. There is only one way to make the boy into something with human behaviour and to do that the clay requires instructions. Words.

The final ingredient is a book – the only one that survived the looting. She found it before she buried her beloved Jean, safely tucked into one of his inside pockets. During his first madness he had tried to show it to her, but as his sanity returned he was at pains to conceal it. Occasionally she would wake up before the sun rose and see him by the light of a candle, flicking through the pages with a smile or a frown, but it was by his graveside that she first began to understand its significance, for here was the closest thing to Jean's soul still remaining on Earth. The leaves of the pages were like those of the old bibles she remembered from church, so thin that they might dissolve in a raindrop. The text was impossible to read; dense with black, like a night sky spotted with tiny white stars where the original colour of the page shone through. She never solved the code, but her baby will be able to: it will be imprinted on his soul.

The boy doesn't protest as she makes the incision in the back of his head. He simply stares forward unthinking and unfeeling.

She stops abruptly with the knife buried deep. Blood. The clay boy is bleeding, but how? It must be some reaction between the blood of the cambion and the philosopher's stone that makes up so much of the clay mixture. Whether an aberration or a hallucination, it doesn't matter – she must continue. There is only one way to give the golem its humanity, and that is with Fulcanelli's diary pages, written in their inscrutable scribble, and so she prises the opening wide enough to fit a single page, and shuddering, withdraws to see what she has done.

The boy finally wails its first wail.

CHAPTER 16
H VULK

The first years with the boy are painfully slow. It spends too long as a baby – about ten years in all – and she wonders whether it will ever actually grow, though she does eventually begin to see a difference. It takes almost a year thereafter before hair begins to appear on its head. Perhaps the clay is still learning to live.

As the years pass, the boy learns to speak, then to interpret the words in his head and then tell his mother about them. In relating Fulcanelli's story, however, he does not parrot back the words now inscribed in his mind because with each word comes a concept and each concept is new to him. Progress is slow. To give him more than a page at a time confuses the boy, his eyes become dark and he refuses to talk. After trying this once, Petra never risks it again.

And so every evening they share another single little piece of Fulcanelli's past. Sometimes it continues a story, while at other times it is full of lists and allusions that Petra cannot help the child to understand. The diary starts in the 1800s and it's peppered with characters who tread a thin line between genius and insanity. Eugène Canseliet figures prominently, and earlier, Auguste and Louis Lumière alongside a string of inventors, occultists, chemists and alchemists. Jean himself, however, never seems to be at the centre of his stories – more on the edge, looking in and looking on. The diary reveals his calm, grounding nature and hints at his ambitions, his dreams for humanity.

Through the diary she learns more about the alchemist than he ever told her himself, and she notices Hávulk's personality developing along the same lines as the Fulcanelli she once knew – abstracted, thoughtful and calm – although she can't be sure whether he takes these characteristics from the diary or the clay from which he's sculpted. He also has a personality trait that clearly hasn't arisen from the meeting of Fulcanelli's words and the material substance of the clay. The boy has an insatiable curiosity that Petra recognises as her own.

Hávulk takes a great interest in the world around him, fearlessly prowling the woods just as she did as a little girl, and even going further afield to the fringes of Svart to spy on the people doing their daily chores. When he returns from his expeditions, pouring out the myriad descriptions of what he's seen, she feels a mixture of motherly pride and fear for her son's safety. She can't help but think back to the fate of Fulcanelli at the hands of the people of Svart, and again and again she warns him about the dangers of trying to integrate with the rest of society.

"If strangers start talking to you, just run and hide, okay? Hide in the woods. They're scared to come here."

"I know, I know. And I don't talk to anyone anyway. Sometimes I want to though."

It's at times like these that she feels pangs of regret: why couldn't she just give him a normal life? Let him go to school or something? But he isn't normal. The teachers would notice when birthdays come and go but Hávulk doesn't appear to have aged. He learns at a different pace, like one of the girls she knew when she was little. Always a bit slow to understand, the girl was an outsider until finally she was found dead from bee stings. She'd been trying to get the honey from a beehive in a tree, but what really killed her was the neglect of everyone around her. That's how Hávulk would appear to the everyday people of Svart. He would stand out and that would lead to trouble.

All she can do is to try to sate his curiosity by giving him second-hand paperbacks to read and allowing him the freedom to go and spy on the people that so fascinate him. Sometimes, through no fault of his own, the boy reminds her of how lonely she is, after all, the boy is not Jean Fulcanelli – he cannot support her with his enduring wisdom. All she has is this child, who is sometimes frustratingly simple-minded and slow to develop, to remind her of what she's lost. She often asks herself what she's doing. Why is she bringing up this child? Keeping herself alive even? When answers fail, a bottle of tzuica fills in the gaps. She wakes up the next day nursing a cocktail of regret and shame. Is this what it is to be a mother? To feel the weight of responsibility for a child's upbringing while at the same time knowing that you are powerless to change the world? To know that bringing him up you will always have to shelter him from those who won't accept him?

Even in their seclusion the alchemist and her son can't help impacting the world around them though. This becomes clear after she notices Hávulk's towel draped over the back of a chair. She's never really paid any attention to it before, but now she notices an odd detail: the white towel is stained a light yellow-orange. She blinks until she's sure she's seeing it right.

"Hávulk." she calls lightly.

"Yes, Petra." He trots in from outside, a perfect boy with a crop of thick blond hair almost covering his eyes. He's completely naked despite the chill of the hut. Looking at him, she feels genuine pride: he's handsome and fearless; already he's explored corners of the forest that she never dared approach. Sometimes he takes her to them, through strange grottoes and along high ridges. The mountains and the forest seem so much a part of him, like brothers and sisters he's known all his life; he's familiar with their every bend and wrinkle.

"Hávulk, what happened to the towel?" she asks, remembering what she called him in for.

"Oh," he says, seeing it as if for the first time. "I don't know. I dried myself. Was that not right?"

"Certainly that's right, but why is it all orange?" And then it clicks. The clay boy is shedding his skin. It's curious – as she looks him over, he doesn't seem to have suffered – the skin is just as it was, but maybe a tiny layer has been washed off in the water. She's momentarily worried, but it's not as if he's dissolving.

It's two weeks later when she discovers the side effect of his morning ablutions. The market stallholder, Madam Valk, who only a short while ago looked so close to death that she could have shaken its hand, is now alive and well after almost a year's absence from the stall that she runs in such an exacting manner.

"Madam Valk, you're well!" says Petra in astonishment.

"Certainly I am. Certainly. Now I'm hoping my useless husband hasn't raised our agreed sum for gold leaf."

"No, no – the gold leaf is still the same price – the paints too, but tell me how you're up and about again."

Madam Valk looks her closely in the eye as if defying her to disagree with the following pronouncement: "Why, the same reason you still don't look a day over thirty. It's the mountain air. I was feeling terrible – I'd lain in bed for weeks so I decided I needed some fresh air. Almost as soon as I'd got outside I was feeling better. A little stroll to the river and a drink of fresh Valta water – well, now I'm a new woman. All you need in this life is a little exercise. I must admit I thought it odd that you lived so remotely, but I expect it's the mountain air, isn't it? Keeps you strong."

"Yes. Yes indeed, Madam Valk."

Madam Valk leans in, confiding. "There are people here who take you for a witch, you know. I laugh at them – for one, I would not do business with a witch and now of course I know your secret! Health and beauty are natural gifts – I've always said so. A little air and a little water!"

After concluding their business the older woman even smiles at her.

During her very brief city visits over the next month she hears more and more about the curative properties of mountain air and water straight from the Valta – even Hávulk, who has become adept at spying on the population of Svart, has heard rumours of miracle cures and starts to see the elderly people throwing away their walking sticks and practically striding down the streets.

Then one day, he and Petra suddenly realise that Hávulk himself is the cause.

It's a cold winter, as they often are in Izvalta, and the mountain stream is frozen over. Cold water is no deterrent for the clay child who doesn't feel the chill, but he simply can't get through the ice. For three weeks he doesn't go through his ritual morning swim. Then, when Petra next visits Svart, Madam Valk is dead.

"One day she was there – the next, gone," says her husband who, with his shaking hands and loose, pasty skin, looks far from well himself.

That evening sees Petra and Hávulk forcing their way through the thick layer of ice, chopping into it with axes, levering up great chunks and hurling them downstream so that Hávulk can get into the water. Within a week, the old man looks rather better.

The causal chain makes sense to Petra – she has remained young by mixing and consuming an elixir from the philosopher's stone each solstice and equinox, following the natural patterns of the universe, and Madam Valk's exposure to the stone was not so very different, though the dose was much smaller. Hávulk is partially made from the stone itself; its energy is the source of his life and as he grows, so does the stone, so even the tiny rinse of it that floats down the mountain stream after he's had his morning swim is enough to invigorate anyone who drinks that water – and most of Izvalta drinks that water eventually.

"Hávulk," she says to him. "Every day now, you must wash in the stream. It's not our fault – we didn't mean it, but if you stop now, people will die. They've started to depend on the elixir. On you." Internally she chides herself for letting this happen. There should have been no influence on Izvalta – no abnormalities that might one day bring curious people knocking on her door as they had before. What is done is done though, and now that she has interfered with the natural lifespans of the Izvaltan population there is no way of telling how many now relied on the stone to stay alive. She couldn't know that this change in Izvalta's average life expectancy would result in a set of British soldiers knocking on her door many years later.

When the soldiers come to her hut in the woods the first time, she knows that the crisis point had arrived, just as Fulcanelli always told her it would. He always said that there would be a time when the world would discover Izvalta and ferret out everything of value here. The known, documented, charted world would eventually fill even the furthest wilderness reaches; every hidden mote of beauty and wonder would be extracted and swallowed like the delicate nooks of a lobster's claws being sucked up by a greedy gastronome.

And now it seems that her own actions will be to blame as the world turns its probing eyes and fingers in the direction of Izvalta, in the direction of the Wolf Wood. She should never have recovered the interpreter's body – by bringing him back from the brink of death she has supplied the British soldiers with evidence of alchemy that points right back to her own home, and her own child. That's the thing that keeps her awake – that she might have endangered Hávulk's life. It no longer matters whether he was born or put together piece by piece; he is her son and the one thing in her world worth saving. Nevertheless, she doesn't feel regret at having saved Terry. His was an open mind ready to be filled – much like Hávulk in that respect.

When she rescued Terry from the wolf's belly, it was no accident; there are no accidents. Something beyond coincidence brought him to Izvalta and that same thing saw to it that he would stumble into her life for whatever purpose – good or ill. She knows that the soldiers will find Terry, then find his scars and trace them back to these woods, with or without his help. They will be back once more, and this time they will take her for an able alchemist rather than a mad peasant.

Perhaps she and Hávulk have just enough time to escape. The idea fills her with an uneasy thrill. The larger world is a place she learned to fear through the words of the old alchemist, who warned of its small-mindedness and the dangers that lie in wait, but Petra has come to doubt those warnings. Perhaps there are also people like Terry out there, and perhaps Fulcanelli was wrong and maybe the world still has corners dark enough for an alchemist and her clay son.

She tries to rouse Hávulk to the task of packing up a few essential belongings – enough to get them through to the end of the winter – but the boy is absorbed in one of the ragged paperbacks from the market. She watches him sitting perfectly still on the floor, his tongue curled slightly over his top lip, a habitual indicator of intense concentration. She doesn't want to disturb him, much less uproot him from his home, because the outside world may be a bold new adventure for her, but who can tell what it holds for him? He's strong, but also vulnerable.

"Hávulk." He registers nothing. "Hávulk, I need you to pack your things." He slowly turns his head, though his eyes linger on the page for as long as they are able before following.

"Do we have to leave?"

"I've told you already, yes."

"Will we see the soldier again? I liked him. Will we see him again?"

"No. No, I don't think so – but maybe we'll meet people like him. Nice people that we can trust."

"How will we know that we can trust them?"

"I don't know."

He turns to his chest of odds and ends and begins to pack them into an old sports bag that Petra bought at the market.

"Hávulk, we can't take all those books. Pack lots of clothes instead – it'll be cold."

"But I don't get cold. Can't I take them? Not even one?"

And she sees a younger version of herself back in the same hut years earlier, with strange men outside the door. She's asking Jean Fulcanelli that same question – couldn't they save one book? Just one?

"Very well. Take your favourite." Jean had saved one book after all – not that there's much left of it now – just a few last pages. The rest have been torn out – they've become part of Hávulk. She's been avoiding these last entries, consciously avoiding reaching the diary's conclusion because she knows how she's going to feel. But it's time – time to leave Izvalta and time to leave Jean Fulcanelli behind.

Once they're prepared for their journey, she takes the pages, brushes aside Hávulk's light hair and he feels more than sees the hand of the writer. Finally, she hears Fulcanelli's last thoughts before the poison took his mind and before she helped to bring him back from madness. She falls asleep with a sense of completion and relief.

It's now that Hávulk notices the scrap of paper – the ripped out diary page with its one ragged edge. In the dark he picks it up. He's never put the words in his own head before, but why not? He won't disturb Petra that way. His fingers seek out the place at the back of his skull where he can fold the clay skin back and bury the words.

The words hit him, more intense than the others. There's something different about this page. The writer is that same man – the same Fulcanelli whose life he now knows so intimately, but the words feel different; taste different. In the darkness he feels the anxiety of the writer and also his anger. The readiness to kill to survive – a readiness verging on desire.

6 August 1939, Austria

I need to write this down. It might be the only way I can make sense of it. Yesterday I reached Linz. The river is so wide now that I feel conspicuous and vulnerable. In rural areas it's still possible to avoid drawing attention to myself. Not so in those built up towns where a solitary rowing boat is a curiosity. Perhaps I also attract suspicion because of the haste with which I endeavour to put such places behind me.

Soon after I entered Linz I heard a shout from the bridge up ahead. My German is fair, but I couldn't understand what the man was saying. I didn't wish to look up, preferring to assume that the shout was not directed at me and hoping to be left alone to go on my way, but then a bullet hit the water in front of me – I was to be given no choice in the matter. There were three young men in military uniform on the bridge and they shouted at me to draw into the river bank.

Though I have been passing for a mute wanderer, I was unsure of the wisdom of maintaining this mask in front of these men who were little more than boys. I thought perhaps they could be reasoned with.

I greeted them in German. The one in front marched up to me and shoved the butt of his gun into my stomach so that I doubled over in pain. "Heil Hitler," he said. I stayed down close to the floor – I had no idea what was happening. All I was aware of was my racing pulse and a head full of unfamiliar animal emotions. Fear and hatred had sprung from nowhere. I looked up into the face of a freckled boy in his late teens. I remember his mopped hair. It occurred to me that he was probably a country boy attracted to military service in the city. The other two were slightly older; he kept turning to them like a puppy looking for approval in the faces of its masters.

The other two nodded at him once, finished their cigarettes and started going through the boat. There was nothing for them there. They took a bit of bread and ham I had left, but I was running low on supplies. They clinked around in the carefully packed boxes with curious glances at each other, then they started opening up the books. The golden edging on some of the pages made them curious – I think perhaps they thought I was a dealer in religious texts – or a church looter – but then they saw the Aurora Consurgens. Seeing the image of male and female united in the rebis they finally turned to look at me. Clearly they had decided that I was some kind of deviant. They upturned all of the manuscripts on the deck and started flicking through clumps of pages, pointing and laughing. They told me I was disgusting – I had no difficulty in interpreting those words. For each insult, the boy above me gave me a kick as if to check that I had understood properly.

By the time they started throwing things into the river, I was bloody-lipped and wretched. I saw what they were doing only out of the corner of my eye. I think when I turned my head to look more directly at them, the boy hit me with his gun again. Hate was suddenly there in great fistfuls – I could feel it as a physical sensation more potent than any I have felt in my life. In that moment these stupid boys appeared completely inhuman. They were destroying my most valued possessions: my very identity. In my eyes they had no right to live.

I don't think the boy understood what was happening when I turned around his gun and slit his throat with the bayonet. It took the other two a long time to react. By the time they realised something was wrong, I was already at the boat. They had left their weapons leaning up against its side and were helpless without them. I ran through the first, then as the other reached for his gun, I withdrew the bayonet and swung the butt of the rifle into his face. Then I stabbed them both several more times each. By the time it was over I could barely see through the tears in my eyes. I don't know what it was. Anger? Relief? Hatred? Self-hatred? I have often said that I don't understand the minds of men. This apparently includes my own.

Thank God they didn't scream, for not only would it have sickened my wretched soul; it would have also drawn attention to the scene. There was blood everywhere. I dragged the three bodies under the bridge so that they could only be seen by someone walking the path directly underneath it, but anyone looking over the side of the bridge could have seen the pools of blood. Oh God, what have I done?

It was early morning and traffic was thin, and it is due to this fact alone that I remained unseen. Even as I finished hiding the last soldier from sight, I could hear feet on the bridge. I stayed in its shadow, reeling with fear and sickness, hoping that they would somehow pass me by. And they did. I took the boat and rowed hard for safety. As I passed the place where the books had been thrown, I looked into the water, but saw only an impenetrable murk. What use is mourning a drowned book? Better to mourn a life cut short. I didn't look at the dead faces and yet they are somehow present in my mind, where they appear distorted, but fundamentally innocent. That's what keeps occurring to me – they were so unprepared, so shocked, so surprised to find themselves dying.

I thank God that He has preserved me through this ordeal, and yet part of me wishes He hadn't. I have rowed through the night knowing the impossibility of sleep while these nightmares are running through my head. I'm incredibly tired – I only hope that when I do finally sleep I won't be discovered. My own life suddenly feels sacred to the point that I will do anything to defend it. I now know in a way that was once entirely academic, what mortality is, and that I will cling to life like a newborn to his mother's breast. If necessary, I know that I would kill again to see a new day.

The boy shivers and looks at the floor, clutching his sides and stomach as if to keep himself from physically falling apart. For the first time he feels anger. Adrenaline, or something like it, fills his being. There is no chance of sleep now – he will seek revenge. Against whom and for what reason he does not know or understand; all he knows at this moment is the words, their drive, their determination and their blind destructive fear. It is this feeling that leads him to step out of the hut and into the night.

Petra stirs, her sleep disturbed by something in the hut. There's a tentative light outside, pawing softly at the ground and giving the world just a little warmth. A sobbing comes from the boy's bed, and she turns blinking eyes to him in the semi-darkness, strikes a match and touches it to a candle. The light illuminates the boy lying at a curious angle in his bed, his hands above the covers. Her eyes examine those hands – they're stained a colour that in the yellow light appears brown, but isn't. It's red. Her mind races. Blood? Has he cut himself? Had some accident?

"Hávulk! Hávulk! Are you okay? You're bleeding!"

The boy's eyes open slowly. "I killed someone," he whispers.

"What?" He has to repeat it twice before she starts to understand.

"A soldier. He was pointing a gun at me. The words told me to do it."

She can't believe what she's hearing. "Which words told you?"

"I... I found new pages – the pages from Mister Fulcanelli's diary that were ripped out. You were asleep so I put them in myself, but they were from the same book – they were Mister Fulcanelli's words. They were frightened. They said I'd die if I didn't... if I didn't... that someone would take something from me. So I killed him."

"Jean's words made you kill someone?"

"It's the same writing, the same book. I can feel it's the same man's words that have been in my head all this time, but they were so... They feel different. I don't like them. I can't take them out. Help me, Petra."

Petra thinks about the pages. Ripped out? She hadn't noticed them. Perhaps Jean hadn't wanted to remember their contents, though she never suspected for a moment that his diaries could contain a malicious sentiment – he was always so balanced and gentle. Perhaps the boy is confused, made some mistake, ripped a page from one of the paperbacks with their war stories. Is such a thing even possible? Is Hávulk so susceptible to the words in his head? Perhaps only as susceptible as any human is to a persistent thought.

Either way she must know – what were these words? But the boy won't tell her. He just keeps repeating, "I'm scared of the words. Take them out," and looking at her with begging eyes.

"Hávulk, you know I can't take them out. They're part of you now." It's true, but her voice has an edge of impatience borne of a curiosity that even the blood on Hávulk's hands does nothing to divert: she has to know what happened to Fulcanelli. She wants to be reassured about the man she once loved – even the blood doesn't faze her. But no end of pleading will get Hávulk to tell her the story the words told him. Eventually she persuades him to rinse the blood off his hands and go to sleep for the final few hours before daylight – they both need to rest.

She can hear him tossing and turning, his sleep disturbed by nightmares. There's nothing she can do for him except to take him away – and that's just what she'll do. Right now. She's nervous to leave her home, but really this day has been a long time coming. The outside world has already crossed the threshold, an unwanted guest bringing gifts of doubt and danger.

She begins to pack, gathering provisions for the journey in a stout sack. When she's done with the food she goes back to rouse the boy, but Hávulk is gone. There's a note written in scratchy hand – Fulcanelli's hand.

Dear Petra,

I have decided to carry on the work of Monsieur Fulcanelli. I have little choice. He's in my mind. His ambitions are my ambitions. He came here to build a better society for people and I think there is a way that I can make it happen. Monsieur Fulcanelli knew how horrible the world can be, but I can make it better. I'll go to the king. I'll persuade him to make me his heir. I'll promise him the secrets of alchemy, then after I'm named as his successor I'll do whatever I need to do. I can do it, Petra. This is what Monsieur Fulcanelli wants. Please don't try to stop me.

Goodbye,

Hávulk.

She puts down the letter with tears in her eyes. "No," she mutters under her breath. How could this happen? In a freakish twist of fate, her son is going to try to become Monterek's. She has told Hávulk nothing of Monterek's baby – the one she brought into the world then so quickly dispatched to the next. Hávulk was to be hers and hers alone, and now he will go to Monterek and Monterek will pass him off as his son – assuming he doesn't simply torture Hávulk. Either way, she will have lost both Jean and Hávulk to the mad king.

Her mind whirls with possibilities – she sees her beloved boy coming under Monterek's influence, going to live in the castle and forgetting all about her; she sees him trying to kill Monterek, failing and being executed in the high town square.

Above all, she sees that Monterek will give nothing away. His selfishness has endured throughout his reign. Never has he shared power with anyone – not the mistresses he's kept, nor the girls he's raped in dark alleys, let alone their illegitimate children. Fulcanelli was a wonderful man, but naive and too eager to trust in the goodness of man, and this blindness will be Hávulk's death.

She must go to intercede – to demand the return of her poor deluded son – and there is only one way she knows to do it for sure. A way that will force Hávulk to abandon his suicide mission and Monterek to disown the boy. Petra grabs a shovel and heads out to a solitary clearing in the woods to start digging.

CHAPTER 17
FATHERHOOD

Monterek rests a knotted hand on the boy's silk-smooth hair. So this is fatherhood – or rather, this is what it feels like to pretend, though it does seem somehow... right. After so many solitary years in the company of squabbling title-holders and the twig-dry bureaucrats who badger him with dull questions every time he goes on foreign visits, this almost tangible sense of connection to another person is something of a tonic. Just being in the boy's presence fills the old man with a new sense of purpose; pride drives his every movement and he feels compelled to get up and walk around the parapets, to point out to his new son all of the wonders of his kingdom. He almost has to remind himself that he's doing this for appearances only, that he doesn't know this boy from the uncontrolled progeny that tumble in the gutters of the low town, that he wouldn't be anywhere near this castle – or Monterek's throne – if he hadn't promised to the king the answers he's been seeking for so long – the secrets of alchemy.

It was no parlour trick either – whatever the boy gave the king's oldest husky, it certainly had an effect. To see a creature that had spent the last four months moping around and falling into its food suddenly jump up and chase the bitches around the yard, cock standing to attention like an iron rod – why, it was more than a miracle – it was magic.

And it's so simple – just a quick mixture and hey presto! To think of the convoluted claptrap that Gregor's been feeding him for so many years – absolute nonsense about the need to apprentice himself to a master and the stars that were never quite aligned. The erudite patriarch was tasked with discovering those secrets over half a century ago, but to this day he has nothing to show for it but a bad cough and a convulsive shakiness from sampling too many poisons. If only he knew that his miserable act had been upstaged by a mere boy. Gregor will never discover the boy's abilities of course – those must remain secret until Monterek himself has learned to create the elixir. At that point the boy's usefulness will have to be re-evaluated, but for now he will pose as the king's son and heir, and it's the kind of make-believe that could almost be truth: those deep-set eyes and folded ear-tips could be evidence of the boy's Turkish ancestry, the pride of his bearing a hallmark of high birth. He can only be ten years old or so, and already he has that majestic walk, not pretentious, but confident of everything around him, confident of his place in the world and in his place at the pinnacle of the natural order of things.

"And how long do you propose to keep him, King?"

There's something about the way Gregor has started pronouncing 'King'. He speaks perfect English with a very mild accent, but every time he says that word nowadays, it comes out twisted, like he's gargled and chewed it around every cavity in his body before finally spitting it out.

"I don't propose to keep him at all, Gregor. He will be my heir. I expect him to outlast me."

"But he's a bastard."

"Patriarch, your words are too frank. You forget yourself."

"You don't need an heir – I almost have it – I swear." The strain on his voice makes him break into a ragged cough. The king doesn't wait for it to subside.

"Just days ago you declared to me for the thousandth time that the pursuit of alchemy was hopeless without a master. Have your efforts been so inspired by the prospect of the lad's accession?"

The other is silent – as silent as the boy, who sits so gracefully at the king's right hand that he could be rooted there – no, not rooted but carved in place. His new clothes almost look like decorations on a statue.

"My boy?" Monterek is slightly relieved when the boy's head moves in response. "How do you feel about being king, eh?"

"I would like that, father." The word freezes Monterek momentarily.

"Of course we will have to change your name. 'Hávulk' is no name for a king. Marek perhaps, like my father. And then you can live here – you'll have this whole castle to yourself and..."

"And the library too?" It's the first time he's shown any hint of real excitement.

"Certainly. Even Gregor's alchemy books if you can read them. After all, he can't." He never misses an opportunity to remind Gregor of his failings.

"But, King – why now?" Gregor is beginning to annoy him. "You have had other offspring."

"Yes, Gregor – and your point is?"

"Well, why did you not settle for one of them?"

"Gregor, I don't know if you recall what happened to those boys born out of wedlock, whose mothers so much as whispered the royal name, do you?"

"I recall. And I am mystified as to why this... child should be any kind of exception."

The king sighs, bored. "I did not want an heir at that time – I wanted eternal life and the last thing I needed was a litter of peasant brats trying to poison my tea to hasten their accession. But..." He pauses to clear his throat. "Time has changed my priorities – if nobody succeeds me, the vultures will swoop in and take apart my kingdom piece by piece. Yevnik will claim the castle, Frisk will declare himself President, and their wives will bicker over who gets the candlesticks."

"But the mother...."

"What of the mother?"

"Well precisely – would we rather not call attention to any... unfortunate incidents of your past?"

The suggestion gives Monterek pause. Until this moment he hadn't considered that this boy could genuinely be his son, but now he thinks of it, there's a possibility – or at least a possibility that someone might claim him. There have indeed been incidents over the years. Times when the ripe young daughters of Izvalta could be collateral for favour in the king's court, and times when the king simply took his due wherever he happened to find it. Just a few days ago there was a peasant girl in the Verkaz fields. Nothing to write home about, but certainly convenient. He'd been randy all day.

Who is this boy with his magic powders? Lean, healthy and with an air of knowledge and mystery. Perhaps he's some orphan of the high town, left to fend for himself in the woods. It leaves much unexplained, but there will be a time for questions. For now, the boy is a gift from above.

"There is no mother. The boy told me she is dead, didn't you, lad?" The boy nods, taking direction well from his new father. "You like books, don't you, my boy?" Again he nods and the king reaches for a small silver bell. The door to the great hall swings briskly open in response to its ring. "The butler here will take you to the library, where you can read as much as you want."

"Will you come and read me something, Father?" The butler

looks up at Monterek in surprise – Monterek's new 'son' is going to be news very soon, but for now the king's stony look is enough to discourage questions.

"Uh, yes. Later maybe. Now off you go – follow the butler."

When the door closes, the king addresses Gregor. "I... imagine it's quite possible that someone might mistakenly believe that the boy is theirs – perhaps a mother, even a father. I don't want to hear of such people. I don't want anyone to hear of them. Understand?"

"Very well, but there will be questions. There is simply no proof of his identity. He could be any common child off the street. Perhaps a pauper who fancies himself a prince."

"Enough of this!" Monterek stands. "I will allow no doubt on this score: he is my son because I say he is my son. Will you call the king's word into question?"

The older man offers a near imperceptible gesture of contrition.

"And to allay the doubts of the rest of the populace, you will arrange a naming ceremony to take place in three days' time. Understood?"

"Certainly."

"And now I will join my son in the library." Monterek leaves Gregor in the hall, alone but for the uneasy feeling in his gut.

CHAPTER 18
BOGEYMAN

Terry has been set free from the confines of the medical centre, but outside its walls he feels somehow more caged: watchful eyes follow him wherever he goes and he has been told in no uncertain terms that he's not permitted to set foot outside the perimeter unaccompanied. So no hope of making contact with Petra – not that it seems like a clever idea anyway. He only hopes that she's managed to leave Izvalta or hide somewhere the soldiers will never find her. He wouldn't wish the barrage of tests he's just been through on anybody. His arms still ache from injections and his legs are only just remembering what it's like to stand.

All those tests and for what? Even Ethan Smith can't seem to tell him what they found. Perhaps he genuinely doesn't know, but it's hard to trust anyone now. After private Jim Sale's grizzly death, the camp is not in a sharing mood.

At least for most people there's not much doubt about what killed him. It's on the informational video that they all sat through before coming out here, and they've been speculating about it since they first set foot in the Carpathian forest: bear attack. It's generally acknowledged that a bear could rip off a man's head – and it would, too, if it thought that man were threatening it. Shooting at it might reasonably constitute threatening behaviour, and a big bear could take a few bullets, assuming that Sale actually managed to hit it, which is by no means a given. Case closed for most people, and an end to joking about the local wildlife. Only Neil won't accept it, and his protests are conspicuous. Terry wonders what exactly he can't accept. Perhaps he has a problem understanding death itself – after all, he's what? Eighteen? Nobody needs to see that.

Or perhaps he did need to see it. The shock of real violence has vaporised his bravado, but maybe it's too much: last night Neil sobbed himself to sleep while Terry lay on his bunk wishing himself a million miles away and trying to think of something to say. Neil barely even acknowledged his existence this morning.

But it's not just that he won't accept Sale's death; he won't accept that it was an animal attack. He thinks it was a kid.

That possibility has Terry worried – because he did see Hávulk that night, and with his distinctive hair-colouring and curl-tipped ears there can be little doubt it was him. On the other hand, Terry was drugged and woozy. Seeing pink elephants wouldn't have been out of the question. And to imagine Hávulk killing somebody? It just isn't possible – even if he wanted to, how could he actually decapitate a fully-grown man? And why would a soldier shoot at a 10-year old boy?

Neil opens the door and steps through, his movements clipped and precise.

"I was just thinking of you," says Terry.

Neil says nothing. He puts his gun on the low table and mechanically begins to clean it. The silence is pendulous.

"Look, I'm just going to say this – I'm sorry about Sale and, well, if you want to talk about it, I'm here."

Neil carries on cleaning the rifle. When he's finished, he stares through the sight, aiming so intensely at an imaginary target that Terry can't help looking to see if there's actually something there. It's just a bit of wall.

"I saw it," says Neil quietly.

Terry studies his room-mate. "What did you see?"

"The god-damned bogeyman."

He's so certain, so rigid. It might be madness, but there's no question that Neil believes it.

"What did it look like?" asks Terry.

"What did it look like? It – well, shit – it just looked like some kid. But then it moved. Moved like I don't know what – not like a kid anyhow. It was almost like it was some kind of liquid more than a person. You know like Terminator 2 – that metal cop, y'know? It was over at the edge of the woods. Sale shone a light at it. Nothing like a bear. No fur. Smooth skin. It was upright, walking, but it wasn't like walking. Like it kept changing. It got bigger as it got closer – I mean, not like that. Not like it was just getting closer. It changed."

"Bears walk upright sometimes, you know."

"Are you listening? This wasn't a fucking bear! It was a kid. Some freaky, like, shape-shifting kid"

"Okay, okay! Well what did he look like?"

"Jesus, man – I don't know. These kids all look the same. It was just a kid. A boy. Hey, how'd you know it was a he?"

"Can't imagine a female bogeyman." Terry cracks a little smile, which is almost shared.

"Yeah, well. Everybody thinks I'm nuts. Fucking bears – it wasn't a bloody bear. But if I see it again I'll nail the little shit."

"You're gonna kill a kid? I mean, jeez Neil – listen to yourself. A kid that can rip a guy's head off? A kid that can just run through a camp of armed soldiers and out the other side without a scratch?"

"Yeah. Yeah, that's exactly what we're talking about. Dunno whether you noticed, but there was some guy supposed to have been eaten by a wolf and shat out the other side. Three days later, all he's got to show for it is a few scars. This whole place is like an extended X-Files, and you know what? Call me Joe Abductee, but the thing I saw was not human and everyone's gonna thank me when I blow its fucking head off."

There's a party setting out for the alchemist's hut. Rogers tells him to tag along – not explicitly as a hostage, but that's certainly how it feels.

As it happens, there is no trouble at the hut – it's deathly quiet. The black walls crush in all around, sucking up light the way a desert sucks up water. It feels dead in here, like a tomb.

"No sign of the alchemist."

"You check the furnace? That's what happens to witches, right?"

One of the soldiers tugs gently at the huge door, pulling it slowly open with a drawn out horror-movie creak. He pokes his head in.

"Nah – nuthin' in here. No bones or bodies, but wait – what is... aargh!" The soldier thrashes his arms around wildly. With uncanny speed, Neil is at the ready, pointing his gun at the furnace, his gaze locked in a maniac stare. Then the soldier pops his head back up above the furnace door with a grin. "Nah, just kidding," he says.

"Hey, Davis – quit screwing around. Spencer was ready to fill you full of holes," says Rogers. "Right, boys – look sharp – I want a full inventory – we're looking for chemicals, minerals – anything you could mix up in a cauldron. Any interesting looking papers too. Might be a secret formula hidden here somewhere." Rogers plucks a paperback book from a shelf – one of about a dozen similar titles. It isn't what he was hoping to find, but he leafs through it nevertheless.

"Hey – I've read that one. Alistair MacLean. Do you think it's a clue?"

"What, something buried deep in the text? Somewhere behind the Nazis, the lone gunslinger and the mad scientist?" says Rogers. "Keep looking." He turns to Terry with a sigh. "Anything coming back, Morton? Any secret passages around here you remember?"

"Yeah – where's she keep the gold?"

"I – I'm sorry – I wasn't in this room at all – I was next door." They push open a door and see a wooden table dark with dried blood.

"This yours then?" One of the soldiers sniffs at it. Terry walks away, feeling faint. The soldiers look around. The hut is sparse on personal effects, but there is one thing: a sketch of a boy set in a handmade wooden frame.

Neil snatches up the picture, studying it so hard his gaze threatens to ignite the paper.

"It's him," he says. "It's the bogeyman. That's what killed Sale."

Rogers takes the picture gently from him. "Neil, it would be best if you let this go."

"Bull-shit. This is the fucker – I saw him."

"You're out of line."

"But..."

"Spencer. Shut it."

"Funky bauble," says Ethan at Terry's side. He's picked up a nasty looking glass ball. It's only small – a couple of inches across – and grey and lumpy. Terry takes the thing from him and inspects it. It really is horrible, but for no obvious reason. It's repellent in the same way as a dead mouse that's been left to rot and moulder behind a cabinet. He almost drops it which, it occurs to him, would be an exceptionally bad idea. And then the light of recognition dawns: this glass ball is what Petra described in Tirig Og Kam. The by-product of an insane hangover cure, complete with the sickness inside. Is it his imagination or can he almost feel it trying to break out? Just touching it is enough to make his stomach rise up into his throat, an acid bile washes up the back of his mouth and into his nostrils.

"Ugh. Check this out. Skid marks." One of the younger privates is holding up a white towel stained yellow-orange. "You into this weird shit, Morton?"

Terry doesn't dignify it with an answer. He pockets the glass sphere without really thinking – mostly as a way to break contact with it.

"Fascinating." The doctor is searching through the miscellaneous collection of jars and dishes. He pokes his nose in to sniff at them, prods them with a glass stick and then decants them one by one into screw-topped bottles, which he places into a padded case.

"Got anything, Doctor?"

"Maybe – I'll need to get these back for analysis."

Terry looks around the hut and the soldiers' faces smirking at the squalor. At this moment, he begins to understand Petra's words: these people will never understand what this place is, what alchemy is – they see the world in terms of subject and object – man acting upon the world to shape it in the way he sees fit, without giving anything of himself. He wonders where she is and if she's safe. He hopes beyond all hope that she and Hávulk have gone away, that they've found a safe haven elsewhere. It would help him feel less guilty. He can't know that at this moment, the king is busy preparing for the ceremony in which he will name Hávulk as his heir, and Petra too is preparing – in her own way.

CHAPTER 19
CEREMONY

It's quite a crowd – it almost looks like they're invading the castle. Thousands of upturned faces like so many stones on a beach, all waiting for the king to step out onto the battlements with the next Prince of Izvalta.

Everybody has been invited, from the farmers dressed in patched-up jackets, to the neatly attired citizens of the high town, as well as the visiting military, Terry among them, who are diplomatically showing face. The place is thick with murmur – it spreads like a creeping vine amongst the crowd: new theories as to the boy's identity take root around the square, until speculation becomes certainty. His mother is a foreign queen, a common prostitute, a victim of war or amnesia or crippling illness.

And then they appear – the great bear of a king and a comparatively thin, diminutive creature to his side. Terry feels his heart stop as he recognises Hávulk – and Terry is not the only one to recognise the boy golem.

"It's the bogeyman! That thing! That kid! The picture at the alchemist's hut – it's him. That's what killed Sale!" Neil is shouting as loud as he can but his words are lost in the jubilant roar of the crowd. Finally, he starts to shout in Rogers' ear and Terry watches as the superior officer quietly puts Neil in his place. This time though, Rogers looks interested, because Hávulk is at the epicentre of a web of coincidences that are hard to ignore: the death of Sale, an alchemist with miraculous healing powers, and now he's a prince. There's something going on here that begs investigation.

The crowd cheers while the two incongruous characters wave from the castle battlements, and then gradually the noise dies down. The king is speaking – in English. Terry wonders if anyone's translating for those who don't understand, but maybe the effect of his booming voice and upward-swinging fist needs no interpretation.

"Citizens of Izvalta, today is a great day for our nation. As we all know, a small country like ours has an uneasy relationship with the world outside. Without a strong and unyielding king, our great land might fall prey to foreign interference. The Europeans" – he spits it out with disgust, like a fly he's swallowed – "would take away our livelihoods – they would repossess our farms and they would force us to pay them taxes with which they would furnish their expensive summer homes.

"Izvalta must have a strong king, and, while I have no intention of dying, I am growing old. In order to safeguard Izvalta, I have decided to name an heir: my son, believed lost, but just recently returned to me by divine providence. His mother, sadly, is no longer with us. But she would not want us to mourn her passing – we must celebrate Izvalta's new heir – Marek Al-Lazari."

Hávulk waves a bashful wave, growing gradually bolder until he's beaming a huge smile on his people. But now the roar of the crowd is diminishing – something else has grabbed their attention.

"Look!" Ethan Smith grabs Terry's arm and points toward a dark figure standing fully upright on the peak of a rooftop. Petra. She looks up at the king and Hávulk, her hair and coat billowing out behind her. The crowd is quiet, waiting for something to happen, for some cue from their king, but Monterek looks as perplexed as anyone.

Finally she breaks the silence in a voice that rasps through the air. "Give me back my son."

If Monterek recognises her, he never lets it show. "Do I know you?" he says simply, raising his voice only enough to make it travel the distance to the rooftop.

"That's my son," she says.

"You are mistaken. This boy's mother succumbed to a fatal illness – but here, let's ask Marek." Monterek turns to the boy, who stands strangely impassive at his side, like his soul has momentarily retreated from his body, leaving just a sculpture behind.

"Marek?" he says. "Do you know this woman?" but the boy keeps his silence.

"I am also known to you, Monterek, but that's not important now – now I just want the boy back. Whatever he's promised you is a lie – a cheap trick that I taught him. I'm begging you – give the poor boy back to me."

A heavy body presses past Terry, grunting something that doesn't sound like an apology. It's moving in the direction of the house on which Petra is standing. He's about to shout out a warning, but Ethan whispers in his ear.

"Careful now – don't get yourself into more trouble." So Terry waits, fidgeting with impatience to know what's going on.

"Marek, is this your mother?" asks Monterek again, finally grabbing the boy's head and turning it in Petra's direction.

The boy's eyes meet Petra's. "She's not my mother," he says, and she visibly sags, momentarily almost losing her footing on the rooftop. She regains herself to some extent, although her voice starts to take on a tone of desperation.

"I am not truly the boy's mother, I admit."

"Well then, why are you here interrupting this ceremony?"

"Because you are not his father. Nobody is."

"What rubbish! Explain yourself."

"He's not human – he's a clay boy – a golem. He has none of the usual hallmarks of birth – not even a belly-button."

"What? Well that's easily disproved! Come on boy – I know it's chilly but you can show us your belly button and we'll get rid of this madwoman."

Hávulk shoots Petra a wild look. She's undermining his plan, discrediting him – and for what? So that he can run away with her to continue a feeble life of pointless alchemical works? There's a perfect plan in his head to take Izvalta by right. Once the people know that he is their king he can finally shape the kind of society that Fulcanelli dreamed of – one of equality and justice. Izvalta will be a utopia at last, but only if the crowd believes that he's the king's son. Hávulk backs away from Monterek, instinctively clutching his belly.

"Boy? Let's see it."

"Uh. I can't."

"He's not human, Monterek – but he is my son nevertheless. Please – please give him back to me. He's all I have."

Monterek isn't listening. He has Hávulk by the wrist and he's wrenching up his shirt. He sees the perfectly smooth belly and takes a step backward. The crowd below is almost forgotten – they're just a backdrop of faces set against the uncanny silence of thousands waiting to see and hear what will happen.

A moment passes before Monterek retrieves his command of the situation. "Is that all? It will take more than a minor birth defect to prove he's not human. Come on now – do you really expect me to believe this nonsense?"

"I... I suppose I didn't expect you to believe me so easily.

That's why I brought this." She takes something from beneath her coat – it's hard to see from the ground – it looks like a cylinder or something, made of glass and greenish, with something inside.

"What is that?" the king demands.

"It's yours, Monterek. Your baby." She looks at Hávulk, and Hávulk looks back, his gaze arrested by the cylinder. "Hávulk," she shouts "This is the shape that brought you into the world. One night in the low town the man next to you raped me. I don't expect I was the first to bear one of your children was I, Monterek? But I guarantee that this one had the shortest life. When it was born I used its spark of life to make you, Hávulk. In a way, you are his son as much as mine. But you were born out of love, while this thing..." she holds the tube above her, "was born of hate, of arrogance, born of the man who drove Jean Fulcanelli to poison his own mind. The man standing there is both your father and his murderer. He will never let you become king despite all of his promises. You want to be the instrument of Fulcanelli's work? Be his revenge!"

Three men try to grab her at the same time – they've been creeping slowly across the roof over the course of the conversation. Petra shrieks and thrusts an elbow into one's face – he rolls back off the roof and Terry hears a crunching landing and a cry of pain from the other side of the building, but the other two have her arms. As they struggle, Petra's grip on the cylinder loosens and it arcs forward off the roof, slowly spinning down to the street below. It lands with a sound of shattering glass around where the crowd is thickest. There's a moment when the only noise is that of Petra's struggling – then a scream rises from where the cylinder smashed and the crowd opens up in a circle around it.

The scream is like an explosion in Hávulk's mind. He looks down at the pink and red smudge on the cold cobbles and once again the words crystallise in his mind. He has the capacity to kill. And he must. He looks to Monterek but the king has turned tail and covering his retreat two lines of broad-shouldered guards close ranks. They level automatic rifles at the boy, who bares his teeth and runs at them, casting them aside like cloth dolls, their faces sewn into an expression of surprise at the strength and speed of this thing that appears to be just a boy. Shots are fired in haste and fear, serving only to further injure the beleaguered guards. In the space of just a few seconds one man's throat is ripped out, bullets puncture another's shoulder and chest, an arm is severed at the elbow, ribs are cracked under the force of Hávulk's thin, gentle hand, and then it all comes suddenly to a halt.

Hávulk stands rigid and immobile, like a photograph of a tidal wave, its mammoth crest of kinetic energy instantly stopped. Captured. In the beat of silence, the guards each step backwards and a man sprawled on the ground in the shadow of Hávulk's now frozen descending fist rolls away with the noise of a frightened animal.

Gregor, the patriarch, wizened by years and riddled with maladies, is the man who victoriously steps out from behind the boy. In his right hand he holds a bloody mulch of what appears to be paper. A thick wedge of the stuff, marked up with script that, though almost illegible before, is now so soaked in blood that it's impossible to make out a single character. Some of it has practically become a paste. Gregor walks slowly around the golem, satisfaction gleaming in his face.

"It's like your heart, isn't it, boy?" he says. "It's like I've ripped out your heart and here it is in front of your eyes." He coughs a long, hacking cough. "What are you without these bits of soggy paper, eh? I wonder." And he pushes Hávulk with his extended left index finger. The boy falls slowly backward, the back of his head with its gaping open cavity hitting the stone rampart. The boy registers no pain. He just lies there, eyes open, looking up at a sky that he once understood so well. The movements of heaven and earth are now strange to him, though he remembers that once they had meaning. Once. Clouds roll by and he is content to watch them. He is content to do anything really. There was something more... Something important, but whatever it was it doesn't matter now.

The boy folds his hands over his chest as he calmly gazes upward, his ears deaf to Gregor's victorious taunting or the cries of the wounded, or the shouted orders of the king who leers warily over him. Nothing makes an impression at all – until he hears his name. His name. He has a name. Of course he has a name.

"Hávulk!" Petra is screaming at the top of her voice. "Háv..." A blow to her stomach makes her swallow her last syllable.

The boy raises his head very slowly. He can see her behind a wall of people all with... what are they? Yes, he's recalling it now. Guns – that's right. He can see the pain on her face and he can see that it's not physical pain, though there's that too. And he wants to go to her and comfort her, but someone is taking his hands and binding them. He's upright, moving slowly, thinking slowly, and he remembers a time when he could think so much faster and the thoughts had more meaning.

A man with a big black beard is talking now. His... father? No, that seems wrong. He has a gold band on his head. If only he could remember what that meant. The man is talking to Petra. He's saying "Oh yes – I remember you. Long time ago. You had a mouth on you then too. Needed a man to set you right, didn't you?"

Hávulk smiles when Petra spits in the bearded man's face, though he couldn't say why. Then he shuts his eyes as she is beaten down. When things are quiet again he opens his eyes.

Through a forest of legs he can see Petra on the ground, and he can see blood on her face.

He begins to wail, howling like an animal he remembers from the woods – from his home. And then the butt of a gun hits him in the face, and there is a moment of silence as everyone around him tenses, awaiting his reaction. But he can't remember how he's supposed to react, and so he stays quiet. The bearded man lets out a short laugh and turns away from the whole scene.

Gregor, his hands still bloody, dismisses the crowds below, citing an assassination attempt as the source of the chaos. The people begin to depart, muttering question after question to themselves. Questions shared by Terry Morton and the soldiers, none of whom could see what occurred on the castle ramparts, but all of whom can recognise gunshots when they hear them.

In the great hall, Monterek orders away his best hope for realising his dreams of gold and immortality. "Lock him up," he says. "And the bitch."

He consoles himself with a hot brandy. This particular disappointment is a bitter pill and a distasteful one. When the boy came to him, promising to share the secrets of alchemy, for a few precious days, time seemed endless and free – there was no need to worry about the future because it was limitless, and in a future with no conclusion, anything is possible. Now it feels like there is no time left.

He looks at his left hand, which over the last year has begun to shake with alarming regularity, occasionally upsetting his aim and letting a target run free, back into the woods. Perhaps the woman and her boy do hold the secrets he's looking for – but it's clear that they will die before giving them up. And then a solution presents itself as Captain Rogers appears at the door led by two royal guards.

"Sorry to disturb Your Highness," says Rogers, approaching

224 | J W MURRAY

the throne. "But there's a matter of some urgency to discuss. I hope you can make a little time for me?" The king nods and sits back on his throne.

Rogers continues. "You are aware of the recent attack on our camp, resulting in the death of one of our men – a Private James Sale, who was violently killed. Decapitated."

"Indeed?"

"Well, Your Highness, we initially believed it to be a case of animal attack, but there is evidence to suggest otherwise."

"Oh?"

"We have reason to believe that the perpetrator was in fact a boy."

"I'm sorry? A boy killed one of your men? Did he get in and steal a gun? In which case how could you possibly have thought it an animal attack? Even the Carpathian cats aren't so dexterous."

"No, Your Highness. He seems to have ripped the soldier's head off with his bare hands."

The king pauses, thinking of the scene that he just witnessed and Rogers smiles to himself as if seeing precisely the thoughts in Monterek's head.

"We have an eye-witness account, Your Majesty. Private Spencer, who was also on guard duty at the time of the attack, believes that the boy who was named as your successor – Marek – was the perpetrator."

"He has not been named, Captain, and will not be named."

"My apologies. My mistake. It seemed there was some kind of a scuffle?"

Monterek drains the last of his brandy and stands, enjoying his height advantage over the foreigner. "Let's cut to the chase, Captain. You want the boy. You suspect he has some kind of power. And indeed he does. For the very first time in Izvalta's history, there is blood on the ramparts, and not because of any invasion. Just a boy. Tell me – what will you do with him?"

"We would like to determine whether the boy could indeed be capable of these acts of violence as you say. If we can prove that in fact he is guilty of murder, we would like to see justice done."

"Do you know what a homunculus is, Captain?"

"I can't say that I do."

"I think you do know," the king says. "I'm getting old, but I'm not blind – you're here in search of alchemical secrets. I'm sure you're actually very familiar with the concept of a homunculus – an inanimate object gifted the power of action through various means. I myself have been searching for alchemical secrets for years, without knowing that there was a living alchemist within the borders of Izvalta. I suspect that you have equipment and methods devised to analyse the boy.

"Find his secrets. If I choose to hand him over to you, you will in return share any of these secrets that you may discover. I will be notified immediately. I hear that your interpreter, Morton, was recently returned to life from near death – I presume by the power of an alchemical elixir. Should you discover this elixir – and you will know if you have – then I shall require a supply." He holds up a hand to indicate that he has not yet finished.

"A final word. I understand that the kind of tests that you might run on the boy could be... invasive. We deem this boy no longer a boy – no longer a human being – he is a creation of man, just like a mechanical clock. In order to learn the workings of a clock, one must take it apart. Do with him what you will. What. You. Will."

"And the woman? If you think this boy is a homunculus, presumably she made him."

"She'll try to poison me at the earliest opportunity. There's only one thing to be done with her – and you will look the other way."

"Wait, what are you...?"

Again Monterek raises his hand. "No. No enquiry. No negotiation. This is my country. The boy will be delivered within the hour."

CHAPTER 20
THE CLAY BOY

The issue divides Izvalta, walking a tightrope between ancient religious dogma and the contemporary reality that Izvalta is gradually beginning to face. No longer is this a valley of people who exclusively make their own clothes and food and who marry people living on the same street. Trade is the new reality: jeans and t-shirts from Vietnam, radios and televisions from Korea – even cars. Izvalta is a meeting place of two distinct worlds, one of them rooted in tradition, in belief, in seasonal celebrations, sowing, harvesting and watching their families grow. The other world is tourism, foreign money and a neighbouring country's cast-off technologies. In the high town there is a dwindling interest in tradition as anything but an artefact they can package and sell in a gift shop, which is why the word 'witch' generally elicits a murmur of disbelief.

Yes, they've all heard about the crazed woman who dropped a tiny dead body from the roof of the Hotel Carpathia – the majority had been at the catastrophic naming ceremony watching it happen – but with gradual Westernisation of Izvaltan thought, it now feels uncomfortable to attribute the woman's madness to witchery rather than some more easily explained psychological affliction. This congregation gives such things as witches, werewolves and vampires even less credence than the concept of

God as Provider. There are other providers that are more easily explained and other diagnoses for mental imbalance, and there hasn't been a witch accused in Svart for hundreds of years – it's uncommon even in the smaller settlements in the surrounding countryside. The patriarch, however, is insistent.

"Yes, a witch," he booms from the pulpit in his cracked voice. "Even in this modern age – for evil never does rest. Let us remember to be forever vigilant, dear brothers and sisters, for the snake takes many forms upon this earth, often in the form of other animals and even in the form of man. 'How shall ye know them?' Why, the Bible itself tells of them. They are the star-gazers and potion-makers. Secretly do they practise their arts – in places away from the good people that may taint the pure evil of their deeds. Their resting place shall be the fiery lake of burning sulphur. We must purge the land of this evil lest it drag us all to those nether regions." He usually doesn't put on such a show.

The sermon is a prelude – something to prepare the public for Madame Fulcanelli's grizzly fate, and it goes some small way to dissipating the surprise felt when, the very next day, Izvalta begins its preparations for the first public witch burning in over 250 years.

Hávulk is also safely under lock and key. One of the concrete camp outbuildings has been re-purposed to contain a prisoner – even one with potentially superhuman strength. A solid metal door has been constructed from the shattered skeleton of a nearby structure and secured to the front of the building.

"It's not exactly maximum security," Ethan Smith points out to Terry, but even so it seems more than is needed. Hávulk looks like he's trying to curl up into himself, becoming little more than a small boulder. No longer is he the lean boy full of energy and life – he's lost inside himself. He mutely submits to a barrage of tests, which leave his arms looking bruised and sore. The x-rays reveal nothing out of the ordinary – they're much the same as Terry's were. In fact, doctor Mitchell is beginning to question the whole process. Walking discreetly past the boy's prison, Terry overhears a conversation between Rogers and the doctor.

"It makes no sense, Captain. How he could have done it with only his bare hands? None of these data show anywhere near the necessary muscle development. He's just like all the other kids in the area – he's lean and tough, but he's no body-builder."

"I know, Henry, but we keep him until we have some answers. Sale's head didn't just fly off of its own accord. At the very least we have Private Spencer's sworn word that he saw the boy that night. And then there's the supposed mother."

"Did you hear that she's being executed?"

There's an intake of breath and a slight cough from Rogers. "We can't be seen to intervene. This boy could be our last lead. I need something concrete."

"But there's a limit to the tests I can run. To all intents and purposes it looks like he's just a normal boy – and it looks like he's in pain. These are invasive tests and we're not giving him enough recovery time."

"Of course if he's not a real kid it doesn't matter – if he's not human, he doesn't have any human rights."

"Tristram, what if he is human? That's where the tests are pointing. Some oddities, certainly, but all within the bounds of human possibility. People can be born without a belly button – although it's true that usually there would be a scar elsewhere and I haven't found one. Nevertheless, slight abnormality is no grounds for his classification as anything other than human."

"And his head? The cavity where the patriarch found those pages?"

"Nothing there. Just a sore spot that he seems to have scratched a lot."

"Have you at least got him to talk?" Rogers sounds suddenly tired.

"He seems to have a natural gift for silence." The doctor considers. "Maybe Morton could get him to talk – the boy's been asking for him."

"Morton? How in hell does he know Morton?"

"I would assume that they met at the alchemist's house."

"Hmph – another detail that little rat decided to leave out. I'd rather use someone I could actually rely on."

"Well the boy doesn't seem too happy around soldiers. I could sit in with Morton. Guide the conversation. Find out what's going on here."

"Okay, Doc. Go ahead, but I'm keeping those guards posted outside."

Neil frowns at Terry and Henry Mitchell as they approach. He's not on guard, but his pacing is starting to wear thin a patch of grass just in front of the makeshift prison.

"You're going to talk to the bogeyman?" It's like he's challenging them.

"Well," sighs the doctor, "the tests are getting us nowhere. We're no closer than we were a week ago – there's nothing we've found that suggests that he's anything other than a normal child."

"Oh yeah, apart from that whole murder thing, right? Listen, Mister White-coat – you saw Sale's body. You know I saw this freak do it. That's all you need, right? We're in the middle of nowhere. All you need to do is say it's dangerous – say it's a killer – a... a golem or whatever. It's a machine."

"I'm sorry, Private." They press on.

"You're making a big mistake. It'll break out and get you. You're not gonna know what hit you, but I'm gonna be ready. Don't say I didn't warn you."

The boy is curled up in a corner, facing away from the entrance.

"He's been turning down food. Won't eat a thing," whispers Mitchell to Terry. "Which means that if he's just a boy he'll die shortly – if we can't talk to him – get him to see some sense."

"I suppose we can only try." Terry approaches the cage. One of the guards motions to say he shouldn't get too close.

"Hávulk?" There's no response from the boy.

"Hávulk – I heard you wanted to speak to me."

The boy turns in the cage and looks up at Terry with unblinking eyes that seem older than the face in which they are set. "Part of me did."

"How are you feeling?"

The words are slow to surface, like bubbles through thick oil. "I don't know. Disappointed. I thought I could help people. I thought Petra would understand that. But now I see why she didn't want me to – because now I can see what people are really like – all they've done is hurt me." Again there's that uncanny stillness to his body, like he's barely breathing. "What's happening to Petra?"

"Uh. There's no news. I'm afraid," says Mitchell quickly.

"You're lying," Hávulk replies mildly. "It doesn't matter. I'll talk to you – I'll tell you anything you want, but Terry – I have a favour to ask of you in return."

"What is it?"

"Help Petra."

"But I..."

"I think you'll know what to do when the time comes."

Terry looks frightened and perplexed. How is he going to prevent an execution? Is he supposed to single-handedly spring her from the castle dungeon? Maybe Hávulk doesn't realise how much danger she's in. All eyes are on Terry as he tries to process what this could mean.

"Well?" asks Mitchell, testily, in an obvious hurry to get to his questions. He gives Terry a look as if to say 'just promise already – does it really matter?'

"Okay. I'll help her. Somehow." It comes out as a mumble, but it's enough to satisfy Hávulk.

"You'll know what to do. I'm... glad."

The doctor clears his throat. "Hávulk, I found a strange bump at the back of your head. It looks like you've been scratching it. Do you know where it came from?"

"Petra gave it to me. It's where she put the words."

"Words?"

"What more do you want to know? Words. On paper. Otherwise, how would I know what to think?"

"You mean you put the words in your head?"

"She did. You don't listen."

"When this happens – does it hurt?"

"Um. I don't know. I don't really know what hurt means."

"Well, er – is it like burning your finger or maybe getting pricked by a thorn?"

"I don't know. It's like going to sleep, then waking up in a different place. Not very different, but there's more of it. I don't think you would understand. You keep on trying to treat me like a boy, but really I'm not."

"If you're not a boy, then what are you?"

"I've told you before. You just don't believe me." Mitchell looks ready to continue the argument, but Terry steps in.

"Hávulk, will you eat some food? We're worried about you."

The boy smiles at him – an old smile. "I suspect you won't have to worry for a good deal longer – but yes, I will."

"Well young man, this is progress at least," says Mitchell. "I just want to ask you one more question and then we'll get you some food, okay?" He digs around in a pocket and pulls out a photograph. "Do you recognise this man?" Hávulk's spirit seems to depart his body, leaving just the shell there, sitting ghostly still. Terry and Henry Mitchell wait for an answer in the same way that two lost tourists might wait for a train at an abandoned platform.

"The... the words told me to," he whispers.

"Told you to what?"

"To kill him." Hávulk's eyes fix on the unsmiling image of Jim Sale – a headshot taken when such a thing was possible.

Terry can't believe what the boy is saying and tries to get him to change his story. "No – you must be confused. Wasn't it just a bear? An angry bear, Hávulk? Hávulk?" But the boy is quiet. Minutes pass. Terry tries again and again, but Hávulk appears not to hear. Terry gets up and walks outside feeling dizzy. The doctor finally follows, trying to process the boy's brief confession. They don't notice Neil, who has been listening at the entrance.

"I... I don't believe it – I think he must be confused. I mean, he's been abandoned by everyone."

"I don't know, Morton – he seemed pretty clear. What I don't understand is..."

Three shots cut the air. Then another three. Then a single final bang. Looking back at the prison, Terry knows that it's over, even as the guards shout at Neil to drop his gun. Hávulk is dead and Sale's death has been avenged.

CHAPTER 21
THE WITCH

All other news is trivial: the only topic of consequence is the impending execution. From the elderly and God-fearing, who can only imagine that it's a good thing to purge an evil spirit from the land, to those that pick up 24-hour world news who can't fathom how anyone can be burned as a witch in this day and age. Depending on who's talking, one might get the impression that Petra is either a dangerous terror ready for the fires of hell, or a sad alcoholic who's been living on her own for so many years she's gone stark raving mad. After all it's a fairly frequent and mundane occurrence to run into a drunk in one of Svart's dark little alleys late at night; it's absolutely unheard of to bump into a witch.

It's a beautiful day in spite of the tense atmosphere that pervades the backstreets and talking corners of the city. The sun seems particularly bright for winter and the morning mist has lifted unusually quickly. From the military camp, Terry can just about see the tallest peak of the castle, and it's on this point that his eyes are fixed.

There was nothing he could do for Hávulk and there's probably nothing he can do for Petra, but he has to try – he promised. And now, unbelievably, the boy he made the promise to is dead. And there won't be a memorial because officially it didn't happen. Terry hasn't been instructed to keep his trap shut. The location of the unmarked grave is secret – not even Rogers knows where it is. The whole thing is so horrific that Terry is tempted to just forget – let Hávulk and his promise disappear from his mind like the scars that have just faded back to normal skin. The same normal skin he was born with in a quiet hospital in the English countryside 24 years earlier.

But he remembers the scars, and Petra, and he can't forget his promise. Though he's not sure what he can do. The soldiers won't intervene – they're staying out of sight, perhaps hiding their embarrassment at having lost their test subject.

There have been rumours that the expedition is drawing to a close; that maybe the data that brought them here were just a statistical aberration. Old people have started dying again in Izvalta.

He grabs his coat and swings it over his shoulder. Ethan Smith stops him at the gate.

"Where you headed?" he asks.

"Just thought I'd take a look around."

"You're not planning to watch are you?"

"God, no. I just – I just need to see the square. See that it's real. Then I'll walk away."

"Can't say I understand. Just watch out up there. Don't want to hear you got burned alongside the witch."

"She's not a witch."

"See? That kind of talk might land you in trouble. Public opinion is not a thing you mess with – not out here."

"I'll be careful."

The soldier makes a doubtful sound. "One last thing. Recording equipment. Gimmie. Don't want this on YouTube."

Terry hands over a long-dead phone that he's been carrying out of habit, then he starts the ascent.

236 | J W MURRAY

This gathering is different from the others. Whereas the bear festival was drunken and raucous and the naming ceremony was laced with a tantalising draught of expectation, this one is sombre, bleak. A clutch of well-dressed observers gather around the wood pile in the square beside the castle. They shuffle nervously from toe to toe, twitching like birds as they glance towards the gate. These aren't glances of wild anticipation, rather they look hopeful of disappointment.

Terry's approach raises eyebrows and a threatening murmur. Feeling the chilly mood of the crowd, he skirts the square, pretending to look in the firmly shuttered shop windows. It's not the execution scene he had pictured, straight out of a textbook on the French revolution, with mobs and flags and yelled slogans. Here he feels like an uninvited guest at a funeral – and he has the uneasy feeling that someone is about to challenge his relationship to the deceased.

Over his shoulder he hears the tap of shoes breaking away from the shuffle of the crowd and a deputised hand touches his upper arm, gentle but firm.

"Today is a holy day in Izvalta. You should not be here," says the owner of the hand. Terry turns to see a stern moustached face with tired, sagging eyes.

"Oh? I didn't know. What are you celebrating?"

"You need to leave."

"You can't stop me being here."

The moustached man's retort goes unheard as the funereal atmosphere is rent apart by the sound of a demonic engine. He glances away and Terry takes the opportunity to duck into an alley from which he can watch the proceedings unchallenged.

There's an uncanny theatricality to Monterek's entrance. His trike doesn't seem to be any less noisy even though it's proceeding at a snail's pace. His facial hair has been combed out to the sides, where it sticks wirily despite the breeze and there's that same determined, murderous expression on his barbarian face.

But if this is a barbarian king, he's chosen peculiar friends: following the trike in slow unified step are a full choir of singers clad in bright red. Their voices are barely audible over the thrum of the king's motor.

Finally, there is a prison wagon – a slightly makeshift affair constructed from a cart to which have been attached four sturdy posts wrapped in chicken wire. Sitting inside is Petra.

As she comes into view, the crowd stirs. One woman breaks away and makes a beeline for the edge of the square, shaking her head and holding her stomach as if she might vomit. Others look away. The whole procession is followed by a wave of confusion and bemusement. Terry moves unobtrusively closer, edging towards where the crowd is thickest. Nobody seems to care about him now – their eyes are fixed on the condemned prisoner, who is now passing close enough that Terry could reach out and touch the wire. He barely recognises her; she just looks like an ageing woman, tired and beaten and in need of help. There are bruises on her face, her arms and her legs, all of which have been exposed to the cold. Her clothes have been ripped and she's sitting on a stone in the middle of the cage, shivering. She doesn't look like the woman he talked to in the bar, nor the woman who nursed him back from the brink of death. She's aged so suddenly; her bones seem to have withered, shrinking her frame and causing her tough, smooth skin to hang loose and wrinkled, so that she now looks like a woman in her seventies.

All of the fairy-tale norms surrounding witches call for something entirely different: a creature twisted, gnarled and knotted like the bark of an ancient and hate-filled tree; she's supposed to crow and scream and rattle her cage; she could even appear young and deceptively beautiful by casting some spell on the crowd, but the woman in the cage is none of those – she's just another old lady of Svart, the quintessential picture of a grandmother.

Terry sees the shock on a hundred faces as they turn away – handfuls of people at the fringes of the crowd drift off quietly and self-consciously, muttering to themselves.

Very slowly the procession reaches the stack of logs and the patriarch steps forward. "Brothers and sisters!" he shouts as the king finally cuts the engine. "Do not be fooled: this woman is verily a witch." The speech has a biblical theatricality too, as the old man unleashes the full Old Testament box of tricks, accusing the shrunken and defeated old woman of any kind of unholy communion he can think of. "Though she looks like a woman now, her true form is that of a wolf. I say again, do not be fooled," he adds a little desperately over the muttering.

Petra sits impassive in the cage while he declaims. "See my people, the wolf-witch is subdued by the glory of the king and by the symbols of holiness!" The patriarch, his voice strained by the effort, has to pause for a fit of dry coughing. He struggles to pronounce his command. "Judgement has been passed. Purify this vessel in the sacred fire."

Two royal guards come forward to lead her into the square and up the wood stack, where they tie her to the vertical centre pole of the fire.

Terry watches while a voice inside him screams at his inert body to do something, but he can't – he's rooted to the spot. His mind struggles to make sense of the picture his eyes are showing him: are they actually going to burn this woman? It should be a fictional character in front of him – a badly drawn medieval stereotype witch, with a cauldron and a jar full of newts' eyes – this kind of thing doesn't happen in reality. He knows that. He must know that. He wants to suddenly notice the reassuring black plastic edge of a television screen framing the whole scene, but there is none.

"Christ," he says to himself, finally turning away from the horrible spectacle, thrusting his gloved hands deep into his pockets in preparation for the chill of the walk home. There's something in the left pocket – something spherical about two inches across. It takes a moment of blind fumbling to get his gloved fingers around it and when he yanks it into the scrutinising sunlight he almost drops the thing onto the cobbles. The alchemist's trapped hangover.

What had she said? The essence of the nigredo, condensed into a glass ball. He takes off his glove and reaches out to it. As he touches the gritty surface, his fingers recoil; he feels sickly and faint, and it's not the thought of someone being burned alive: it's something inside the ball.

He has a thought – a fantastical thought that seems to him at the same time utter nonsense and a perfectly well reasoned course of action. He stops and fingers the ball, proving the effect to himself, trying to be sure of the horrors trapped the other side of the glass like a child forcing himself to feel ill so he can skip school. This is real though. It has to be real.

The patriarch and choir have started to intone in Latin – a sonorous low sound amplified by a set of speakers mounted around the courtyard. They stand facing Petra as she is tied into place. She doesn't protest – she just looks downwards, like a rag doll with some of the stuffing taken out.

Terry watches from the edge of the square, considering his next move, still paralysed by indecision. If he steps forward now there's no telling what kind of trouble he might land in. What does he think the glass ball will do anyhow? What is it? Some kind of magic? Ha! He doesn't believe in magic. And yet, not so long ago, he was ripped apart by a wolf and stitched back together by an alchemist. *Really?*, asks Lucy's voice in his mind's ear. *Did that really happen? Whose word do you have for that?*

It's been so long since he's even thought of Lucy. She's so far away – to the point of inhabiting a completely different reality. In her world, people drink vast mugs of tea for breakfast and slather hot crumpets with knobs of butter; in Izvalta people die, and sometimes they come back to life. Not Hávulk though.

The men on the wood pile have finished tying Petra in place and are descending to join a circle of guards around the great fire. And then he sees the flame: a huge wooden torch stuck fast in Monterek's thick fist like a giant holding a flaming telegraph pole. Surrounded by an increasingly bemused and conflicted public the king marches slowly towards the bonfire, his thick top lip curled upwards like a burning leaf of paper, into a full sneer.

And with Hávulk's image in his head, Terry makes his decision. He elbows his way towards the front of the crowd, where he looks up at Petra – a crushed garment on a brittle, twiggy frame, starkly contrasting the fleshy presence of the king.

"Hey!" he shouts, but she doesn't look up. People around him are talking at him in serious, warning tones, and he feels hands pushing, shaking, prodding.

"Look up," he says again. "Look up!" he shouts but he can't make a dent in the wall of noise. The people either side of him are now gripping his shoulders. He glances at them and shoves away, but this only redoubles their efforts. He's being pushed backwards.

There's a fizz in the air as torch is touched to kindling. The fire has started.

"Shit shit shit," he mutters to himself. Petra is still looking practically comatose, her head lolling, not looking anywhere but at her own feet. Then there's a gap; a drop in the volume of the crowd as the fire catches their attention, and Terry makes his move.

"Petra!" he shouts. Finally, her head stirs and she looks vaguely in his direction. As she sees the object that Terry's holding above his head her stature changes; her back straightens and she smiles. She takes a deep breath, then nods at Terry.

Terry too takes in a deep swallow of air, following suit. Then he hurls the glass ball towards the foot of the fire.

Time seems to slow as the heavy ceiling of reality comes crashing in on him, the precarious supports of hope and credulity suddenly gone. His fantasies have fooled him into believing the mad tales of a crazy old alcoholic who once claimed to have trapped sickness itself inside a glass ball. In this terrible moment he knows it's not true and he's about to watch that same poor, damaged alcoholic burning at the stake – an image that will scorch itself on his retinas and haunt his dreams. The nebulous mass of people around him resolve themselves into hands and arms and fists. They have him now, locked in their grip moving him roughly away – they very nearly knock out the breath that he still has stored away in the pits of his lungs, but for some reason he holds on.

And then the nausea hits. It feels to Terry like a tongue of humid, sickly air is trying to force its way in through his open eyes and up his nostrils. He recognises it only too well – that revulsion of the body reacting to poisonous spirits, the feeling of needing to rid himself of everything trapped there in his guts, to turn himself inside out and start again, except that the feeling won't go away and he can't imagine it going away – ever.

Without breathing, all he feels is the nigredo's presence, though he can see its full effect on the faces of the men and women on either side of him. Their eyes water as bile rises in their throats. The fists fall limp, they release their grip on Terry's arms and soon almost everybody but Terry is down on their hands and knees, holding their aching heads, moaning and nursing their sick stomachs. Some have already started to vomit, the shockwave of nausea engulfing everybody in sight and a horrible electric squeal as the speakers in the square start gushing feedback, causing the writhing crowd to groan as one.

Without stopping to consider what's just happened, Terry forces himself forward, blinking against the nastiness on the air. He's stepping over and through a rolling, groaning mass of humanity on his way to the quickly spreading flames.

As Terry reaches the edge of the pile of bodies, the patriarch's liver-spotted hand stretches out and tries to clutch at his foot. Continuing to grit his teeth, Terry aims a kick at the old man's head, and he falls backwards, heaving out a spatter of sick down his cassock. The flames are coming dangerously close to Petra, and Terry is aware that he's not going to be able to hold his breath forever: time is running short. He looks up at her and she nods furiously in the direction of one of the soldiers sprawled on the cobbles. Terry takes a second to realise she's looking at his ceremonial sword. He snatches it up, but by now he feels like his lungs are about to burst. Desperately he tears off his coat, bunches it up and tries to breathe through it. He breathes in deeply, taking care to cover his whole nose and mouth, but still he feels a twinge of the worst sickness he's ever experienced. With great difficulty he climbs up to Petra with the sword in his hand. He swings at her bonds, but he's half-blinded by the vile fumes and instead of cutting the rope, he slices a gash in Petra's arm. Her eyes register the pain, yet the blow doesn't break her concentration – she's still managing to hold her breath.

The second swing is better aimed. Her hands are free, she takes the sword from Terry, chops once and twice at her feet and steps forward, taking Terry's hand as she does so. Terry is now beginning to succumb to the toxic air, and is so dizzy that he has great difficulty following her. Foggily he wonders how far they will have to go to escape the sickness – has it perhaps spread through the whole city? With an immense effort he raises his head to look for a way out. All he sees are reeling, puking people – even up to the edge of the square. Going that far looks utterly impossible in his state, like sprinting up Everest. The sickness it getting so bad that he feels almost ready to give up, assume a foetal position and let the fire take him. Petra, however, seems to have no intention of succumbing. She pulls him off the flaming pile, an elderly lady supporting the gangly youth with her withered shoulder.

King Monterek is rolling on the floor, leaning up against his trike, which is such a bright shade of red that even looking at it is painful for Terry. When Petra starts it up, he thinks he really is going to die – as does everyone else around them – within seconds a wide circle is cleared around the stomach-churningly noisy little vehicle. Only Monterek hangs on, stretched out on his belly, head raised, looking up at Petra with bloodshot eyes. She guides Terry to the back of the trike, where she sits him carefully down.

"Al... che... mist," the King croaks, fingers groping at the air, pitifully failing to grasp the hem of Petra's coat. "Please... please help me. Forgive me."

Petra is silent – she doesn't even seem to see his face, which has turned a hollow green. Putting down one still naked foot forcibly on the back of his neck, forcing his face into the same gritty cobbles that bludgeoned the bear's face some weeks before, she looks up into the sky. Terry's eyes follow hers, but fail to see anything but clouds – the sky reveals no message from God, no celestial emperor commanding her with a downturned thumb, to end this man's life. She releases her breath and breathes deeply the rancid air. This, then, will be her own decision. The world and

God will take no stance, and so she will decide for herself to take her revenge. She lifts up the sword, and with a log-splitting swing she separates the king's head from his shoulders.

CHAPTER 22
A PREVIOUS LIFE

The scream of the trike's motor is so unbearable to Terry that he notices nothing of his surroundings; he's only aware of constant motion, like he's being gyrated in a paint-mixer – his particular shade, a lurid yellow-green with touches of orange.

Finally, the horrible contraption shuts up, though the ringing in his head persists. They've come to a stop in front of a little cluster of houses – the kind of picture-postcard image that looks like it's been untouched for centuries, until you notice the power lines. The place is crowned by red-tiled roofs with fluffy curls of smoke rising gently from the chimneys. Petra stares at it sadly.

She dismounts and takes a couple of paces towards the houses while Terry nervously finds his feet again. The nausea has almost passed, but he's shaking all over, taking great gulps of fresh air to try to drive the bad air out of his system. The stillness of the valley closes in. Birds sing while the river gently trickles on its way to the lower flats of Romania. At this distance from Svart, there's not even the sound of barking dogs. Then just when the world looks like it's calmed down, Petra turns to him.

"Where is Hávulk?"

It takes him a moment to process the question. Doesn't she know? Perhaps she was spared this piece of knowledge out of mercy – or perhaps it was being saved for a dreadful climax to her suffering on the pyre.

"Petra... I'm sorry." He looks at her helplessly and explains. "The attack at the camp – when Hávulk killed the soldier. The soldier had a friend who wanted revenge. He killed Hávulk."

"He's dead?" She flies into a rage. "Why didn't you do something? You idiot! Why did you save me and not him?"

"Whoa, whoa." Terry tries to calm her.

"I'm not important – I'm just an old alchemist. He... He was my son. My son. Why didn't you save my son?" She hits him hard in the chest, so that he falls back against the trike and his headache starts to throb back again. "You fucking idiot! Do you know what you've done?"

"What? I don't understand."

Tears stream down her face, welling in newly defined wrinkles. "No, you don't, do you? Your soldier friend has destroyed a truly perfect being – not just some lump of flesh and blood. Of course you don't understand. Perhaps you still think he was just a little boy."

"Well, wouldn't that be bad enough? Look, there's nothing I could do."

"And yet you manage to save me from execution. Nothing you could do? I wonder how true that really is."

"What did you want me to do? Take on the army? For what? Wasn't he made out of clay?"

She looks at him coldly. "Yes."

"Then can't you can make another one?"

For a second, it looks like she's ready to kill him.

"Do you tell a mother who's lost a child to just give birth to it again? Do you?" She sits by the side of the road – a road with tarmac breaking away in chunks and no traffic. She rests her bloody arm in her lap and makes a bandage for it from a sleeve while she cries. Terry stands uneasily, not knowing what to do or say. After some time she speaks.

"Ten years ago I was cursed with a child," she says, her tone icy and detached. It isn't clear to Terry whether she's really talking for his benefit or for the sake of reasoning out a personal trauma. "It was not my child and I did not choose it – it was forced on me. But I saw how it could be used."

"Used?"

"I make things change from one thing to another. That is what alchemy means at its most basic level. But in order to create something new, there is always a form that is subsumed – whether it be sulphur or charcoal or quicksilver, or life. When I decided to make my boy of clay, I knew the Work would require sacrifice – it would not be enough to simply add the philosopher's stone to a clay model. There had to be a spark. Blood. A soul."

"You sacrificed your baby to make another baby out of clay?"

"Yes." She's matter-of-fact.

"What did you sacrifice to bring me back?" He's suddenly worried.

"Nothing so dramatic. You were still alive. But for Hávulk I needed a life. That life was transferred from one form to another. A more perfect form. The child I created was a gift from God; the thing I slaughtered never deserved life."

At one point Terry had felt so close to Petra, like he had understood her and she him, but now a man is dead in the city square; now she's confessing to murdering a helpless baby, and whatever powers brought Terry back from the brink of death probably have a similarly dark source. He feels complicit. He *is* complicit. He let loose whatever poison the people in the square just ingested. What if it's fatal?

But then again, maybe this is just Petra's coping mechanism: her insistence on pseudo-magical events just a mask to dull the edges of the real world where her son is buried in an unmarked grave.

"Hávulk was a good kid," he manages to say.

"He was much more than that – he was the embodiment of the philosopher's stone and... and he contained the last remnants of my beloved Jean."

"But... Petra. He was a boy – he had a boy's physiology – there was no difference between him and any other boy. The doctor checked – ran tests. I'm really sorry about it, but maybe if he hadn't thought he was some kind of monster then maybe he wouldn't have got mixed up with the soldiers or tried to kill Monterek."

"Really Terry? You don't believe in homunculi? In golems? And that sickness you just released in the castle square? Was that not real? And the healing of your scars? I see none left – can you deny that?"

And he can't – the scars have faded to the point where he's almost forgotten them.

"If you accept these effects of alchemy, you must also accept that Hávulk was not human. It doesn't mean I didn't love him."

"But you put words in his head, right? I mean, you cut his head open and put in paper. It's... It's..."

She looks at him pitifully. She looks around her at the hard lines he must see everywhere, where she sees fluidity and change.

"The details aren't important, Terry. I was his mother. He was my son. I loved him and I tried to show him the path I thought was right." Sorrow hits her once more and she begins to sob. "But I couldn't protect him."

Terry clears his throat, racking his mind for some word of solace. "I talked to Hávulk... before he died," he says. "I think he knew what was coming."

"Oh?"

"He made me promise to save you."

Her brow wrinkles and she sniffs. "Save me? For what? I have no grand purpose, no plan. I'm just an old woman whose last hope is gone."

There is a distant wail. It travels some way down the valley, taken up by new voices, coming in tiny waves as the wailers take their breaths. Petra Fulcanelli follows the sound and recalls when she was not Petra at all, but a little girl called Elze, hearing the same sound.

The door of one of the houses opens up in front of them. An old man pokes out his head and gazes up the valley with sleepy blinking eyes. The wailing lasts for about a minute. By the end of it, Petra is looking up again, with a stiff smirk.

"It didn't last very long at all – didn't even make it to the lower valley. A small comfort, I suppose."

"What was that?"

"They wail for the passing of the king. I remember it from my childhood. When the last king died the women cried until there were no tears left in their bodies. Few will shed a tear for Monterek."

The man from the house turns his attention to the two strangers on the road stood next to the bright red trike, and hobbles toward them, one hand on a doughty stick topped with a cloven hoof. His face bears age the way that knotted wood bears polish; it gives him character, adorning his face with a suggestion of wisdom and honesty. As he approaches, he stares intently at Petra.

"Elze?"

The word almost knocks her over. "I'm sorry – I don't know you, do I?"

"I knew it! That was your home once." He points to a house slightly smaller than the one he's just left, set in the middle of a snow-covered field. There are boards over the windows. "Don't tell me you've forgotten."

"Ivan?" she says.

Terry's eyes dart from one to the other – they're speaking Izvaltese and it's the first conversation he's heard in that tongue without someone trying to translate for him.

"I'm surprised to see you alive. And the wailing – the king can't have passed, can he? Or maybe..." he says with a dark smile, "that explains how you're here. That red machine – that's the king's too, isn't it?" Then he sees the gash in her arm. "Elze, you're bleeding. Let me help – come inside and I'll get you fixed up."

After a moment she relents – the wound needs to be tended to. "Okay, but I'll have to be quick – and we'll have to do something with that trike. It's too obvious just stuck there."

He frowns at it. "I have a grandson who's handy at stripping those things down to sell. Nice new parts like that should make good money – that is if you don't have a use for it. We do a lot of trade with Romania nowadays. The young men like their specialist parts. Doesn't matter what they do as long as they're shiny!"

"But Ivan, I can't let you help me – Monterek is dead – I killed him. There will be people looking for me."

"How...?" he begins to ask, and then thinks better of it and reverts to his previous attentive demeanour. "Well. Just a quick stop then – you can't go on with your arm like that. Don't worry. Your young friend can put the trike in the wood shelter – the wood's almost finished now anyway. We could do with a nice early spring this year, don't you think?"

Directed by Ivan's gestures, Terry rolls the trike into the shelter. As he ducks through the neatly curved doorway to the house he sees an ageing couple – an elderly man looking fondly at an elderly woman. It takes him a moment to realise that the woman is Petra. She appears so very different from the way she was when he first saw her – as if perhaps she's always been an old lady but just today she removed the make-up – the faerie glamour that made her young. She looks like the rest of the old women of Svart, just a little paler maybe.

Ivan busies himself with some antiseptic and a bandage while Petra sits at a kitchen table scuffed and nicked by countless generations of diners.

"What are you going to do?" asks Terry, who is now feeling more lost than ever, like he's walked in at the end of a foreign film with no subtitles.

"You could stay here," Ivan suggests with his head inside a cabinet. Apparently he understands some English.

Petra looks at him curiously. "Ivan? But I can't. I... I just killed the king."

He removes his head from the cabinet and looks at her seriously for a few seconds.

"That's true. Not a popular man, Monterek, but I suppose there might be repercussions." His brows knit into bushy knots, which, once they fathom their answer, gradually untie themselves again and a smile appears on his face. "I think we can hide you," he says. "Just a second. Young man, take a seat – you're making me anxious with all your pacing."

As Terry sits, Ivan heads upstairs. A few minutes later he is back with a bundle of busily patterned clothes. Pinks and greens leap from the folds – all kinds of gaudy flowers, petals, buds – a chaotic counterpoint to Petra's simple monochrome rags. He hands them to Petra. "Try those. Trust me," he says in response to her sceptical look.

She goes upstairs and soon returns with the light, soft clothes trailing behind and around her. She's unrecognisable as the woman who, less than half an hour ago, exacted her terrible revenge on the king. Ivan grins, every wrinkle of his brown, weather-worn face beaming satisfaction.

"You look... different. I'd barely know you," says Terry.

"These clothes are strange. Won't someone suspect something? People will ask who I am."

"And you can tell them truly that you are Elze Veshnik, the girl who used to live in the neighbouring house. You could even move back in. Everybody knows you ran away, Elze. They thought you ran away from Izvalta." The old man chuckles. "Though few know that you did it to avoid marrying me."

"Ivan..."

"Oh don't worry – I've had time enough to get over that. Will you stay? All you need do is make up some stories about your life outside the valley. You'll be believed – after all, Izvalta hasn't grown wise in your absence – the people are just as credulous as they always were. I convinced Markus the other day that the mountain goats sometimes dance when they think nobody's looking."

Petra still looks uncertain, but the gravest doubts would melt away in the warmth of Ivan's reassuring presence. Tears well up in her eyes.

"I would like to lie down," she says, choking on the words.

"Wait – Petra, what's going on?" Terry feels that lump in his throat that signals that an end is close at hand – that point at which two paths must diverge. Two paths that will never reunite.

"What is happening?" she replies. "The world is turning. I've spent a lifetime standing aside to watch it turn – more. I think the time has come to let it carry me. Time to live the life I never lived. And you must do the same, Terry. We should both return to the lives that were meant for us."

"You don't mean that, do you?"

She looks back at him with the eyes of an old woman. Even

her stance suggests less a ball of strength than something more nebulous and circumspect, resigned and slightly stooping. "I think so, Terry."

"And what about me? They'll put me in prison. They'll torture me to find you. They'll..."

"The wisest man I ever knew," she interrupts, "believed in a kind of providence – a God or a guiding force that he acknowledged even as he strove to be master of his own destiny. We cannot run, Terry, and I don't think you're ready to hide. We can only pray to providence. I think you'll be alright. Foreigners get away with a lot," she adds with a smile.

"So we have to say goodbye?"

"Yes." She steps forward and hugs him. "I'm pleased to have met you, Terry. You're a good man, but not wise. Maybe the world will teach you wisdom."

"What do you mean?"

She just smiles.

Later that evening, Ivan leans forward to prod a healthy-looking fire with a soot-blackened poker. Finally, he sits back in his chair, satisfied with the blaze. Petra takes a seat opposite and glances around the interior of the house. It's so different from Jean Fulcanelli's hut – it seems excessive with its decorative wall hangings and the purposeless trinkets lining the mantelpiece.

She's drawn to a picture with a frame made of bound sticks. Inside is a colour photograph in which she sees a middle-aged version of herself with an arm around a middle-aged version of the man settled in the chair beside her. Minutes of scrutiny confirm her suspicions – it really is her.

"How...?" she starts to ask.

"You recognise the woman in the picture? You should. It's Eva."

"And these clothes?"

"Eva's. My wife's."

"You married my sister?"

"You ran away. The marriage was decided by your father and mine."

"Where is she? What happened to her?"

Ivan's face is clouded by painful memory. The mention of Eva halts his tongue and chokes his throat, leaving him in a kind of paralysis of thought. Petra asks no more questions. She and Ivan sit contemplating the fire until the embers drown in a sea of ash.

Before Petra falls asleep she peers into the darkness, trying to imagine what the future might hold, and she mourns the loss of a son that wasn't truly hers. She should have reconciled herself to the idea of death some time ago, as a passing from one form to another – from human shape to the shape of the earth, the woods and the mountains. Death is after all, just another transmutation. Hávulk was made from clay and he's returned to that form. The passing is all in her mind; it's not a true reflection of how the world is. That doesn't stop her tears.

She sees the new path of her life with an unprecedented clarity: it's the same path she left so many years ago – the one where she simply grows old and dies, satisfied with Ivan's companionship. There are children and grandchildren in this future – her sister's; there are household chores and harvests and seasons. It's simple and comfortable and incredibly inviting – as inviting as sleep. One could just... fall into it.

CHAPTER 23
RETURN

Ethan Smith nods at Terry as he passes the gate. "You've been gone a long time."

"Went for a walk."

"Lot to take in, huh?"

"Yeah – couldn't stomach it in the end."

"Probably for the best, mate. Don't want to be haunted by those kinds of images."

"Right," Terry says, the image of Monterek's rolling head entering unbidden into his mind.

He makes a beeline for his room. He just wants to lie down, close his eyes and let his mind process what he's seen and done, but when he reaches the room it's in darkness. The tiny windows are curtained over, trapping in the damp, earthy smell of the old shed. He goes to turn on his lamp, but stops short when he hears breathing from the bottom bunk. It's the kind of heaving breath that might give way to sobs at any moment.

"Neil?"

The deep breathing continues. Terry switches on the light, revealing the motionless figure of Neil sitting on his bunk, his eyes hollow and red. He looks a wreck. A moment passes before Neil acknowledges that there's someone else in the room, and when he speaks it's as if he's continuing a conversation he's been having with himself for the past few hours.

"I... I shot him."

"Yeah. Yeah, well I guess you had your reasons."

"Damn right I did. Damn right. He killed Sale. Head... Ripped it off, you know? Off."

"Neil, have you..."

"But he was just a boy. I mean, I shot a kid. I thought maybe he'd break or something – green blood, or maybe he'd heal back up and that way we'd know it was some fucking alien in disguise or some monster."

"The bogeyman?"

"Right. Right – the bogeyman. They said he was made of clay. Like pottery right? But he didn't smash. Just died. Like a kid. He just slumped over, y'know? And the doc says, 'He's dead.' *He's* dead. Not 'It's dead.' And I realised it was just a little boy all along. And I killed him."

Terry can't think of anything to say. He stands in the middle of the room for a long time, just looking down at Neil, who isn't looking up. He wonders what will happen to him. Will he be disciplined somehow, or will there be some kind of understanding reached? It's not like Hávulk will be missed by anybody but Petra, and she herself is a fugitive. So might he be, although by some miracle apparently the news hasn't reached the camp yet – only tomorrow will tell. After a little while, he turns out the light and climbs up to the top bunk, where he largely fails to fall asleep.

He is awoken the next morning, not by Neil's ear-splitting reveille, but by the low rumble of trucks. The noise interrupts uneasy dreams and he feels like he's only just been able to get to sleep, but the trucks are unbearably loud – there's no way to block them out. He swings awkwardly down from the top bunk. Neil is nowhere to be seen and his bag is missing too. Terry draws back an ancient scrap of curtain and is momentarily blinded by the light of a bright grey morning.

Outside the trucks are being loaded. The tents are already well on their way to being packed up into their sturdy green sacks and the soldiers look ready to move out. They're standing around smoking and chatting.

"The fuck?" says Terry out loud as he starts searching wildly for some clean underwear and a pair of trousers. "Are we leaving? What the hell is going on?"

"Knock knock, civilian – time to move out," Rogers says as he barges through the door.

"What's happening?"

"Developments, son. Cutting short the holiday. Seems there's been a bit of an uprising. Wouldn't look good politically to stick around. Anyway, we're out in thirty minutes – that's three zero." He bangs the wall twice and strolls off.

"Shit." Terry chucks his disordered stuff into a bag and with a quick glance backwards to see if he's left anything behind, he charges out of the door. He really doesn't want to be left on his own in Svart – not after what he did yesterday. He recalls one of his dreams in which he was being burned on a bonfire. No – it wouldn't be good to stick around.

Outside, with a badly packed rucksack trailing in the mud, he finds Ethan Smith smoking a cigarette and gazing up towards the peaked roofs of the castle.

"So what happens now?" asks Terry.

"Now we leave. I don't know about you but I'm ready to get back to the real world – back to a place that has real coffee, running water and an internet connection, you know?"

"But what about the mission?"

"What mission?"

"Well – you know, the mission we've been on. The Izvalta mission."

"I think you'll find it was just a manoeuvre – a bit of foreign field training."

"But..."

"But what? We still get paid for training – even the failed interpreter probably gets something. Maybe a dictionary. Here – let me grab that bag for ya."

Terry knocks gently on the frame of Rogers' rickety wood door, which is standing open as he packs up a final few papers. He looks up and then returns to his packing.

"Morton. All packed up?"

"Um – just one thing I wanted to clear with you."

"Stop right there, civilian. Don't say anything you might later regret."

"What's going to happen to Neil?"

"I expect he'll want a short vacation – time to think. But then I expect he'll go back to regular military service."

"There won't be any disciplinary action?"

Rogers stands upright. "For what?"

"For uh... Hávulk."

"For what? Is that one of those phrases you picked up? I'd be really fucking careful what foreign phrases you sling around in the real world. They could so easily be misinterpreted. I mean, I don't know if you heard but the King of Izvalta was decapitated yesterday." He pauses, eyeballing Terry as if maybe he's deciding whether he's likely to say something stupid in a pub one night, or to share a particular story on the internet. After a moment or two, Rogers seems as satisfied as he's capable of being. "I'm putting it down to a bear attack. They're dangerous, those bears. People should be more careful. Anything else, Morton?"

"No, sir."

The rest of the day passes in a blur. Suddenly he's going home. The bumpy road to Bucharest seems to fly by beneath him;

the wilderness of the countryside gives way to solid brick cottages, and then they finally embrace the grey tower blocks of the city. Young guys walk the streets in packs, close haircuts and sports clothes marking out their uniform, steam gushing from their mouths like recently quenched dragons as they watch the convoy pass by.

They leave Terry at the airport – he's boarding a civilian plane back to London. He feels like he's been whisked away, just at the point of understanding something. He's touched the surface of a weird anomaly: the last bastion of a lost art – and now he's gone, hopelessly removed, robbed of a real end to the story. What will happen to Izvalta? And to Petra? Their goodbye seems so woefully inadequate – so many things were left unsaid. Where yesterday he could only wave a hand, today he would pour out words in a torrent. But today is too late.

The airport lounge is mundane. Dull duty-free shops with a gleaming array of fundamentally samey shit. 'Romanian experience' shops stocking generic souvenirs made in Thailand and catering stalls churning out a stream of blandly reliable foodstuffs. It all seems so unreal. He sits in a chair that squeaks at his smallest movements and watches as ordinary people pass by: businessmen chatting casually and answering tinny-tuned mobiles, early-season backpackers wearing shorts and looking cold but irrepressibly optimistic, mothers guiding young children around various obstacles and steering them away from the sweeties. This, he realises, will become the norm again – and sooner than he thinks.

In an effort to retain what he's just experienced, to lodge its details in some kind of reality, he buys a fresh notepad and a biro from a kitschy stationer, orders a coffee and sits down, chewing the end of the pen and planning to write down everything he's seen, starting at the beginning.

As he does so, Terry's uncertainty starts writing itself into his words. His hand, initially clear and legible, becomes less so as he sketches out his impressions of the feast of the bear. The paragraphs that relate the details of being maimed by a wolf and then miraculously healed are practically unreadable.

He stops to review his account, scratching his unkempt head, and concluding that it just doesn't hold up. He doesn't remember being attacked – just being stiff and achy. He never actually saw any alchemy, apart from what he's termed the 'hangover bomb' – and that now seems like a dream – he's not certain it wasn't. Surrounded by so much pedestrian normality, the idea of capturing a hangover is just absurd – just as it was when Petra first told him that story.

"That story!" He almost jumps out of his chair. He digs at the bottom of his backpack. After some searching he fishes out the recorder. With hands shaking, he plugs in a set of earphones and plays back the interview with the alchemist. It's the only thing he recorded during his time in Izvalta, and the sound quality is pretty terrible – with lots of background laughter from the locals in the bar, but he can just about make out Petra's slurring words.

He listens. 'A simple glass ball, but into it is injected the essence of the nigredo – corruption and dirt and shit and sick.' He stops the playback. This is madness. Everything around him screams that it's impossible, that it doesn't exist, that you need chemicals to produce the effects he saw in the square. You can't just blow into a ball. People make home-made chemicals all the time. Mix a few household items together and you can get some pretty potent stuff – infinitely more probable than the version of events she relates in the recording.

You've been had, Terry, he tells himself. *All this stuff is bollocks. What about her son? Yeah, what about her son? Figure it out. She said it was Monterek's son. He raped her.*

If he assumes Petra was telling the truth about that, what sounds more plausible? Woman digs up some clay, models it into the perfect likeness of a human being and plants in it a bunch of magic words and brings it to life, or; Woman gets knocked up in a violent encounter that she would much rather forget, then, when she pops out a little baby nine months later, invents something about a 'golem' that she's made and convinces herself it's true because she can't bear the alternative?

If only he had a picture or two – some kind of evidence. A newspaper maybe – a copy of *Valta* that describes, in whatever language, what exactly happened: the sudden sickness and the king's decapitation. But he has nothing except for a fuzzy story from a drunk woman and a few memories that his mind is already busy explaining away with scientific, rational thought.

He sighs and thinks of home – a place where everything is connected, where each describable item has a Wikipedia article. A world that can be understood and categorised. Izvalta isn't part of it; Izvalta exists outside the network and outside his reality – the two places are somehow incompatible. He looks down at the recorder and presses down the record button, overwriting the fantastical nonsense on the tape with the sounds of wheelie bags and last calls.

There's a little more time before his flight departs so he settles in a plastic chair while lethargy, in turn, settles on him. His mind wanders back to the high-sided valley and the long cobbled march up to the castle, the slit-eyed houses peering at him to remind him that he's a foreigner under scrutiny. Soon all of it will be far behind him and he will no longer be a stranger. He'll be known and understood, maybe even loved? It's been a long time since he thought of Lucy. The boarding call pulls him out of his trance and he scrabbles to get his things together and join the queue.

It's his feet that betray him: they leave the queue and take him with them. Curious how sometimes the body does things without the mind's involvement.

He finds a phone – one of a cluster of old-fashioned coin-eaters made up to look like something more than a phone. He's thankful for a pocketful of change. On his third attempt he manages to reach Lucy on her mobile. She sounds distant – and of course she is – but the air around her words is irritable, irritated, as if he were cold-calling from an insurance company. He wonders – not for the first time – whether this assignment her father found for Terry was designed to drive a wedge between he and Lucy, social climber and social misfit – and whether it has succeeded. And further still, whether he should perhaps be grateful.

"Hi Lucy. Just calling to say that the mission's done. Or whatever it was. The training. The military thing. Done."

"Really?" She doesn't sound excited.

"Yeah, but... well... I met someone. Here."

Lucy barely misses a beat. "*There*? In what-was-the-place-called?"

"Izvalta. You see, I... I think I need to, you know – see the world."

"Play the field, you mean?"

"Not really."

"And when were you planning to get an actual *job*, Terry? How about a place to *live*?"

"Well that's just it – I think before finding a place to live I might need to find a reason to live." He can hear the glottal 'ugh' of disgust quite clearly at the other end of the phone.

"That is possibly the most abhorrent, idiotic, hippy bullshit thing I've ever heard come out of your mouth – and that's no mean feat."

"Yeah, well. It's true. Goodbye, Lucy."

He has the small pleasure of hearing her start to protest as the phone clunks back into its cradle.

Behind him, an accented voice calls final boarding for his flight. He takes out his ticket, deposits it in a chrome bin and strolls towards the exit – back out into the cold, back out into a world full of tiny pockets waiting to be explored and experienced. More than he could possibly see in a single lifetime.

CHAPTER 24
BUCCO

It's strange that she so perfectly fits everything her sister once wore. The neat and practical shoes she wore around the farm when she was feeding the chickens; the warm shawl that matches Petra's hair so well – everything fits. Even Ivan, who transparently dotes on her, seems so kind-hearted and genuine that she looks back at him and starts to wonder if she really did run away from him all those years ago. Was it all just some fever dream? Hasn't she really been here all the time? Did she even have a sister at all?

Ivan is reluctant to talk about Eva or her death, but finally relents and tells her what happened.

"She loved to wander in the forests. Bucco followed everywhere she went." He gestures to the black and white dog lying on the rug. "On summer days she used to take a basket out with her and bring it back full of bilberries. And then one day two summers ago she didn't come back."

She had fallen while crossing a stream and cracked her head open on a rock. The dog dragged her up the bank and began howling – which is what brought help, but of course it came too late.

Everything fits – apart from that dog.

After a month in her sister's shoes, her new life feels so real that she's almost convinced herself that this is the way it always was: she and Ivan in a little house, tending the land, surrounded by family, telling the grand-children stories (hers largely based on anecdotes from the books she's read).

The neighbourhood, gossip-laden as it is, is curiously silent on the subject of Elze's return after so many years; it's just accepted. This is partly due to the respect the community feels for 'Grandpa Ivan', but there are also bigger issues facing Izvalta now that the king is gone. The high town dignitaries are proposing plans to continue the royal line from amongst their number, but the Izvaltan church – in particular the patriarch – has refused to back the move. The low towners are also pitching in, and placards have started to appear written in block letters of Izvaltese proclaiming slogans like 'Palaces are Public Property', 'Lazy High Towners do some work' and 'Democracy for Izvalta'.

There's also the problem of the dead: for years, the people of Izvalta have been at the pinnacle of high health. Until just recently, the one run-down hospital has been very quiet, but now its handful of doctors are starting to see cases of influenza, measles and even cancers that haven't been seen for almost a decade. Even more disturbing, the elderly have started to die off in great swathes. The doctors are blaming foreign diseases carried by the soldiers, with the result that Izvalta is for the first time considering closing its borders to its main source of income – tourism.

The *Valta* newspaper has been reclaimed and re-purposed as a mouthpiece for Izvalta's first nationalist party, calling for a redistribution of wealth. If the world's press were in any way interested, it would see the start of a revolution on a microscopic scale – but of course, it isn't interested. For the first time, Izvalta is starting to think for itself, although its thoughts are largely confused and contradictory.

There's so much to talk about that Petra and Ivan have faded into the background noise; even Ivan's family accepts her – it's just the dog that doesn't. Bucco can tell the difference: every time he sees Petra wearing something that belonged to her sister he goes wild, and given that she has little else to wear, he spends several hours a day railing against the stranger who's taken the place of his mistress.

"I'd like to talk, Bucco."

She's sitting on the stone steps of the house with the dog growling low at her feet. Spring has begun to tint the landscape with a rich palette of greens and the air has a pleasant flowery scent. It's warm, no need of a shawl, but still she is wearing her sister's clothes – she almost can't imagine what her own once looked like. In a wardrobe somewhere in the house hangs the shapeless woollen coat she used to wear – a present miraculously retrieved from the castle, which is being gradually sacked. Peculiarly lavish gold ornaments have started to adorn the mantelpieces of Svart, alongside the existing cheaper plaster of Paris ones. She's been thinking about that coat.

"I think you're right, Bucco. I fit in here so well, but it's not my life. It's my sister's life – the one that I chose not to live. I can't end my days like this, nodding off to sleep in a rocking chair. Most of all I can't stand feeling so old.

"You know, Bucco, there's a solution to that – I can fix the aches and pains. My equipment is all stolen or smashed and it would be so much work to make it all again, but I've heard that these days you can go to a shop and buy almost anything you can imagine. Not in Izvalta, obviously – but other places." She stops to listen to the sound of her own words. She's lapsed into a part-Latin, part-French, part-Izvaltese crossbreed language – not that the old sheepdog understands, but Jean would have. The dog continues to growl at her, and she knows that he'll only stop when she's gone.

With some difficulty she finds her old coat. It's been hung by hand unknown at the back of the less-used wardrobe. The touch of the material brings back memories, to say nothing of its smell. The coat is dense with peculiar smoky fragrances: the smell of open fires, metal and earth. When she puts it on, it feels like a suit of armour. It gives her a feeling of purpose and an identity.

When she tells Ivan, tears spill over his deep laughter lines. Although he has been expecting this for some days, he can't help but mourn her as though her leaving were a second passing for his wife.

She leaves more quietly than she arrived, with nothing more than a coat, some sturdy boots and a parcel of food. She has no books, no burners or alembics, she has only a will to live – to be a simple, enduring strand in the knot of humanity.

CHAPTER 25
EXODUS

Gregor, the patriarch, is panicked. When a witch is able to step off a bonfire, kill a monarch and then simply drive away it can look suspiciously like divine punishment. If he's honest with himself, he really hasn't handled the backlash very well and his authority has certainly suffered.

On top of that, it seems that revolution is in the air: the high town is under constant political attack by the peasants in the valley, and because of the spate of deaths he's even had to go back to performing last rites. It's time to get out of Svart, out of Izvalta; time to find a place where he can be assured of his status, and for that he's going to need cash. The exchange rate for the Izvaltan akche was never good and in these turbulent times a metre-high stack of notes might only convert to a few Romanian Lei. The only thing that still has value is gold and thankfully he has plenty of it put aside. The rainy day has finally come and he congratulates himself on his perspicacity years before. Few men could claim to provide for themselves so effectively seventy years in advance of their need.

One spring day, the usual bell ring to signal the morning service fails to sound. When the members of the congregation reach the church door they are puzzled by a sign pasted across it: 'The church is closed today. I am sorry that I will not be able to guide you in your prayers. Let this be a time for individual contemplation. There is much to contemplate.'

One or two rich high-towners, deciding that this must be some kind of joke, rattle the door and shout the patriarch's name. Nobody comes to the door. From inside there is only a recurring noise: *Clink-clink. Clink.* The church door remains closed. The priests who come to assist the patriarch later in the day are also surprised, but also rather glad to be spared the old man's gloomy presence – besides, there's plenty to do. They too turn around and walk away. The doors remain closed throughout the day and into the night.

As the morning sun cracks the horizon, Gregor makes the final preparations for his departure. The horse and cart are both old, but should get him far enough. He's looking for a fairly large settlement – probably Craiova to the south, judging from the map. He loads the cart with some difficulty. Until recently he has benefited from incredible good health, especially for someone in his nineties, but now he's struggling – yet more proof of God's indifference to his plight.

The cart is packed and covered with a tarpaulin. Streaks of orange and pink cross the sky, a projection from a world much wider than he has ever known. Apart from a brief mountain crossing as a boy, exploring the Saxon churches and cobbled streets of Sibiu, he hasn't travelled at all. Svart has been his life – in many ways the king himself was his life, selfish brat though he was – even until the end.

As he descends the hill, the going is fine, but as soon as he reaches the valley floor and the path levels out, the old horse begins to wheeze with the strain. It's not long before he sees the first of the villages that border Svart. They're simple things, nothing to compare to the grandeur of the high town, but the disdain he initially feels turns to sadness. Wouldn't it be pleasant to have that life, surrounded by family and home comforts? An old man – possibly around his own age – nods at him without recognition. He's feeding scraps to a horde of chickens that are now whirling around his feet. Gregor looks at the man without deigning to nod back.

Following the road to the south he watches the sun rise in the east, illuminating the flat green expanse of Wallachia in front of him, with the Olt River tumbling down on his left towards the Danube. From the edge of the Carpathians it's a beautiful sight and he's filled with the sense of a world replete with possibility once more – just like it was in his youth. But of course the going is slow. Cars overtake him one after another, honking at the old cart and, on several occasions, Gregor fears for his life as a driver only barely manages to brake in time.

After a day of plodding south, night descends. This is the part of the journey he's been trying not to think about, but now he has to face it. He has no money, just a pocket full of akches that are worth nothing at all, and apart from that, he simply can't stop – that would mean parking the cart somewhere, and if he did that somebody might look under the tarpaulin.

The old horse is slowing. After six years spent making short trips up and down the diminutive high street of Svart, it's not prepared for a full day's journey towing this weight. Gregor kicks at the poor beast's flanks and it manages a little more speed. By the dead of night, however, the horse is practically at a standstill. Frustrated, Gregor kicks again and again, but only succeeds in making the horse whinny. It simply won't go any further.

The clouds have obscured the moon so that the only light is from a tiny patch of stars. The road is briefly flooded with light as a car passes him, swerving to avoid the unexpected blockage in the road. It honks as it fades into the blackness. It would be a comfort to believe that God will help him in his time of need, but that hope can only spring from naiveté. He watches the dark line of the trees. Beneath the prickling branches there is a tiny flash of light – the eye of some nocturnal animal. Or maybe a tooth. He must carry on – with or without the horse.

He climbs stiffly down from the seat – it's been a very long drive and the night will only get longer. One hand on the cart, he walks around to the back and lifts the tarpaulin. The thin light glimmers off a heap of finely sculpted gold. On the top, a breath-taking golden Jesus looks up at him, his jaw dropped in moaning agony. Gregor covers the face in a cloth and inspects the cart. There's no way he can take everything here, no way to take even a fraction of it. Cursing, he looks into the distance. Perhaps there is a house up there where he could find some help. *Ha!* he says to himself – *they would just take everything.* If he wanted to be a pauper he might as well have stayed in Izvalta. He knows what he's going to have to do. He bends down and picks up the cross, fitting his bony shoulder underneath a golden armpit.

About half a mile down the road, Gregor hears a scratching in the trees to his right. He looks around. Nothing. Then out of the corner of his eye that glimmer again – a brief, devilish sparkle. He hurries his pace, hearing only his footfall on the tarmac and an occasional scrape as the base of the cross begins to drag on the ground. He begins to wheeze like the horse, but every time he stops he sees that glimmer of an unknown thing in the darkness, and so he carries on.

When the Romanian farmer finds him in the morning, the old man is flattened beneath a massive golden cross. It's hard to say what he died of, but his eyes are opened startlingly wide. There is a trail of gold scratches on the road extending a full mile behind him. It's quite the oddest thing the farmer has ever seen.

"Daddy, Daddy."

He manages to cover the dead man's face before his son sees it.

"Is it gold, Daddy?"

The farmer chuckles grimly to himself. "No, my boy – gold isn't like this. You can find small bits of gold sometimes, but for churches and so on people just use bits of other metal and coat them to make them look like gold, you see?"

"Oh."

"Looks like this man robbed a church, thinking it was all real gold. I suppose he got what he deserved in the end. Now go fetch your mother, there's a good boy."

As the boy runs off to the house, the farmer tries to pry open the dead man's stiff fingers, which are still wrapped tightly around the cross, but with no success. Finally he gives up.

"Keep it," he says to the dead patriarch. "You've paid for it."

EPILOGUE

There is an unmarked grave not far from the place where the military camp stood earlier in the year.

The buildings now lie empty and the wind likes to play in amongst the wooden beams, whistling its tune of merry desolation throughout the spring and into the summer. On a stormy August evening, the rain batters down on the patchy wood-shingled roof, sloshing in great sheets across the front of the old building. It etches paths of loosened soil down the shallow hill, washing away stubs of ill-rooted weeds down onto a flat where the stream muddily puddles and gurgles until it finally overflows and continues its journey.

When the stream reaches the grave, it disappears into a thick crop of luscious green grass populated with vividly coloured flowers of blue, red, purple and orange. A local might tell you that it's curious to see them all together in the same season; they might also tell you that there's something almost magical about the place, although only one person could say why – a woman who once lived in the valley who could, if you bought her a drink, tell you a story about a clay boy who would wash in the mountain stream next to his home. She could relate how every day a thin layer of the clay boy's skin would wash off in the water, trickling down the stream and joining the river in the valley below. The water would swirl the boy's skin around and around until the skin became part of the water itself and the water would dance all the more merrily for its presence. While the boy lived, the river would breathe with life that it had never known before; fish would jump and play; the plants by its banks would grow lush and dense and every resident of Izvalta that drank from the river would feel a new surge of life.

And although that boy is gone, some small part of him is buried here, under the flowers. The earth in this place remembers a beauty that mankind is all too quick to forget.

The woman visits the place once in a while. Sometimes in ragged clothes, sometimes like a lady from the city, neat and trimmed. Each visit she picks a flower – a different type and colour each time – and puts it in her hair. And then she is someone else: venerable, fearsome, young, innocent. Perhaps the flower decides or perhaps she does – the only thing that matters is her will to carry on.

THANK YOU

To all of those friends and family who read Izvalta and gave feedback at various stages, thank you so much.

Thank you to my family: Maman, Papi, Nick, Granny, who sped through the first draft in minutes. Thanks to Leah, Chris, Ian, Hamish, Nat and Jenn for being a proper audience and telling me what they really thought, and to Lyndsay and the Boston Speculative Fiction Writing Group – the hunting scene is just for you guys.

A huge thanks to my editor, Flora Napier.

Ash, of course, is the person I couldn't do anything without.

CREDITS

Cover font: Linux Libertine
Designer: Philipp H. Poll

Author name font: Vremena
Designer: Roman Gornitsky

Chapter heading font: Butler
Designer: Fabian De Smet
CC BY-SA 4.0 licence (unedited)

Body font: Charis SIL
Designer: SIL International

Cover images:
Der Wanderer über dem Nebelmeer (1818)
Artist: Caspar David Friedrich

Opus Mago-Cabalisticum et Theologicum
(1719)
Artist: Georg von Welling

Basilica Philosophica (1618)
Artist: Johann Daniel Mylius